THE FAITHFUL

.ll.

DON MACDONALD

THE FAITHFUL

A MICHAEL SHELTER MYSTERY

Prepared for the Press by
Deanna Radford, Rivkah Groszman, Jennifer McMorran, Barbara Rudnicka
Cover image: Laura Boyle
Cover design: Debbie Geltner
Author photo: John Kenney
Layout: Daniel Ursache

Library and Archives Canada Cataloguing in Publication

Title: The Faithful / Don Macdonald.
Names: Macdonald, Don, author.
Identifiers: Canadiana (print) 20260174629 |
Canadiana (ebook) 20260174645 |
ISBN 9781773901985 (softcover) |
ISBN 9781773901992 (ebook) | ISBN 9781773902005 (PDF)
Subjects: LCGFT: Detective and mystery fiction. | LCGFT: Novels.
Classification: LCC PS8625.D6265 F35 2026 | DDC C813/.6—dc23
Printed and bound in Canada

Legal deposit—Library and Archives Canada and
Bibliothèque et Archives nationales du Québec, 2026

We are grateful to the Canada Council for the Arts, the Canada Book Fund, and SODEC for their support of our book publishing program and to the Government of Quebec through the Société de développement culturel and the Programme de credit d'impôt pour l'édition de livres—Gestion SODEC.

Montreal
www.lindaleith.com

Also by DON MACDONALD

Omand's Creek

And all who believed were together and had
all things in common. And they were selling their
possessions and belongings and distributing
the proceeds to all, as any had need.
Acts 2:44 – 45

For out of the heart come evil thoughts, murder,
adultery, sexual immorality, theft, false witness, slander.
Matthew 15:19

In loving memory of my parents

Donald Ardell Macdonald
Patricia Ann Macdonald

ONE

BEFORE HE REACHED the yard, Jacob Waldner heard the clanging of metal on metal and knew his brother was having a problem with a combine. Approaching the huge green machine, Jacob nodded to his cousin Johannes, who was watching Amos working deep inside the rig.

"What's going on?" Jacob asked.

"A stuck bearing."

Hammer in hand, Amos stepped away from the combine and cursed under his breath. He glared at Jacob and shook his head. Amos wore a handmade shirt, black pants, and suspenders, just like the ones they all wore. From the dust on Amos's pants, grime on his hands, and ill temper, Jacob could tell the repair job wasn't going well.

They'd been running the combines hard late into the night over the thousands of acres belonging to the colony. The machines cut, threshed, separated, and stored the grain in a hopper until it could be offloaded onto a dump truck. It wasn't surprising for a combine to break down. Still, this dirty, annoying job would pull men away from harvesting on this sunny late August day, ideal weather for getting the wheat crop off.

"You're on your way, then?" Amos said, wiping his filthy hands on a cloth, his voice sour.

“I’ll be back in the early evening. Sorry for the trouble. Do you need anything from the city?”

Amos shook his head and was about to say something when a chime sounded in his brother’s pocket. A WhatsApp message.

“Hold on,” Jacob said. He pulled out the phone and glanced at the screen. A two-word message: *call me*. Slipping the phone back into his pocket, he felt his face grow warm as adrenaline hit his system. Looking up, he realized Amos was watching him. “I need to make a call,” he said apologetically.

Amos gave him a dark look before turning back to his work. Jacob walked over to the other side of the gravel yard and scanned the area. When he was sure he had privacy, he tapped an icon on the screen and brought the phone to his ear. There was no need for preliminaries.

“When will you be here?” The words were spoken in the same German dialect Jacob had used to speak to Amos and Johannes.

Jacob felt a surge of excitement. He struggled to calm himself. “I’m leaving at nine.”

“It’s the same place. Call me when you get there.” The line went dead.

Judging there was nothing more to say to his brother, Jacob made the short walk to the house where he lived with his wife and three children. He sensed the light had become softer and the morning air cooler, a prelude to the early prairie autumn. Their home was the middle unit of five identical, two-storey, connected houses built by colony men, and, like everything else on the property, was owned by the community. He picked up the case containing his laptop and slipped on a backpack where he'd stored a change of clothes and some toiletries for the day ahead.

With everything ready, he glanced in the mirror. He wore a trimmed beard, as most men in the community did. He was only thirty-three years old, but he'd noticed the beginnings of a paunch from the hours spent in his sedentary job, keeping the colony's books and presiding over the shopping for supplies. The elders had sent him to community college to learn bookkeeping. He'd hated it at the time, but the training had proven useful in managing the colony's accounts and investments, and the shopping took him to the city. Those trips gave him perfect cover for a rendezvous like today's. This time, he also had two urgent meetings to attend, hoping—and fearing—he'd find answers to the suspicions tormenting him.

It would be tight, making it back to the colony on time. Of course, he could return immediately after the meetings, but his heart had decided otherwise. He'd once again prayed for the strength to resist temptation and even considered seeking advice from the minister. But the persistent strum of desire deep within him was too powerful. He was again about to defy the will of God and his community.

Before leaving, Jacob found his wife mopping the dining hall floor, where the colony's adults took their meals together, men on one side of the room, and women on the other. Children under fifteen ate in a separate dining room. It was Rachel's turn that week to work with the other women cooking for the community. It meant rising early, joining them to prepare breakfast, then working through the day on the rest of the meals.

"Do you want to take some sandwiches?" she asked.

"I'll get something in the city." Jacob took his wife's hands in his and squeezed them.

"Are you feeling any better?" she asked. From his moody silences, she knew something was bothering him, but he'd refused to tell her what it was.

"I'm fine. I'll be home in time to kiss the children goodnight."

Heading to the large parking lot, he checked his watch. He'd reach the city around 10:30.

Jacob drove northeast past small farming villages, examining the grain fields on either side of the black pickup. The golden wheat was stunted and sparse. The weather was constantly on his mind and that of every other member of the colony at this time of year. The drought had persisted through the summer, but it was too late for rain. It would only interfere with getting the crops off the fields.

He'd been wondering how bad the drought might be for the colony's income, but he let that worry go for now. He had bigger things on his mind, and nothing would be sure anyway until the grain was in the bin. Even then, they would face difficult choices about when and how much to sell. It was in God's hands, like everything else. A Chris Stapleton song came on the radio, and he felt the tension in his neck and across his shoulders release for the first time in days.

Traffic was heavier near the outskirts of Winnipeg. He glanced at his watch. His meeting with the lawyer was set for 11:30 a.m. He'd given himself an hour to navigate the city traffic and leave his stuff at the Airbnb on the northern edge of the Saint Boniface neighbourhood. The expensively renovated house wasn't his choice, but he'd been fascinated on his first visit there by its luxurious touches. Besides the high-end furnishings and linens, there were thick terry towel dressing gowns in the master bedroom and expensive toiletries in the bathrooms.

Jacob found a parking spot half a block from the house. Before exiting the truck, he pulled on a windbreaker to cover his suspenders and avoid sparking the neighbours' curiosity. Walking to the rental, he surveyed the park across the street, and, in the distance, a patch of forest along the banks of the Seine River. They'd taken a walk in those woods once, and it had felt like entering a secret, hidden world in the middle of the city. Being outdoors together had brought back childhood memories and the freedom they'd had then to roam the countryside. Now they tried not to be seen together, though there was little danger of word getting back to the colony.

He punched four numbers into the keypad, pushed the door open, kicked off his shoes, then made a quick tour of the place. He felt his feet sink into the thick beige carpet in the living room, where the furniture was upholstered in leather. In the adjoining dining room, an oak dinner table was surrounded by high-backed chairs, and the kitchen had a massive island, granite countertops, and stainless-steel appliances. The place had the same enticing aroma he'd smelled on his other visits. He'd been told it was sandalwood.

Upstairs, in the bedroom, he took his backpack into the en-suite bathroom. He washed his face and hands and returned to the main floor, ready to leave, when he was surprised by a knock at the back door. He glanced at his watch. It was hours before they'd agreed to meet, and Jacob had appointments to keep.

He glanced in the mirror over the mantle before hustling to the kitchen, anticipation growing in his chest. It had been weeks since they'd been able to see each other. He didn't bother to glance through the peephole before opening the door.

It was a mistake.

TWO

AT A RED LIGHT on Portage Avenue, Michael Shelter gave his head a hard shake and opened his eyes wide, trying to stave off the overwhelming desire for sleep. The exhaustion was intense. How the hell was he going to make it through this shift?

Raising his head, he glanced to his left and found his partner watching him from the driver's seat.

"You okay?"

"Just another night of bad sleep."

Gabriel Traverse hit the gas, in his usual relaxed slouch, two fingers and a thumb on the bottom of the steering wheel, his Ray-Bans on to filter the mid-afternoon sun.

Shelter had never been a great sleeper, but for the last couple of weeks he'd been tormented by a vivid nightmare. He found himself back in the dimly lit hallway, the young woman lying on her back in a pool of blood, her brown eyes pleading for help. The scene was terrifyingly real. It jolted him awake each time, leaving him breathless, covered in sweat, his heart racing.

"You call the doctor about that dream yet?"

"It'll pass."

They'd been partners for years, longer than any other detective team on the homicide unit. They could read each other's moods as well as any married couple, and it hadn't taken long for Traverse to pick up on changes in Shelter—his irritability and low energy. After hearing about the nightmares, Traverse had recommended a trip to the doctor.

Shelter was worried about it too, but he couldn't see what his GP could do for him except prescribe a different sleeping pill. The ones he already had made him groggy the next day, so he avoided taking them. He'd considered the possibility that a neurological problem was the source of his insomnia, dark moods, and more frequent headaches. His wife had died of brain cancer a decade earlier, and that had started with headaches. He thought about it again, then said under his breath, "It's not a tumour."

"What?"

"Nothing. I think I'm losing it."

"Ya think?"

They both smiled at that. Shelter was grateful for what had been a slow day. It was only a couple of hours until quitting time. Traffic was light, and Traverse was driving fast, heading to the North End to talk to a source. They hoped the guy—a low-level gang banger—would give up something useful on the murder of a drug dealer, but it was a long shot.

Shelter let his mind wander to the previous night and the couple of glasses of wine he'd downed. He knew alcohol wouldn't help his sleep, but he'd needed a drink.

He'd expected a regular, relaxing dinner with his girlfriend. But what began as a light-hearted discussion about the joys and miseries of having a kid had somehow escalated into a full-blown argument.

Penny had knocked off early that afternoon to see her sister's newborn daughter. As Shelter chopped vegetables for a salad, she told him about the wonder she'd felt at seeing the baby, musing about how great it would be to have a child together. Shelter, going along with her breezy tone, laughed and said, "Been there, done that."

The temperature drop had been sudden and unmistakable. He realized too late that he'd misjudged the situation. Still, the vehemence of Penny's reaction shook him. He was tired and quickly lost his temper. She insisted on how important this was to her. Shelter demanded more time to think about such a momentous decision. They went back and forth until she stormed out of the house. He opened a bottle of Cabernet Sauvignon and struggled to calm down.

Shelter was pulled from the memory by the buzz of his cellphone. It was Sam Breska, a staff sergeant at the police communications centre.

"We've got a body in a house in Saint B," Breska said. "A male. His throat's been cut." He paused a beat. "The victim's a Hutterite."

"You're kidding me."

"Nope. David Orest is the sergeant over there. He says he's sure from his ID and the way the guy's dressed."

"Okay. That's strange."

Shelter ended the call, took a moment to consider what he'd just heard, then relayed the news to Traverse, giving him the address in Saint Boniface.

"A Hutterite?" Traverse said, with a shake of his head. "Get outta here."

"Definitely a first."

"No kidding. And here I thought you'd seen it all at your age."

Shelter rolled his eyes and gave Traverse a knowing smile. It was a running joke between them. At forty, Traverse was only a couple of years younger than Shelter, but that didn't stop him from treating his partner like a fossil.

"What do you know about Hutterites?" Traverse asked.

"Like everybody else, I know one when I see one."

Shelter had been fascinated by Hutterites since he first saw them as a boy. They came in from the country on shopping trips and were impossible to miss. The women wore ankle-length dresses, white blouses, and black kerchiefs in their hair. The men were bearded, solidly built farmers in suspenders.

What little Shelter knew about them came from a university sociology class. They were deeply religious and lived apart from mainstream society in close-knit, largely self-sufficient rural communities known as colonies, scattered across southern Manitoba, the other prairie provinces, and the northern United States. He recalled that they shared Anabaptist beliefs with the Amish and Mennonites—principally adult baptism and strict pacifism. Unlike those other sects, though, the Hutterites lived communally, with all property owned by the colony, and all members' needs provided for from common resources.

It was useless to try to anticipate where the investigation would lead, but Shelter wondered how in the world a Hutterite could end up killed in a house in the city.

When they arrived, several cruisers and the forensic team's box truck were parked in front of the two-storey house, and yellow crime scene tape had been stretched between trees and fencing to block off the property. The homicide hadn't yet hit the local news, but it wouldn't take long for one of the neighbours gathering in the park on the other side of the street to alert the media to the police activity.

From the box truck's presence, Shelter knew technicians from the Forensic Identification Unit, known informally in the department as Ident, would already be working the scene. Ducking under the tape, he nodded to the uniform keeping watch at the door.

"The paramedics have already come and gone," the constable said.

At the top of the front stairs, Shelter turned so Traverse could see a rectangular black-and-silver doorbell video camera mounted to the moulding to the left of the door. The door jamb and lock appeared undamaged. He stepped into the entrance hall.

The stairs were on his right, and an expensively decorated living room was on his left. The victim was sprawled face up beside a glass coffee table a few metres from the arched entrance to the living room. A crimson oval stained the carpet, where blood had spread from the man's neck wound.

David Orest, the sergeant in charge of the scene, looked up from his notebook and gave the detectives a curt greeting. They'd met many times in these kinds of circumstances. Orest was in his late fifties, with a beer gut under his uniform, a shiny bald head, and a silver fringe cut close to the skull.

"Throat slashed?" Shelter asked.

"From behind, under the beard." Orest drew his pen across his neck at the level of his Adam's apple.

"Forced entry at the rear?"

Orest shook his head. "Uh-uh. The door was unlocked."

Shelter glanced at Traverse. The absence of forced entry and the attack from behind suggested the victim knew his assailant and might have turned his back, unaware of the danger.

"What have we got for ID?" Traverse asked.

Orest consulted his notebook. "From his driver's licence, his name is Jacob Waldner. The address is the Round Rock Hutterite Colony. That's near Krefeld. Thirty-three years old."

Shelter knew Krefeld well. It was a small farming town about an hour and a half southwest of Winnipeg.

"What do you think?"

"Not sure, but it doesn't look like a robbery. There's sixty bucks in the guy's wallet and a credit card in the Hutterite colony's name. No drugs that we've seen."

"Any sign of the weapon?"

"Not so far."

"How about a cellphone or computer?" Traverse asked.

"No sign of either. Do they even use them?"

Traverse shrugged.

"There *is* an empty briefcase on the dining room table." Orest passed Shelter three police-issued Ziploc bags marked Evidence. "Besides his wallet, this is all he had on him." One bag held a bulky black vehicle key, another a plain ring with half a dozen keys, and the third a small silver key no longer than a paper clip.

"That's not a house key," Shelter said, bringing the bag with the small single key close to his eyes before handing it to Traverse to examine.

Passing it back to the sergeant, Traverse asked, "Who owns this place?"

"It's an Airbnb," Orest said, his eyes returning to his notebook. "The owner's name is Abbas Khalil. He called it in."

Traverse took down the name and address.

"He says the guy who rented the Airbnb phoned him to report the body."

"Sorry?" Traverse said. "The victim didn't rent this place?"

"Apparently not. It's someone named Elias Stahl."

"He found the body but didn't call 911?" Shelter asked.

"That's the story."

Shelter glanced at Traverse, who gave him a mystified look. "Where's the owner?"

"Outside in a cruiser. He's pretty freaked out. He's waiting to talk to you guys."

"We saw there's a doorbell camera. Have you seen others?"

Orest shook his head. "Not so far. The owner says there's only the one. Nothing inside or covering the back."

"Have you looked at the video?"

"Uh-uh. Left that for you guys."

Approaching the corpse, Shelter's eyes went to a spray of blood across the coffee table and the couch cushions. The pattern was typical of blood spurting from a severed artery. It had dripped down the base of the couch. More blood had pumped from the angry neck wound and seeped into the carpet. With this much blood, he was hoping the assailant had stepped in it, but he couldn't see any tread marks or other disturbance. Whoever had slashed this guy's throat had been careful where they stepped.

Shelter bent at the waist to examine the wound more closely. The throat was a wet, crimson mass of exposed crescent-shaped tissue, over two inches at its widest. He noted the cut started close to the jawbone under the left ear and ended near the collarbone on the right side of the throat. That suggested a right-handed assailant.

In that moment, Shelter felt his pulse race, his gut tighten, and a chill run down his spine. He'd examined dozens of corpses and had always been able to quickly bring his physical reactions under control, but this time was different. His face grew hot, and he felt sweat beading on his brow. He should've been able to assess the body objectively, but he found himself panting, trying to get air into his lungs. He had the strange impression that he was both participant and observer of the scene playing out before him. He watched Traverse peer at the body beside him and suddenly felt light-headed. He staggered sideways, bumping into Traverse hard and almost falling.

Traverse gripped his shoulder. "Whoa!"

Shelter gave a quick, hard shake of his head, embarrassed, took a step back and looked Traverse in the eyes. "I got dizzy there for a sec. I'm okay."

Traverse studied him, his brow wrinkled with concern. "You're not looking so good, man. You better sit down."

Shelter raised a hand. "No. I'm okay." But he was shaken. He'd never experienced anything like what had just happened.

Traverse still had his eyes locked on him. "You sure?"

"Yeah. No. I'm good."

After a moment, Traverse returned his attention to the body. Shelter took a step forward to stand beside him. But he still felt woozy, and his face was warm. He forced himself to hold still, discreetly taking deep breaths and struggling to focus on the body in front of him. Over the next minute, he sensed his heartbeat slow and felt himself regain control.

He returned his full attention to the corpse in front of him. From his elementary knowledge of anatomy, Shelter could see that Jacob Waldner's carotid artery and windpipe had been severed. The precision of the cut, made from behind in one movement, showed expertise. He wasn't a pathologist, but it seemed unlikely the victim could have cried out. With blood cut off to the brain, he suspected loss of consciousness would have been almost immediate, death just a few minutes later.

He took a step back to stand in front of the picture window overlooking the street, where he was joined by Traverse. Together, they surveyed the scene. Except for the blood and the corpse, the room seemed undisturbed. Shelter's reading was that the killer had attacked Waldner from behind as he entered the living room. The weapon, method of attack, and otherwise undisturbed room didn't point to a frenzied murder driven by rage or fear. It looked planned.

Traverse apparently had come to the same conclusion. "Clean job," he whispered.

There were three bedrooms upstairs, all with new, high-end furniture and finishes that made them look like expensive hotel rooms. In the master bedroom, Shelter nodded to a female Ident technician dusting a nightstand for fingerprints. The king-size bed was neatly made, with white pillows propped against the headboard and a ruby blanket neatly folded at the foot. Sunlight filtered through sheer curtains covering the windows. He peered into the bathroom and noted a hand towel thrown on the sink, but no other signs of use. He'd only ever stayed in hotels and had never rented an Airbnb. He wondered how much it would cost for a place like this. Certainly, it wouldn't be cheap.

A small backpack lay unzipped on the bed. He used a pen to lift the corner of a neatly folded shirt to look underneath and saw nothing but a pair of underwear and socks. Apart from that, the room looked unoccupied. A selection of current magazines and a TV remote were neatly arranged on a chest of drawers under the large screen mounted on the wall.

"Let's go talk to the owner," Shelter said.

At the top of the stairs, Traverse touched his arm. "Hold up a sec. What happened to you down there?"

"It's nothing. I just felt a bit dizzy all of a sudden." He wasn't going to tell his partner or anyone else about the bizarre out-of-body experience.

"Has it happened before?"

"No. I'm fine."

"I mean it. Maybe you should go home. I'll finish up here."

Shelter sensed anger boiling up from his gut. "Hey, I said I'm good. Let it go."

Traverse raised his hands and cocked his head. "You're the boss."

Shelter felt instant regret. He knew Traverse was just concerned for him. The sleeplessness, nightmares, and now this scary experience—he had to admit it had all begun after the shooting, and it seemed to be getting worse by the day.

Was he becoming a danger to his partner and himself? Traverse might be asking himself the same question.

THREE

IT HAD STARTED with a tip about a young woman who'd shot and killed her boyfriend the day before. Shelter and Traverse had tracked her to a rundown house in the West End. Once the tactical team had searched the place and determined it was empty, the detectives moved in to look for clues to the woman's whereabouts.

Shelter was going through the kitchen drawers when he thought he heard a thump upstairs. The sound had been so faint that he questioned whether he'd actually heard it. Traverse was in the basement, and no one else was supposed to be in the house.

Shelter drew his pistol and crept toward the main hallway. He'd just passed through the kitchen door when he heard a stair creak to his left. He looked up and locked eyes with a young woman on the staircase. She was carrying a long gun.

"Police! Freeze."

The woman leaped down the stairs two at a time. At the bottom, she pivoted toward Shelter and brought the double-barrelled shotgun to her shoulder in the same motion.

Shelter squeezed the trigger three times. The sound of the Glock firing exploded in the silent house. The force of the bullets threw the woman onto her back. The shotgun clattered to the floor beside her.

His ears ringing from the blasts, Shelter gasped for breath. His heart pounded so hard it felt like it would jump out of his chest. He heard Traverse banging up the stairs from the basement behind him.

His pistol raised, Shelter approached the woman and kicked the shotgun away. She had greasy black hair and was dressed in jeans and a grey T-shirt. Her face was swollen and badly bruised—evidence, Shelter assumed, of a recent beating.

He heard Traverse blurt, "Holy shit!"

"Call an ambulance!"

The woman's eyes were closed, and she was struggling to breathe. Kneeling beside her, Shelter smelled the distinct copper odour of blood. Pink foam bubbled from her mouth. Her shirt was wet from the blood pumping out of her wounds. It began to pool on the floor under his knees.

He was preparing to administer CPR when the woman's eyes opened and locked on his face. He whispered, "I've got you."

She drew in a deep breath and let it out in a long stream. Her lips moved. She tried to speak, but no sound came out.

He touched her shoulder. "Stay with me."

Her head lolled to the side, and Shelter knew in that moment she was dead. Still, he went on administering CPR for long minutes until the paramedics took over.

As other cops arrived on the scene, Shelter stumbled out of the house in a daze and stood on the front sidewalk, drawing in the cool spring air. He hugged himself to stop shivering as the adrenaline jolt to his system slowly dissipated.

He tried to process what had just happened. He went over the shooting, moment by moment, trying to think of what he could have done differently. Before heading out that morning, he'd read through the woman's file. She was just twenty years old, the same age as his daughter. Since earliest childhood, she'd endured a grim, poverty-stricken life. Her mother had been addicted to drugs and alcohol, and the girl had been shunted from one foster home to another. When she aged out of the child welfare system, she'd followed her mother into addiction and became involved with the violent abuser she eventually killed.

Court records showed the man had been convicted two years earlier for an assault that put the woman in the hospital with missing teeth, a broken nose, and fractured ribs. Apparently, she'd returned to the man sometime after his release from jail—a sad but not infrequent occurrence.

Shelter knew it was far more common for violent men to kill women, and he thought about the terrible physical and mental suffering this woman must have endured to take the step of killing her abuser. Now she too lay dead.

Traverse came down the front steps. He put a hand on Shelter's neck and drew him close until their foreheads were touching. "You did what you had to do, buddy," he said, giving Shelter's neck a gentle squeeze.

Pulling back, Shelter met his partner's eyes. "She never had a chance in life."

"That's not your fault. None of it's your fault, okay? You gotta get clear on that."

Over the next several days, Shelter's professional life was controlled by rigid procedures following a critical incident, as it was called in the police department's sanitized, bureaucratic language.

He was required to go on leave and undergo a mandatory assessment by a department psychologist, who turned out to be a grey-haired woman in a cardigan and a knee-length, pleated skirt. She reminded him of the ladies in his mother's bridge club as she gently questioned him about his feelings about the shooting and what else was going on in his life. He assured her that he'd seen many terrible things during his career, and while he regretted being forced to take the woman's life, he'd come to terms with the reality that he'd had no choice. The psychologist cleared him to return to work the following week.

As was the case for all "police-involved shootings," the civilian Independent Investigation Unit conducted a probe. A search of the house found an open trap door to the attic in one of the upstairs closets. That's where the woman had been hiding. The shotgun she'd pointed at Shelter was the same one she'd used to kill her boyfriend. It'd been ready to fire—loaded and the safety off—when Shelter shot her. The investigative unit's final report wouldn't come out for months, but the circumstances left no doubt that it would conclude the shooting had been justified.

At home, Penny was horrified by the incident and worried about the toll it would take on Shelter. But he'd insisted he was fine and cut short her attempts to discuss his emotional reactions to what had happened.

When he was cleared to return to work, he assured her he was ready to go back, and he fully believed it himself. He wasn't a delicate flower. He'd always been able to keep an even emotional keel and move on from distressing scenes he'd witnessed. He kept his focus on the job at hand and did his best to maintain a mental boundary between his professional and personal lives. This time should have been no different.

It was a month after the shooting when he began to have trouble sleeping. When he finally drifted off, he'd find himself back in that hallway, staring into the young woman's pleading eyes. The nightmare was terrifyingly real. And once, in the past week, the images had even replayed in his mind while he was awake. He found himself reliving the shooting in real time, in the same vivid, frightening detail. He'd kept these haunting episodes to himself, pushing away the anxiety and telling himself he just needed time to get his head straight.

Now, back on the main floor of the house in Saint Boniface, Shelter should have been focused on the discussion Traverse was having with Orest about canvassing surrounding houses for witnesses. But his thoughts kept returning to the strange out-of-body experience and dizziness he'd suffered earlier. It felt like he'd come close to fainting. As he left the house, he touched Traverse's arm on the front stairs. "I know I don't have to say it, but I'm going to say it anyway. What happened earlier stays between us, okay?"

Traverse raised an eyebrow and shook his head in exasperation. "You got it."

After so many years working together, Shelter knew his partner would be hurt by the suggestion that he'd ever betray his confidence. But Shelter couldn't help himself. Doubts in the department about his mental health would mean sick leave or worse—being forced into a desk job or even retirement.

But asking Traverse to keep quiet was out of character. It would be another signal that something was wrong.

The Airbnb owner was in the back of a cruiser. Shelter opened the door and asked him to step out of the vehicle. The man looked to be in his late forties with wiry, neatly trimmed black hair and a beard. He wore beige slacks and a blue Oxford shirt with a button-down collar. His black loafers were polished to a high shine. His eyes darted from one detective to the other through steel-rimmed designer glasses.

"I'm Detective Sergeant Michael Shelter, and this is Detective Sergeant Gabriel Traverse. And you are?"

"I am Abbas." He spoke with an Arabic accent.

"Abbas is your first name?" Traverse asked.

The man looked from Traverse to Shelter.

"We need your full name, sir."

"Yes, of course. It is Khalil. Abbas Khalil." With an embarrassed smile, he added, "I'm sorry. It's been a hard afternoon."

"We can speak in our car just over here," Traverse said, pointing to their sedan a little way down the street. Once they got Khalil in the back seat, Shelter and Traverse slid into the front and turned to speak to him.

"Our colleague says you found the body," Shelter said.

Khalil looked down at his clenched fists in his lap. From his furrowed brow and hunched shoulders, Shelter assumed the initial shock at discovering the body had given way to worry about being drawn into a murder investigation.

He enunciated each word precisely. "I receive call from the man who rents the house."

"What did he say exactly?"

"'There is dead man in the house. Call police.' This is all. He hanged up."

"But you didn't call the police. You went to the house instead?"

Khalil paused. "I really could not believe it was true. I live close to here and work at home. I came right away."

"What did you do then?" Traverse asked.

"I knock on the door. No answer, and I open it. Going into the living room, I see man lying on floor." Khalil started wringing his hands. "A very terrible thing. Much blood."

"And you called 911," Traverse said. The call had come in just before 3:00 p.m.

Khalil laid a palm over his heart and looked out the car window toward the park.

Shelter struggled to make sense of the story. Elias Stahl rents an Airbnb where Jacob Waldner is murdered. Stahl is at the house at some point, flees the scene, but then calls the homeowner to tell him about the dead man.

"You have a doorbell camera. The other officer told us this is the only camera inside or outside the house. Is that correct?"

"Yes. I respect the privacy of my guests."

"Did you see Elias Stahl today or anyone else going in or out of the house?"

"I look at video from doorbell camera. I saw a first man come and then, later, Mr. Stahl enter and leave. No one else."

"Show us the video, please," Traverse said.

Khalil dug his cellphone out of his coat pocket and tapped on an app icon. After a few moments, he passed the phone to Traverse. The detective held the device at arm's length so both he and Shelter could view the images.

The camera was motion-activated, and the first clip was time-stamped 10:37 a.m. It showed Jacob Waldner, wearing a windbreaker and a baseball cap, climbing the front stairs and using the keypad to let himself into the house.

"Play it again," Shelter asked. This time, he kept his eyes on the street behind Waldner, looking for anyone who might have been following him. No one was visible.

The next clip was time-stamped 2:07 p.m. It showed a young blond man in a beige open-collar shirt and jeans arriving at the house. Traverse stopped the video and turned the phone to Khalil. "Do you recognize this man?"

"It is Mr. Stahl."

"You've met before?"

"No. We communicate by text and email."

"So how do you know what he looks like?"

"From a photo in the newspaper. I know where he works."

Shelter looked up from his notebook. "Where?"

"He's in charge of the Reservoir Art Gallery on McDermot. For Airbnb, there is also a photo of the person who makes the reservation."

Shelter let out an audible sigh as he made a note. This was getting stranger by the second.

Four minutes after Stahl entered the house, he came back into the frame, scurrying down the front walk with a hand to his mouth. From there, Traverse played clips of Khalil's arrival and the first uniforms showing up at 3:13 p.m.

Khalil reached for his phone, but Traverse told him he'd keep it until a technician could download the video after they finished talking. Khalil's mouth tightened in annoyance, but he made no objection.

Shelter asked, "Do you have Mr. Stahl's home address on record?"

"No. Just his phone number and email."

"What were the arrangements for the rental of the house?"

"Mr. Stahl books it usually a week before, if it's free. This time, he contacted me yesterday and asked if it was available."

Shelter glanced at Traverse. The last-minute booking suggested that something had caused Jacob Waldner to come to Winnipeg unexpectedly. Something within the last twenty-four to forty-eight hours.

"I replied the house was free," Khalil said. "Check-in was at 10:00 a.m."

"A check-in time in the morning?" Traverse asked. "Is that unusual?"

Khalil fidgeted. "This is the check-in time when you take the room for only daytime hours. Mr. Stahl always takes it only for the day. He told me it would be free at five o'clock today."

"You communicated by email. So, it's not rented through Airbnb?" Traverse asked.

"The first time, yes, and then we took it off the app to save fees on both sides."

"How many times has he rented it?"

"I would have to look, but from memory, three or four times in the last year."

"And Mr. Waldner? What was the relationship between him and Mr. Stahl?"

"I do not know Mr. Waldner."

"Did you try to call Mr. Stahl this afternoon about what happened?"

"No. I have been with the police."

Another detective would supervise the collection of any video footage from neighbouring houses and from the nearby main arteries that Waldner might have taken to get to the house. That would mean collecting footage from security cameras used by stores along the route, traffic-control cameras at main intersections, and cameras on city buses, trained on the road ahead.

They sent Khalil downtown to give a formal statement. His alibi would be checked in the hours to come.

Once he'd left, Traverse said, "So, he's running an afternoon delight service on this street?"

"Times are tough," Shelter said. "But why the last-minute booking?"

Traverse shrugged. "Good question."

It hadn't taken long for the uniforms to find Waldner's black pickup parked on the street and connect the licence plate to the Round Rock Hutterite Colony. Shelter peered into the truck from the driver's side window and saw nothing on the seats. Ident would tow it to their garage for examination.

Next, he pulled up a database and matched Elias Stahl to an address on Waterfront Drive, a short distance away, on the other side of the Red River. It was just after 5:00 p.m., and Shelter knew they'd hit rush-hour traffic crossing the Provencher Bridge into downtown. They were about to pull out when Shelter's cellphone buzzed in his pocket. It was their boss, Neil MacIsaac. Shelter held the phone up to Traverse so he could see the name on the screen before answering.

As usual, MacIsaac didn't bother with preliminaries. "What's going on over there?"

"We've got a Hutterite in a house with his throat slashed."

"I know that, for chrissake. Making any headway?" Shelter was used to MacIsaac's jittery nerves and explosive temper. He held the cellphone an inch from his ear. "What's he doing in the city to start with?"

"That's what we're trying to figure out." Shelter kept his tone bland. He refused to be drawn into MacIsaac's little universe of stress. "We've got a solid lead. Someone else rented the house—a guy who lives on Waterfront Drive. We're heading over there to talk to him now."

MacIsaac chewed over the information for a second. "Okay. Have you called out to wherever this Hutterite comes from?"

"We've been on it for an hour, Neil. I'm just getting to it. It's near Krefeld. We're going to have to go through the RCMP for the next-of-kin notification." The notification had to be done immediately because of the risk that the news would come out before the family was informed.

"There's going to be hell to pay when this hits the media. Are you heading out to the country to talk to these people?"

"That's the plan." Shelter had already decided they had enough to keep them busy in the city in the coming hours, and, given the distance, a trip to the Hutterite colony would have to wait until first thing in the morning.

"Keep me in the loop, and let's not go crazy on overtime."

Shelter pocketed the phone and shook his head at Traverse.

"A bit grumpy, is he?" Traverse asked.

"When is he not? Let me call the Mounties and get someone out to notify the family."

As he searched for the number for the RCMP communications centre, Shelter thought about how traumatic the news would be for the close-knit Hutterite community, not just at Round Rock but for colonies throughout the province.

He recalled reading about the drowning of a Hutterite teenager a few years earlier. The death had brought hundreds of mourners to the funeral. It was the first spring of the pandemic, and the gathering was blamed for some of the earliest COVID outbreaks in Manitoba. Up to that point, the province had been mostly spared from infection, and the appearance of cases in Hutterite colonies shocked residents of nearby towns. It sparked ugly incidents where Hutterites had insults hurled at them and were refused service.

Provincial politicians and health officials had to appeal for calm and, in response to complaints from Hutterite leaders, stopped identifying colonies as the source of outbreaks. It hadn't taken much for prejudice and simmering resentment toward the Hutterites to boil over.

At the RCMP command centre, a woman answered and identified herself as Constable Sharon Dombrowski.

"Detective Sergeant Michael Shelter. Homicide at the WPS."

"What can I do for you?"

"We've got a homicide at a house in Saint Boniface. He's from out of town, and we need you to go around and notify the next of kin."

"You've got an address?"

"He's from the Round Rock Hutterite Colony, not far from Krefeld."

There was silence on the other end of the line. "You're saying the victim's a Hutterite? You gotta be kidding me."

"I said the same thing." Consulting his notebook, Shelter gave the Mountie the colony's address and Jacob Waldner's name and date of birth.

"What should we tell them about the circumstances?" Dombrowski asked.

"We don't know much ourselves. So, let's just tell them it appears he was the victim of a homicide near downtown Winnipeg. You can say we still don't have many details and that no arrests have been made." Shelter could hear the constable typing as he spoke. "You can also tell them Winnipeg police will visit tomorrow morning and hopefully have more information to share with them at that time. Okay?"

"Yeah, got it. It'll be the Carman detachment. They should be able to send someone right away."

"Thanks. And one more thing: No questions from your guys about what Waldner was doing in Winnipeg, okay? We'll be there in the morning."

FOUR

RIDING IN THE PASSENGER SEAT, Shelter plugged Elias Stahl's name into Google, and a series of news articles and blog posts about him popped up. "He's the executive director and curator of the Reservoir gallery," he told Traverse as they crossed the wide, slow-moving Red River.

He read from the gallery's website, "Dynamic contemporary art from leading Canadian and international artists." Shelter knew the gallery by sight and its reputation for showing avant-garde art, but he'd never been inside. He perused the board of directors and recognized a few names from well-to-do families. "The board and list of patrons look very white and very well-heeled."

Stahl's home address was on the edge of the city's Exchange District, a collection of heritage brick and limestone warehouses and office buildings. Stahl's place was on the fourth floor of a recently constructed brick condo facing the river. Across the street was a walkway that followed the riverbank south for a kilometre to where the Red met the Assiniboine River. The view of the river and Saint Boniface beyond would have made an already expensive condo even pricier.

There was no answer when Shelter pushed the intercom button. He took the three steps down to the sidewalk, where Traverse was waiting, and glanced upward. A call to Stahl's phone went to voicemail.

"The gallery is around the corner," Traverse said. "Maybe he's over there."

The art gallery was in a converted nineteenth-century warehouse. From the care taken in restoring the tan brick facade, wood trim, and limestone, Shelter could see that the building had been expensively renovated. The gallery took up a large space to the right of the building's central door. Three tall, arched windows would provide natural illumination for artwork. There was no sign, just one word in discreet black lettering in the corner of the window closest to the entrance: *Reservoir*.

A woman who lived upstairs happened to arrive and let them into the building. Looking through the gallery's locked glass door, Shelter saw a beam of light reflecting off the ceiling at the far end of the long room. "Looks like someone's in there."

Traverse rapped hard, and after a few seconds, a figure appeared at the other end of the gallery. From the photos he'd seen on Google Images, Shelter knew the man approaching was too old to be Elias Stahl. He was bald and looked to be in his early sixties. He unlocked the door and opened it to the width of his slim body, his eyes behind an expensive-looking pair of oval rimless glasses. "Yes?"

Shelter held up his ID. "Winnipeg police. Is Elias Stahl here?"

The man squinted at the ID, then stepped aside. "Please come in."

In the entrance area, he said, "I'm Leonard Diamond, chairman of Reservoir's board. Elias is here, but he's had a terrible shock and is very upset. We are aware of Jacob Waldner's death. He was a close friend of Elias's."

Diamond wore a fine navy-blue wool sweater over a crisp, open-necked white dress shirt. His grey slacks were freshly pressed, and his suede loafers looked as soft as slippers.

"How are you aware of his death?" Traverse asked.

"Elias telephoned and asked me to come down to be with him. He told me he found the body."

"But he hasn't contacted the police?"

"We were just about to," Diamond said. "I've only just arrived myself, and I told Elias it was imperative he call immediately. But he's frightened and isn't thinking clearly. This way, please."

Diamond led the detectives through the gallery. The hardwood flooring had been polished to a high gloss. Exposed beams ran the length of the ceiling. Abstract paintings of different dimensions were mounted on white walls beneath unlit track lighting. A large installation dominated the centre of the gallery. To Shelter's eyes, it seemed haphazardly put together from discarded construction materials—wire mesh, lumber, and cinder blocks, with an old television set at its centre. A temporary wall stood at the end of the gallery, displaying an arrangement of four small paintings that Shelter took to depict desolate prairie scenes.

Diamond led the way around the wall. Shelter saw a darkened office and a glassed-in conference room where a young man sat, leaning forward in his chair, his head bowed, and his eyes closed.

Elias Stahl remained silent during the introductions. Shelter studied him as he and Traverse took chairs across the table. He was struck by Stahl's red-rimmed, piercing blue eyes. He looked to be in his early thirties, with high cheekbones, full lips, and carefully tended stubble. His thick, dirty blond hair was parted on the side and fell to the nape of his neck. He was dressed in what appeared to be the same attire they'd seen in the video: a cream-coloured linen shirt, jeans, and black canvas shoes visible beneath the glass-top table. There were no cuts or bruises on his face or hands, but he wore a gold ring on the third finger of his left hand.

This was a delicate situation. Stahl was the first and obvious choice for a suspect, and he'd fled the scene of Jacob's murder without calling the police. But he hadn't abandoned the body for someone else to find. He'd called Khalil to alert him and then stayed put downtown rather than trying to evade police. His behaviour was suspicious, but it could have been the result of shock.

For the moment, they'd treat him as a person of interest in the investigation, not a formal suspect. But the moment it looked like Stahl might be the killer, it was imperative that they give him his rights, arrest him, and take him downtown for a formal interview. Otherwise, his lawyer would have a field day at trial questioning their motives and police work, and there'd be a good chance Stahl would walk free. One way or another, they'd need a recorded statement from him, but for now, they'd get the basics.

Once Shelter had confirmed Stahl's full name, address, and date of birth, he turned to Traverse to take over the questioning.

"We're investigating the murder of Jacob Waldner in a house in Saint Boniface," Traverse said. "Mr. Diamond tells us you are aware of Mr. Waldner's death. Tell us everything you remember about what happened, starting from the beginning. Please include as much detail as possible, even if it seems unimportant."

"Just a moment." It was Leonard Diamond, seated at the head of the table. He held up a hand to Stahl and swivelled to face Shelter and Traverse. "I'm a doctor, not a lawyer, but it seems to me Elias should talk to one before he goes on?"

Traverse shrugged in Diamond's direction. "That's up to him. He's not under arrest, and he's free to call a lawyer or stop talking to us at any time." He returned his gaze to Stahl. "But I'd think you'd want to give us all the help you can in finding whoever killed Jacob."

Diamond sank back into his chair and looked to Stahl. The young man nodded that he was ready to go on. Still, Diamond pulled a cellphone from his pocket and laid it on the table, a gesture Shelter took to mean he was ready to call a lawyer at any time.

Stahl sat up, lifted his eyes to the ceiling, and sighed loudly. Not bothering with the box of tissues in front of him, he wiped a shirt sleeve across his eyes and nose. Lowering his chin, he rested his eyes on Traverse.

"I saw him," he blurted, his voice choked with phlegm. "Oh, God." Tears filled his eyes, and he splayed his fingers on the table.

The detectives waited for Stahl to compose himself. "What did you see?" Traverse asked.

"I saw Jacob lying in the living room. He'd been attacked, and there was blood everywhere. I went near. He was dead. No doubt."

"What time was this?" Shelter asked.

"We were supposed to meet at the house at 2:00 p.m. He was going to message me to say he was there, but he didn't. I kept texting and calling him. He wasn't answering. So, I finally went over there."

"At what time?"

"Just after two. Ten after, I guess, by the time I got there."

Shelter detected a German accent, but it was very faint—only on certain words. His hands were shaking. "You didn't call the police or an ambulance. Why?"

Stahl dropped his eyes to his hands and used the fingers of his right hand to spin the ring. "I was upset and scared. I panicked," he said. It came out in an anxious, pleading way. "I just had to get out of there. I went back to my apartment, called the owner, and told him. I knew he'd call the police."

Shelter was skeptical. His working assumption was that Stahl had killed his friend and fled in a panic. He'd failed to call the police because he needed time to clean himself up, dispose of the weapon, and get his story straight. He'd remembered renting the room and been fearful of talking to the police, so he'd called Khalil. Shelter studied the crown of Stahl's downcast head for a moment. "Why were you meeting Jacob at the house?"

When Stahl spoke, Shelter was struck by a change in his tone. The young man became calmer and more assertive, as if he were giving a presentation.

"I've known Jacob since we were little boys. I'm a Hutterite from the same colony." He paused, took a tissue from the box in front of him, and blew his nose loudly. "I was eighteen, and he was nineteen, when we left together. They call it running away—*Weglaufen*—in our language. Some outsiders call it defection. I call it escaping from a cult."

His eyes went to the ceiling as he seemed to muse over the different words to describe his departure from the Round Rock Hutterite Colony. "I read a book once that described it as the most shameful thing you can do as a Hutterite. They may see it that way, but I've never thought of it in those terms. I had no choice."

Returning his eyes to meet Shelter's, he said, "After a few months, Jacob went back. Living in the city, away from the colony, was too hard for him. But we stayed close."

"You met in rented rooms?" Shelter asked.

Stahl's eyes narrowed, and his tone became challenging. "Maybe not the most shameful thing, yeah?" He gave a sad smirk. "What is it you want to know? Were we lovers? The answer is yes, but it was much more complicated than that. More complicated than you could understand."

"Try us," Traverse said.

"We loved each other since we were kids. We left together, and he chose to go back alone, get married, and have children." Stahl went silent for a few seconds. "We met when we could. He has a wife, and I have a husband. As Hutterites, we know a lot about keeping secrets. We're good at it. Many rules, many secrets."

Shelter considered this information. Not only did the two men have to keep the secret from Jacob Waldner's wife and the closed, devout community of the colony, but also from Stahl's husband. Complicated indeed.

As though sensing his thoughts, Elias said, "Jacob was tormented by it. He was a believer, a family man, and a leader in the colony. He knew what we were doing was a grave sin in the eyes of the faith and the community. But he loved me."

Shelter watched Elias closely. If he was the killer, it would have been a crime of passion, unless there was another deeper secret between the two men. But a crime of passion normally implied a struggle, bruising, and defensive wounds. There was no evidence of a struggle at the crime scene or injuries on Elias. He hadn't seen any on Waldner either, though a cursory visual evaluation was far from conclusive at this point. For that, they'd have to wait for the autopsy. Skin under Waldner's fingernails, bruising under his clothing, or other forensic evidence could indicate there had indeed been a fight. Nevertheless, Waldner's killer had slashed his victim's throat from behind in what looked like a decisive motion and then left with the blade. That suggested a premeditated crime.

"Did you kill Jacob?" Shelter asked.

Stahl glared at him in horror. "Oh my God, no. I loved him."

"Then who would have wanted to kill him?"

"I have no idea," Stahl said, his voice rising again with anxiety.

After a moment, Traverse said, "Lead us through your day."

Stahl's face glistened with a film of sweat. He reached for another tissue and patted his forehead and cheeks, giving himself time to gather his thoughts before beginning.

"This morning, I called Jacob at the colony to confirm he was coming. Then I worked on the last-minute details for a major exhibition opening here tomorrow. The launch party is tomorrow evening, for God's sake." He sighed and rubbed his hands over his thighs at the thought.

"When did you reserve the Airbnb?" Traverse asked.

"Yesterday. I was surprised to get a message from Jacob saying he'd be in town today. I really didn't have time, but I see him so rarely."

"Where were you before you went to the house?"

"I was with my assistant at the gallery for most of the day."

"Name?"

"Li-Min Huang."

"You say you were together for most of the day. Why and when were you apart?"

"I went out around noon to pick up some lunch for us."

Shelter made a note. The assistant would be interviewed, and every detail of Stahl's story would be checked.

"Where and what did you buy for lunch?"

"There's a restaurant on the other side of Main Street. I picked up sandwiches."

"How long were you gone for?"

"Twenty minutes?"

It would be a stretch, but in theory it was enough time for him to get to Saint Boniface, enter through the rear entrance, commit the murder, and get back.

"You said you went to meet Jacob at 2:00 p.m. Did anyone see you on the way or when you got there?"

Stahl shook his head.

"Did you remove anything from the house?"

"No. Of course not. What would I remove?"

"Did Jacob usually bring a laptop with him?"

"Yes, in a briefcase with his papers."

"Did he have a cellphone?"

"Yes."

"What was his number?"

He took out his phone and showed them Jacob's number.

"When you spoke to him this morning, was he upset?"

"Not that I noticed, but we only spoke for a second. We agreed he would text me when he got to the house, but I didn't hear from him."

"Why was he in town? Just to see you?"

Stahl shook his head and gave a rueful laugh.

"Hutterites can't just go wherever they please. He had to inform the elders that he needed to go to the city for business."

"What business?"

"I assume he needed to see their lawyer about a dispute they're having over a piece of land."

"But you said it was a last-minute thing. It wasn't planned in advance?"

"No. Like I said, he texted me yesterday, and I made the reservation for the Airbnb."

"Texted you when?"

"In the afternoon."

"Let's see the texts."

Stahl handed over his phone, and Shelter scanned the exchange before taking a picture of it. The late notice of the trip to the city confirmed that whatever had brought Jacob to town likely happened in the last forty-eight hours. Before Shelter could ask more about the land dispute, an idea struck Stahl.

"Have you told his wife and mother?"

"They're being told as we speak," Shelter said. "We're heading out there tomorrow."

A new intensity came over Stahl's face as he seemed to come to grips with the implications. "This is going to be terrible. Don't tell them about us, about our relationship. Please."

Shelter glanced at Leonard Diamond, then back at Stahl. He was about to speak when Traverse cut in, "We can't very well tell the family that Jacob was killed in a house without explaining what he was doing there."

"No, please. You have no idea what this means."

"We have lots of experience explaining difficult things to families," Traverse said.

"A colony is not like the outside world—the English world, as they call it." Stahl stood and paced the length of the table before turning to face the detectives. The anxiety sent his voice a pitch higher.

"It's not just his death. That's bad enough. But for them, what Jacob and I were doing means he will burn in Hell for eternity, quite literally. It means we cannot enter the kingdom of God, cannot join our families there. That will be more painful than you can imagine for his wife, his mother, and the whole colony. I know because my parents live with it every day."

Diamond cleared his throat. "There's more than just the impact on the families. Elias is one of the most respected young voices in contemporary art today. I'm not just talking about Canada. I'm talking globally. He is an extraordinary talent. His expertise is sought by leading galleries in New York, Berlin, Shanghai, and elsewhere. Being publicly linked to this crime would be very damaging to his reputation. Surely, you can understand the need for discretion."

Shelter ignored this. The impact on this man's reputation in the art world was the least of their concerns.

"What's this about a land dispute?" Traverse asked.

Stahl made a visible effort to calm himself and refocus. "It has to do with a piece of land for a new colony, but I don't know the details. Jacob didn't want to talk about it, and I don't care, frankly."

"You mentioned you're married," Shelter said. "Is your husband aware of your relationship with Jacob?"

"Yes, as a matter of fact, he is. We have an understanding when it comes to Jacob."

Shelter considered this revelation. Despite Elias's claim about his open relationship, a jealous husband could be another strong line of investigation. As he mulled over this unexpected twist, Stahl reacted sharply to something in his expression.

"You're shocked by the arrangement Martin and I have, or maybe you're uncomfortable with gays in general?"

Shelter looked into Stahl's eyes and allowed himself a slight smile. The comment was so far off base as to be laughable. He'd had close gay friends since university and no longer gave much thought to it. The world—at least his corner of it—had moved far beyond discomfort about homosexuality. But he felt no need to make a "some of my best friends are gay" speech to this guy.

"What's your husband's name, and where is he now?"

"Martin Garnier. I'm not sure where he is at the moment."

"But you called him and told him what happened to Jacob, right?" Traverse asked.

"No. He wasn't at home. I decided to come over here and call Leonard for advice."

This was odd, Shelter thought, and the way Stahl said it seemed strangely detached from the gravity of the situation. He'd abandoned his dead and horribly mutilated lover without calling emergency services and then didn't even get in touch with his husband. Instead, he called the chairman of the art gallery where he worked. There was also a gap of several hours between the time he would have arrived home and his arrival at the gallery to meet Diamond. What had he been doing during that time?

"I don't understand why you wouldn't call your husband," Shelter said.

"I've been very busy preparing this exhibition, and let's say things have been difficult between us." He looked through the glass toward the empty gallery in shadows. "We haven't been speaking."

"Where have you been since you called the owner of the Airbnb?"

"I was at home, by myself. I didn't know what to think or do. Finally, I decided to call Mr. Diamond. He's been a great mentor to me."

"We'll need your husband's phone number. And you'll also have to come downtown to make a formal statement and give a DNA sample and your fingerprints."

"Now?" The tone was petulant.

"Yes, now."

"I've told you everything I know, and I still have a lot of work to do tonight for our exhibition opening."

Shelter was again struck by this man's disengagement from what was happening here. It couldn't be lost on him that he was a suspect in the murder of his lover. And now he wanted to go back to work? Shelter wondered whether his earlier tears had been a mask and whether the focused, calculating man in front of him could plan and coolly carry out a murder.

Shelter stood up and gathered his notebook. "At this point, it's your choice to come with us. But if it were me, I'd get my story on the record."

"Elias, don't worry about the exhibition now," Diamond said in a low, concerned voice.

Stahl shrugged at Diamond before turning to Shelter. "How long will this take?"

"As long as it takes."

FIVE

THE HOMICIDE UNIT was on the third floor of the new police headquarters built at incredible expense in the former main post office downtown. It had taken forever to convert the building and sparked a huge fraud and bribery scandal over its inflated price tag. But now that it was done, Shelter was relieved to be out of the crumbling Public Safety Building on Main Street.

It was after 9:00 p.m. by the time they'd finished interviewing Stahl on videotape. The story he told them was consistent with the one he'd told at the gallery. He'd left in a taxi, apparently still intent on returning to work.

Shelter and Traverse rode the elevator to the underground garage.

"So, what do you think?" Traverse asked.

"Not sure. He leaves the body, flees the scene, and doesn't call 911."

"The video from the doorbell camera seems to back up his story, but he could have been putting on a show."

"His alibi for earlier in the day seems shaky. The assistant wouldn't have had eyes on him all day, and he left alone to get lunch."

Shelter stopped walking and turned to face his partner.

"The relationship between him and Jacob goes sour. Jacob decides to end it, and he won't accept it," he offered as a possible scenario.

"Yeah, but it looks like a clean kill. Planned. So that doesn't add up."

"Maybe the two of them were involved in something else. Or Elias is protecting someone. Who else would have known Jacob was in that house?"

"Do you believe this guy—Martin Garnier—was totally fine with Elias sleeping with his ex-boyfriend?" Traverse asked.

Shelter shrugged. "How would Garnier know where Jacob was going to be?"

"No idea, but we need to talk to him right away."

Shelter had assigned two detectives to track down Martin Garnier, but so far, they'd come up empty-handed. Garnier hadn't returned home and wasn't answering his phone.

As they resumed the walk toward their vehicles, Traverse asked, "How's your head?"

"It hurts like hell to tell you the truth, but I just need some sleep." Shelter reached his car first. "We'll do the morning meeting and then leave for the country around 9:30. That'll put us at the Hutterite colony at eleven, okay?"

"Take it easy."

Driving through the darkness, Shelter glanced at the dashboard clock. Just after 10:00 p.m. The crime scene and interviews had consumed him for hours. He hadn't texted Penny to let her know he was going to be late and to apologize for last night. Now, he wondered how serious the rift between them was and whether it would have to be worked out tonight. He longed to get to bed.

Penny was the first woman he'd been serious about since his wife died seven years ago. What with the pandemic and long hours at work, it had seemed as though he would never meet anyone. He'd even tried a dating app, but each time he'd been left sad and dissatisfied. One woman had questioned him closely about his work. She was a reader of mystery novels and probed him for grisly details. Another woman turned out to be an anti-vaxxer with an unhealthy belief in conspiracy theories.

Penny was different. He'd met her in the early spring of the year before, when he'd decided to go out for Sunday breakfast. He stopped in at a café he liked on Sherbrook Street, hoping it was early enough that the usual brunch crowd hadn't yet arrived. But the place was packed, and he had to wait in line for ten minutes before being seated at a window table. The diners around him were noisy and animated, enjoying being out after long months of winter. He quickly found the din unbearable and told the waitress he'd changed his mind.

With his eye on the door, he tried to shimmy past a group of women waiting at the host's station. As he took a final, long stride to free himself, his elbow hit a tray hard, sending steaming mugs of coffee flying. Hot liquid splashed onto the waitress's chest. The tray clattered to the floor, and mugs rolled in all directions.

"Oh my God!" the waitress shrieked, holding her stained blouse away from her chest with her thumbs and forefingers. Shelter stood staring at her, dumbfounded, vaguely aware of the ladies behind him clucking their disapproval. A group by the window jumped up and called for napkins to blot coffee from their Sunday best outfits. Shelter became aware, in his peripheral vision, of an elderly woman who'd bent to pick up mugs.

"I'm sorry. Are you okay?"

"I'm fine," the waitress said, but Shelter could see she was struggling to hide her annoyance.

"Here, let me help you." He bent for a mug at the same time she did, and they banged heads.

"Ouch!" she cried.

Shelter's head was stinging too, but he didn't dare touch the spot where they'd bumped. He heard a woman behind him whisper, "What's wrong with that man?"

He picked up the last two mugs from the floor and put them gingerly on the tray. Looking more closely at the waitress's face, he realized she'd served him a couple of weekends earlier. They'd shared a laugh over the antics of a toddler who kept escaping his exasperated mother to visit other tables. She was East Asian, and Shelter put her at around thirty-five. Her shoulder-length hair was parted in the middle. Shelter wasn't much on fashion, but if he had to guess, he'd say her cream-coloured shirt and low-waisted jeans were this year's style. He remembered her name was Penny.

Now facing one another, the tray of empty mugs between them, Shelter saw that she recognized him, too. "Look, I'm really sorry," he said. "Are you hurt?"

"I'm fine. It's okay. Shit happens," she said. Realizing she'd used a profanity, she grimaced and quickly glanced around to see if any other customers were listening. But the group at the host's stand was being led away, and things were returning to normal.

"Your shirt's ruined. Let me pay for it."

"It'll wash out. Don't worry about it. I gotta get rolling." And she was off, back behind the counter, then headed to the bathroom to change her shirt, Shelter assumed.

They shared a laugh about the incident the next weekend, when he returned to the restaurant and made sure to be seated in her section. Seeing no ring on her finger, he ventured to ask her out to lunch. She accepted only after he promised not to bump into her again.

Things moved fast after that, and soon she was spending almost every night at his house. He'd worried that Kelsey, his daughter, would complicate the relationship when she returned from her first year at university in Montreal, but it turned out she and Penny shared an interest in environmental politics and a love of cooking. One night, Kelsey told him she thought Penny was really great. "Don't screw it up, Dad," she'd said with a smile. He could tell she was relieved he'd found someone.

Kelsey was around the house for only a few weeks before she left to spend the summer at her grandparents' house in Gimli, on the west side of Lake Winnipeg, north of the city. When Kelsey headed back to Montreal, they decided it didn't make sense for Penny to keep her apartment.

Driving west on Broadway, traffic was light, and Shelter's mind drifted to the fight with Penny. He shouldn't have been surprised that she wanted to have a child with him. He'd considered the possibility of children when they started getting serious. Still, he was taken aback by how deeply she felt the need to have a baby. She'd told him about the yearning that had always been there, watching her sister's and her friends' babies grow into little people.

She'd known her marriage was a mistake almost from the beginning. Her ex was from a Korean family, as she was, and she'd described him as cold, detached, self-absorbed. It was a relief when she discovered he'd been having an affair and gave herself permission to leave him. It took time to finalize the divorce and recover emotionally, and by then, she was well past thirty.

Even before Shelter married Christa, they'd talked about having kids right away, so they'd still be young enough to backpack around the world when the children were grown. An unexpected pregnancy in their early twenties turned talk into reality.

They'd planned to have more kids, but two devastating miscarriages led them to decide that Kelsey would be an only child. It was an agonizing choice, especially for Christa, who had a large, extended family. They'd talked from time to time about giving it another try, especially after the heartbreaking talks with Kelsey about why she didn't have a brother or sister. When Christa was diagnosed with brain cancer, it was too late.

Now, Shelter was struggling with the idea of starting again. The first year with a new baby had been an ordeal of sleepless nights and disrupted routines. With the stress of police work, the demands had been unrelenting. Of course, there were many moments of joy and wonder as the newborn became a toddler, but he wasn't sorry to see the early years come to an end. At forty-two, he was apprehensive about going through it again.

After his first flippant remark the night before, he'd grown more serious and shared these doubts with Penny.

But she was insistent that she wanted and needed to be a mother. He told her it was a big step and that he needed time to think about it.

"How much time?" she'd said, banging her wine glass down on the coffee table. She'd gotten up from the couch and faced him from the other side of the coffee table. "We can do this."

"I know we can, but I'm not ready."

"Are you ever going to be ready?"

"That's not fair," Shelter had said, his voice rising in anger. "We've never even talked about this until now."

"I love you, but I can't wait," she'd shot back. Before he could reply, she'd turned on her heel and left the house.

They had been arguing more often in recent weeks over disagreements large and small, from his unpredictable work hours to household chores. If he was being honest, Shelter had to admit he'd been at fault most of the time. The lack of sleep and nightmares left him irritable and short-tempered. But this fight seemed much more serious than anything he'd experienced with Penny before.

She'd only returned after midnight and slept in the spare room.

Shelter had been out the door early, before she came down for breakfast. Now, on his way home, he braced himself for another confrontation, especially after failing once again to warn her that he'd be working late. Penny was given to flights of joyous enthusiasm and equally impressive bouts of rage, so the relationship was an exciting but sometimes exasperating change for Shelter.

When he'd met Christa during his second year at the University of Winnipeg, he'd been drawn to her sunny, gregarious nature after his dour Presbyterian upbringing.

Under her influence, he'd become friendlier and more outgoing, but when she died, he withdrew from their circle of friends and from his softball and curling leagues. Raising Kelsey alone through her turbulent teenage years had been difficult, but his daughter had become his only anchor to a normal home life. With Penny, he felt himself coming out of his shell.

Parking outside his clapboard house, he was surprised to find the lights out. Kelsey was in Gimli, but Penny should still have been up. She was a night owl and would normally have been up reading or watching a movie. Shelter switched on the hall light and checked the back of the house. No sign of her. He climbed the stairs, and in the moonlight that illuminated their bedroom, he saw that she was curled up in bed. He wanted to say something, but he was afraid to wake her.

"Hello." She was awake and watching him in the darkness. "What happened to you?"

"I got hung up on a case. Sorry I didn't message you."

"You never do," she said, sitting up in bed, the comforter gathered around her. "It only takes a second. I get so scared something's happened to you."

Shelter felt a dull ache behind his eyes intensify. He was exhausted. "Yeah, you're right. It was pretty hectic today, and the time just flew by. Sorry."

"Dinner is in the fridge." After a pause, she added, "We need to talk tomorrow."

"Okay." He drew out the word to signal his doubts. "I have to go out to the country, but we can talk when I get home."

Penny let out a resigned sigh and turned over. She knew how unpredictable his job could be and had to accept it would be part of their relationship. Still, having their plans hijacked by the latest murder investigation was a constant source of friction, as it had been with Christa.

He made his way down to the kitchen, where he heated a slice of homemade pizza in the microwave and ate it standing up. There was nothing to be done but try to be fully present for her tomorrow evening, despite his dread at the prospect of a serious relationship talk. After rinsing his plate, he made his way up upstairs, stripped to his underwear, and slipped into bed beside her.

They slept with their backs to each other.

SIX

SHELTER WAS UP AT SIX. He showered and dressed quietly to avoid waking Penny. He made coffee and munched on a couple of pieces of toast while checking his email on his phone. He found one from an RCMP constable who'd informed Jacob Waldner's next of kin of his death.

The minister, Simon Wurtz, will be waiting for you in the main parking lot at 11:00 a.m. Once you get to the colony, take the first left off the entrance road. We told them you would want to speak with the wife, the parents, and maybe some other people in the community. He agreed to that.

Shelter pulled up the *Free Press* website on his tablet. As he expected, the newspaper had only a short article about the murder. The piece had clearly been written on deadline from the bare-bones release the communications department had put out. It didn't include the victim's name because the family hadn't yet been informed. Media interest would explode today with the revelation that the victim was a Hutterite from a colony in southern Manitoba. Reporters would be following it hard, and he knew that would ratchet up the pressure on the homicide unit—and the distress the Hutterites would feel.

He spent the next half hour making notes and preparing for the 8:00 a.m. team meeting. As the senior investigating officer on this case, it was Shelter's job to divvy up tasks among the detectives and pull in specialized resources as needed.

Shelter was a stickler for starting the morning meeting on time. When he entered the conference room at 7:58 a.m., he found four detectives in their usual places around the oval table, chatting, with coffee mugs, notebooks, and cellphones in front of them. Traverse's family lived south of the city, and because Shelter was going to pick him up on the way out of town, he joined the meeting by videoconference.

Shelter began with a rundown of the scene at the house, including the lack of a murder weapon and the interview with Elias Stahl. "The killer either knew Waldner would be in the house at that time or followed him there," he said. "There's no sign of forced entry, so we can also assume Waldner let the killer in."

"What about the owner of the Airbnb?" asked Bryce Majewski, who, at six-foot-five, was as thin as a rookie basketball centre. He had brown hair cut close to the scalp and a thick brush of a moustache. He was the most recent addition to the homicide unit after moving over from robbery a month ago.

"He says he was working at his house just around the corner when he got the call from Stahl. You can follow up on his alibi, Bryce." He made a note before continuing. "For now, we'll focus on Elias and his husband, Martin Garnier. But there are a lot of inconsistencies here, so we have to keep an open mind."

"Like what?" Majewski asked.

"Obviously, we'll see what the autopsy shows, but we didn't see any obvious marks of a struggle on Waldner or

Stahl. And the house was immaculate except for the body." Shelter paused for a moment, mentally ticking off items. "Then there's the weapon. It looks like the killer brought the blade and left with it. From the way the throat was cut, I'd say they knew what they were doing."

Shelter glanced around the circle of detectives, waiting for questions or comments. Thinking about what he'd just said, the murder scene pointed to either a strong motive or a deranged mind. Elias Stahl hadn't appeared mentally unstable. What could have driven him to plan and carry out the murder of his childhood friend and lover?

"Someone could have followed him in from the country," offered Jennifer Kane. She was leaning back in her chair, one knee pressed against the edge of the table. Tall, with shoulder-length hair and blond highlights, she'd gone through the police academy with Shelter and was his closest friend on the force after Traverse.

"I guess," Shelter answered. "But that means the killer would have had to know when Jacob was coming into Winnipeg and follow him without being spotted."

Kane shrugged. "Maybe the killer had access to his plans for the day. What about his cellphone?"

"I was getting to that. It looks like his phone and laptop are missing. I emailed you his cell number this morning, Himmat. Let's get the ball rolling on obtaining the records from the phone company."

Himmat Sharma grimaced and said, "Don't hold your breath." Sharma was a detail-obsessed cop who wore a tie and dark jacket even on the hottest of July days, shunning the casual style of the other detectives. He was easy to frustrate, and one of his pet peeves was how long it took to get records out of the big telephone companies. Shelter knew all about dealing with the huge, faceless corporations that ran the telecom system. There was no money in pulling records for the police, and the companies devoted only a skeleton staff to the task. One harried employee had once rebuked Sharma for his impatience: "Yours isn't the only murder in Canada, you know."

"His cellphone would be owned by the Hutterite colony," Shelter said.

"Do we have an estimated time of death?" Sharma asked.

"From what Stahl said, Waldner left the colony yesterday morning around nine. That puts him in the city at about 10:30. Stahl claims he discovered the body about 2:10 p.m. The ME will probably be able to narrow it down further for us."

Shelter had been well trained by medical examiners to know that determining the time of death was far from an exact science. Here, the house's constant ambient temperature would help measure how much the body temperature had dropped since the heart stopped. Rigor mortis and other factors would also be considered when making a rough estimate.

"Let me see if there's anything yet on the autopsy." Shelter picked up his cellphone and found an email from the province's chief medical examiner's office. "Okay. The autopsy is scheduled for this morning at eleven."

Shelter turned to Ian Sim, who was slouched in his chair, doodling intently on a pad of paper. "Ian."

Sim kept sketching geometric figures. He'd tuned out the meeting. "Ian!"

Sim's head jerked up, and he gave a quick, embarrassed nod. With his mullet haircut, Walmart wardrobe, and basketball-sized beer belly, Sim looked older than his forty-five years. He was constantly behind on his paperwork but always had time to share tiresome opinions on everything from immigrants to the latest misguided move by the Winnipeg Jets. Shelter would have loved to see him kicked off the homicide unit, but his expertise in database software and surveillance technology made him invaluable in complex investigations like this one was shaping up to be.

"You're on video again today. Let's find Waldner's pickup truck and see if he was being followed."

Next was Elias Stahl's elusive husband. He turned to Kane. "Jen, you're back on tracking down Martin Garnier. Bring him in, and we'll do the interview when we get back this afternoon."

Shelter pulled up to Traverse's ranch-style house just before 9:30. Traverse was sitting on the front porch, sipping coffee from a large Tim Horton's car mug. Shelter climbed out of the car just as Traverse's wife came through the screen door, holding the hand of their five-year-old daughter.

Janice Harper grew up on a Cree reserve in northern Manitoba, and Traverse was from an Ojibwe community on the west side of Lake Winnipeg. She was an assistant professor in the University of Manitoba's environmental studies program. They had two older boys as well as the little girl.

"Hey, Mike. Getting outta town, eh?" Harper was dressed for a warm summer day in cutoffs and a T-shirt.

"Into the wild," Shelter said, smiling at their daughter, who was now hiding behind her mother's legs. "How're you doing, Janice?"

"Ah, you know, enjoying the last few weeks of summer."

Traverse gave her a peck on the cheek and hugged the girl. "I'm hoping not to be late, but you know who to blame if I am."

"No OT tonight, Mike. I need this guy to cover soccer practice."

"I'll do my best. Take care."

They got onto the Perimeter Highway and cut southwest on Highway 3. Late summer was Shelter's favourite time of the year to get out of the city. Silt left from the prehistoric Lake Agassiz, which once covered this area, made the Red River Valley the province's most fertile land. Great bison herds once roamed where fields of wheat, canola, and soybeans now ran to the horizon on either side of the highway. The fields were perfectly flat, making the sky enormous, with towers of white cumulus cloud against the deep blue.

Traverse was slouched, relaxed, and sipping coffee. For many years, he'd worn his hair clipped close to his scalp, but in recent months, he'd let it grow longer and now had it tied back. Shelter glanced over just as Traverse absentmindedly ran a hand through his hair, revealing a pronounced widow's peak. "Looks like you're getting a bit thin on top there."

Traverse kept his sunglasses trained on the road ahead. "Don't even fucking start."

"Just saying."

"Worry about your own hair."

"They make creams to slow hair loss, you know."

"Too bad they don't make something to stop that gut of yours from growing."

Shelter laughed and took a long sip of McDonald's coffee. He searched for a country music station on the radio. He liked rock, but Traverse was a country fan, and the twangy guitars and sentimental storytelling felt right for this trip. After a couple of minutes, Traverse asked, with all the seriousness in the world, "How are the roses doing?"

Shelter rolled his eyes and shook his head in amusement. He'd been waiting for the counterattack after his hair jibe, and here it was.

"Not bad. One had a blight, but I think it's going to survive."

"A blight? Oh, how awful."

"I'm trying not to lose sleep over it."

He was used to the other cops teasing him about his gardening and didn't care. His British grandfather had been a devoted gardener. He'd turned the backyard of his house on Brock Street in River Heights into a showpiece during the summer months, with a starring role for his beloved roses. Shelter's mother had taken up the tradition at their family house a few streets away, and with her encouragement, Christa had bought a single rose bush called Morden Fireglow from a nursery one May long weekend, along with trays of pansies, impatiens, and zinnias. Under his mother's watchful eye, she'd rehabilitated a flower bed along their garage that had become overgrown with weeds. She covered the roots of the new rose plant with rich, black topsoil mixed with peat moss, then added a layer of wood chips for mulch. His mother had kept up a running commentary that whole Saturday afternoon.

To Christa's delight, her plant had produced a profusion of roses in shades of scarlet and orange, and the other flowers had flourished. From that first rose bush, Christa added more, reclaiming long-ignored flower beds and opening new ones. Around the roses, she planted annuals, perennials, and shrubs to complement one another throughout spring and summer and into fall.

When she died, Shelter couldn't bear to see all her work wither, and he reluctantly took over the gardening duties that first spring. To his surprise, the plants came back stronger than ever. Soon, he was adding more roses and other flowering plants, spending his evenings weeding, pruning, and deadheading. The intricacies of tending the plants and the physical exertion of gardening were a welcome distraction from his job and the trials of raising a teenage daughter alone. When news got out at the office that he'd taken up the least macho hobby imaginable, the ribbing began, led by Traverse. Shelter grinned and bore it. And that's what he did now.

The two detectives were quiet for the rest of the drive until the GPS app on Shelter's phone warned of an upcoming right turn. He turned onto another highway heading west, parallel to the US border. Here, traffic was light, and the only visual distractions were farmyards surrounded by trees planted to protect the buildings from the snow and winds that swept across the prairie in winter. In late August, these shelter belts stood out like green islands in a sea of grain.

Looking to his right, Shelter spotted a billboard: *You Are a Sinner!* It read in stark white letters against a black background. He pointed at it and said, "Check this out."

Traverse looked up from his cellphone and scoffed. "Subtle message."

"Isn't it supposed to be, "*Let he who is without sin cast the first stone*?"

"I guess people who live in glass houses get to throw the first stone out here."

The billboard was one of several evangelical or anti-abortion messages Shelter had seen erected over the years in the southern part of the province. Had anyone ever changed their religious or political beliefs because they passed one of them?

"Something tells me we've entered the Bible belt," he said.

The robotic GPS voice announced they should take the next left onto a gravel road. There was no sign indicating the Hutterite colony was down this road, but Shelter could make out a collection of low buildings in the distance. After a couple of minutes, they came to a wooden sign with *Round Rock Colony* engraved on it.

At the morning press briefing, the media had been informed that the Saint Boniface victim was a Hutterite, and, as predicted, they'd jumped on the story. Three SUVs painted with the names and logos of TV networks had beaten them here and were lined up on the side of the road opposite the colony's entrance. Cameras on tripods pointed at the colony's buildings, and reporters milled around with cups of coffee in hand. As Shelter turned onto the access road, the cameras followed their car, gathering footage for the noonday news. The parking lot stretched the length of a football field in front of a huge corrugated-metal garage. An assortment of farm equipment and pickup trucks was parked on one side of the lot.

Shelter was about to enter the closed world of a Hutterite colony. It was a world governed by religious beliefs, traditions, and customs that had endured for five hundred years, binding the Hutterites together, separate and shielded from the evil of the outside world.

He wondered whether he'd find the key to Jacob Waldner's murder hidden among the grouping of houses and buildings laid out before him.

SEVEN

SHELTER COULD SMELL a faint aroma of gasoline as he exited the car, and in the gloom of the large steel garage, he could see men working on machinery. Two Hutterite men emerged from the garage's open sliding doors and crossed the parking lot to meet them.

The first to extend a hand looked to be in his mid-sixties, with a salt-and-pepper beard and square eyeglasses. He wore suspenders over a blue-and-white checked shirt and black pants. Two pens were lined up in the breast pocket of his shirt. "I am Simon Wurtz," he said, "the minister here. And this is Paul Hofer, the general manager."

He stepped aside to let Hofer, who looked to be in his early fifties, shake their hands. He, too, was bearded and dressed in the same Hutterite uniform. His face was marked by crow's feet around the eyes and deep lines across his forehead.

"I'm Michael Shelter, and this is Gabriel Traverse, Winnipeg police. We're sorry to meet you under these circumstances."

Wurtz studied Shelter's face for a moment. "We can't believe it's true. Nothing like this has ever happened before."

"It's very unfortunate," Shelter replied. "Is there somewhere we can talk?"

"In the dining hall. This way, please."

Wurtz and Hofer led the officers down a sidewalk past buildings separated by mature trees and well-tended lawns. The men walked in silence, and Shelter sensed this was not only because of the grave circumstances but also because the Hutterites were naturally reserved around strangers.

To the right, a group of preschoolers chased each other and used the swings on the playground beside a white building. The girls, wearing black bonnets, white blouses, and colourful ankle-length dresses, were miniature versions of the two women watching them. The boys wore suspenders over checked short-sleeved shirts, just like the men.

"The children are educated in the colony?" Shelter asked.

Wurtz nodded. "This is our kindergarten, which for us means children from two to five years old. You would call it daycare. Our school is farther in that direction," he said, nodding toward the southern edge of the community.

Shelter pointed to a row of modern semi-detached houses further along the sidewalk. "You build your own houses?"

Wurtz glanced at the homes. "Like everything else, built by the hands of our men."

The housing units, like the other buildings, were unadorned but well-maintained. In front of one dwelling, Shelter noticed a pair of Adirondack chairs arranged on either side of the front door. Another had two large planters overflowing with pink flowers.

Shade trees, grass, shrubs, and flower beds—to Shelter's eyes, the community had the look of a prosperous suburban neighbourhood.

They reached a large, grassy quadrangle that seemed to be the centre of the community. "The dining hall is just there," Wurtz said, pointing to a long, single-storey building. "Behind it are our workshops, the chicken house, the vegetable garden, and a factory where we manufacture a type of farm implement. With the mechanization of farming, most of the colonies have added manufacturing to provide work to our men and, of course, bring in extra income."

The minister led the way up three concrete steps to the dining hall. He stopped and pointed to another entrance a little way down the same walkway. "Our church is attached to the dining hall, which allows us to host large gatherings for weddings, funerals, and other special occasions."

Shelter was struck by the absence of a steeple, cross, or any of the other architectural trappings of churches he was familiar with. To his eyes, it was just another plain building.

"We told the people of what had happened to our Jacob this morning," Wurtz said. "I can tell you this was one of the most difficult experiences of my life."

Inside the dining hall, an accordion-style floor-to-ceiling divider separated the dining area from the church. Wurtz directed Shelter and Traverse to one of the long tables lined up in the dining room. They were of the kind you see in school cafeterias, with plastic laminate tops and fold-down benches. Two Hutterite women were working in the large industrial kitchen at one end of the building.

When the two detectives were seated, Wurtz said, "The men eat on this side of the room and the women on that side," pointing across the hall. "It may also interest you to know that each person has an assigned place. Children under fifteen eat separately in a room over there, where they are supervised by the German teacher."

Shelter gave a polite nod in response before addressing the men in a formal way, looking from one to the other. "Yesterday, we were called to a house near downtown Winnipeg, where Jacob Waldner was found dead. He was murdered."

As he spoke, Paul Hofer watched him carefully, but Wurtz's head was bowed, his eyes fixed on his folded hands resting on the table. Shelter decided to spare them the details of the murder—the cutting of the throat. "It's essential to find whoever killed him as quickly as possible. This is why we must trace Jacob's movements—who he met with and why he was in Winnipeg."

Wurtz raised his head and spread his hands on the table. He said, almost to himself, "Who could have done such a thing?" After a moment, he continued, "Jacob was in the city on colony business, to see our lawyer. We have no idea why he would have been in this house."

"What time did he leave?"

Wurtz looked to Hofer. "About 9:30."

"Who was the lawyer he was meeting?"

"William Cameron."

Shelter didn't know Cameron. He noted the name and would call him the first chance he got. "We understand this meeting was arranged at the last minute. What was it about?" Shelter asked.

"We have a legal problem over a piece of land. Jacob has had to go into the city a number of times about it. He informed us on Wednesday that he had to go, and we agreed. But what was he doing in this house?"

Shelter felt the intensity of the men's gaze. He recalled Elias's plea to them not to reveal his relationship with Jacob, and he considered how best to break the news. "We met last night with a former member of your colony whose name is Elias Stahl."

"Elias Stahl?" Wurtz said, his voice rising in alarm. "What could Elias possibly have to do with this?"

"Elias told us he'd agreed to meet Jacob at the house where Jacob was found dead."

Hofer's eyes widened in surprise. "Meet at the house?"

"What are you saying?" Wurtz demanded, his voice rising in alarm. "That Elias killed Jacob?"

"No. I am not saying that. Please try to calm down," Shelter said. He gave the two men a moment to compose themselves. He flipped a page in his notebook and then raised his eyes to meet Wurtz's. "According to Elias, it was not the first time they'd met in the city. They had ..." he paused a beat, searching for a neutral term, "a relationship."

"A relationship?" Wurtz said. As he stared at Shelter, his mouth moved silently, repeating the word, trying to work out Shelter's meaning. Then the light went on in his eyes. "You're not suggesting homosexuality?"

Shelter nodded.

"No. Not possible. Jacob was a married man with three small children. What you are saying is not possible."

"I know it's shocking for you. But this is what Elias Stahl told us," Shelter said. "You were unaware of a relationship?"

Wurtz and Hofer looked at each other in disbelief. "Of course, we know Elias is in Winnipeg, but not that Jacob was seeing him there," Wurtz replied finally.

"What can you tell us about Elias?"

He shook his head and dropped his eyes to the table, as if working out the implications of what he'd just been told. When the minister looked up at Shelter, his expression had darkened.

"He left the colony with Jacob when they were teenagers. Jacob returned and has become a good member of the community. He is—," Wurtz checked himself, "was deeply involved in planning our new colony. Elias has been allowed to return only once or twice a year to see his parents. His running away has been terrible for them."

"Allowed to return?" Shelter asked.

"I will not allow him to come more often," Wurtz said. "He has made his choice to live in the world and indulge in a sinful lifestyle. He will have to bear the consequences for eternity." He paused for a moment, allowing this grim pronouncement to sink in. "I cannot believe Jacob was spending time with him. He knew this would be against the elders' wishes." Shelter noted Wurtz's description of their relationship as spending time together, avoiding the sexual dimensions of their friendship.

"Do you know of anyone who would want to hurt Jacob?" Traverse asked.

"We are a peaceful people. Pacifism is one of our most important values, one that has led to our persecution through the centuries. I can think of no one who would commit such a crime against Jacob."

"What is this legal problem you referred to?" Traverse asked.

Wurtz was silent as he gathered his thoughts. After a long pause, he spoke. "We are one hundred and eighty people here, and this is becoming too many for the land and resources we have. We must establish a new colony, as is the way with our people. We call this a daughter colony."

The minister spoke in a patient way, as if he was instructing members of his congregation in the finer points of their faith. "It hasn't been easy to find a suitable piece of land at a price we can afford. We're talking about a large property, and, like everything else, prices have been climbing so much in recent years."

Hofer frowned and nodded.

"In the winter, we thought we'd found a solution," Wurtz said. "A very large family farm came up for sale about forty kilometres from here. The father had passed away, and we assumed he'd left the farm to his two sons. One lives in Winnipeg, and the other lives on the property. To our surprise, we learned the father had left the whole farm to the son in the city and nothing to the one who farms the land."

A woman came from the kitchen with a tray and set a glass of water in front of each man. She said nothing and didn't look at any of them. Wurtz took a sip before continuing. "It was an unfortunate situation, but the farm is three thousand acres, one of the largest in this part of the province. The land needs work, but we made a generous offer, which was accepted."

"You bought the farm?" Traverse asked.

"We have ownership, but not possession. By now, we should be working the land and preparing the colony. But the brother on the farm refuses to vacate the property under any circumstances."

Hofer added, "And now he has made an offer to buy it back from us."

"An offer to you?" Traverse asked, his eyebrows raised in surprise.

"He says it's his home, and his brother had no right to sell it."

"So, it's a matter of evicting the brother from the farm."

Wurtz looked to Hofer, and an understanding passed between them. He looked back at Traverse, his face tight with tension. "We have tried everything to get him to go in a Christian way. Jacob went there and asked him to respect the sale agreement. But this man threatened Jacob and drove him off the property."

Wurtz shook his head. "Our lawyer advised us to have him removed. We have discussed it among ourselves and with our accountant. The accountant warned us that forcibly removing this man could create a very ugly situation. He says the surrounding community might take his side against us. It's important for us to avoid that. And it's not our way to use the courts. Many in the community see it as a form of violence and against our pacifist beliefs."

"What does your accountant have to do with it?"

"He lives in the area and advises us on certain business matters."

"His name?" Shelter asked.

"James Deacon."

"Mr. Deacon doesn't think you should fight for the land?"

"He advised us to wait. He's heard that the man who refuses to go actually dislikes farming and is mismanaging the operation in his father's absence. What we've seen of the crops bears this out. He may leave of his own accord sooner rather than later. Mr. Deacon believes patience is the way to go."

"But you have to keep paying the mortgage in the meantime."

Wurtz shrugged. "We have savings, and our manufacturing operation is doing well. We have time."

Shelter made a note to contact Deacon. "What was Jacob's attitude?"

"Jacob disagreed very strongly. He said we had seized a rare opportunity by purchasing such a large piece of land, and this man had no right to stop us."

Hofer nodded in an encouraging way, signalling for Wurtz to go on. "He was in favour of eviction. He pointed to historical examples in which the church turned to the government for assistance. For instance, in the Bible, the apostle Paul appeals to Caesar for protection. In the 1770s, when Hutterites were forced to flee persecution in Eastern Europe and settle in what is now Ukraine, they did so with a Russian military escort."

Wurtz paused to take another sip of water. "Jacob also pointed out that if a neighbour drove into our field and started harvesting our crop, we wouldn't hesitate to call the police to stop him. In this sense, we are already participating in the state's violence. He argued that it was permissible as long as we are not the ones carrying out violent acts."

Shelter considered the colony's struggle between their pacifist beliefs and the desire to stand up for their rights against what was clearly wrong and illegal. "What was your position as minister?"

"At the end of the day, I believe that if we are pacifists, forcing this man off the land would be a form of violence. But in a decision like this, the entire community was involved, not just the elders. It was presented to all the male members, and there was a long discussion and a vote."

"Only the men vote?" Traverse asked.

"Yes. In the end, we decided to wait and see how the situation develops. We can always sell later."

"A difficult situation," Traverse said. "How did Jacob take the decision?"

"He was unhappy about it, but the community had spoken."

"What's the name of the man who refuses to leave the farm?"

"Lanny Butler."

"And the brother in Winnipeg?"

"Daniel."

After making a note, Shelter changed tack. "You are connected to the internet through computers and cellphones?"

"We use the internet for business and educational purposes."

Shelter wondered how the Hutterites could keep the outside world at bay when every temptation was at their fingertips.

As if reading his mind, the minister said, "As a people, we've struggled with how to control the use of the internet, knowing it can be the source of great evil. Some colonies try to restrict it, but we have decided it is the responsibility of each person to avoid sin in its use."

"I assume Jacob had a cellphone and a laptop?"

"Yes."

"We haven't found them. If there are records of the calls he made to and from his phone, we will need them immediately. We will also need records for your vehicles, including who was using them yesterday, mileage readings, and gas purchases."

Wurtz's eyes grew wide. "You can't possibly think someone from our community is involved."

"We need to check everything."

Wurtz studied Shelter's face for a moment before replying, "We will prepare the records for you."

"Now, we'll need to talk to Jacob's wife."

Wurtz glanced at Hofer, and there was a long silence before he replied. "Of course, we want to help you in any way we can, but Jacob's wife and the rest of the family have had a terrible shock. We can answer any questions you have."

Wurtz's tone was polite but firm. Still, there was no chance Shelter would accept second-hand answers to his questions. "Jacob's wife was the closest person to him," he said, matching the minister's grave tone. "We must speak to her, and we may also want to talk to other members of the family and your community."

Wurtz's eyebrows furrowed, and his chin dropped as he considered Shelter's words. "Yes, of course, we understand." He turned to Hofer and spoke a few words in German. Hofer picked up his hat from the table and, with a slight bow to the police officers, left the building.

"Paul has gone to speak to Rachel. We will join them in a few minutes."

EIGHT

RACHEL AND JACOB WALDNER'S home was on the opposite side of the grassy quadrangle. Shelter thought the area might be used for sports, although he suspected leisure hours would be few and far between in the summer on a farming operation of this size.

Shelter's mother had grown up on a farm in western Manitoba, near the Saskatchewan border. She was twelve when the family moved to the city, but she'd always remembered the long hours of hard work her father had spent seeding, fertilizing, and harvesting grain with machinery that needed constant repair. Even at that age, she'd been marked by her father's constant worries about the farm's heavy debt load and her own obsession with the weather. According to his mother, the weather was the one thing his grandfather never seemed to worry about, despite all the trouble it could cause from spring to fall—flooding, hail, drought, frost. "That's in God's hands," he would say.

But it wasn't so easy for a little girl to be stoic. His mother had once admitted that she'd stood at her bedroom window, peering west—"the direction the weather comes from"—hoping and praying with all her might for rain clouds to appear.

Either her prayers or her father's hard work hadn't been enough, for he'd been forced to sell the farm, move the family into rented rooms in Brandon, and take jobs as a hired hand before eventually finding a position with the provincial government and getting back on his feet. When he was still a young boy, Shelter remembered his grandfather, by then grey and painfully thin, telling him how his mother had sobbed the day they'd auctioned off the family belongings, including her beloved horse. He'd shrugged. "Desperate times call for desperate measures."

Jacob and Rachel's two-storey home was clean and well-maintained. Even the cement on the front path looked scrubbed. The only thing out of place was a tricycle abandoned on a patch of lawn. A few pansies and petunias planted in boxes under a picture window offered the only visual relief from the building's whitewashed stucco.

Without knocking, Wurtz led the way into the living room, where three women were huddled on a couch. Paul Hofer and another man sat on hard chairs on either side. Here again, the walls were bare except for a small plaque displaying what Shelter imagined was a biblical passage in German. He noted that this simply furnished, unadorned room fit well with the decluttering mania that had swept North America over the past half-decade.

Hofer stood up and edged past Wurtz. "I will get more chairs," he said, disappearing down a hallway.

"This is Rachel, Jacob's wife," Wurtz said, gesturing to the woman seated at the centre of the couch. Like the other women holding her hands, she wore a black kerchief that covered the back of her head, held in place by bobby pins. She appeared to be in her late twenties, with a pale oval face, plump cheeks, and dark brown hair neatly pulled back under her kerchief. She wore an ankle-length tunic with tiny green flowers over a short-sleeved white blouse. Her large brown eyes were dry and clear as she nodded a silent greeting to the detectives.

"This is Jacob's sister, Emily, and his mother, Mary Waldner," Wurtz said, gesturing in turn to the other women. "And Jacob's uncle, Peter," he added. The middle-aged man to the women's left nodded but didn't smile or offer to shake hands. "Jacob's father passed away a few years ago."

Rachel Waldner's composed expression contrasted with the distraught appearance of the women on either side of her. They too wore long dresses, but of different colours and designs. Emily, in solid pink, appeared to be in her late teens. She was slim, with blond hair and blue eyes. Her mother, Mary, was heavy-set and in late middle age, with brown hair, a round face, a bulbous nose, and thick steel-rimmed glasses. She wore a lavender dress and a blouse with sleeves longer than those of the other two women, reaching to the elbows of her strong arms.

Paul Hofer returned with a kitchen chair in each arm and placed them across the coffee table for the two officers. Wurtz took a position standing behind them.

"First, let me extend our condolences to you for your loss," Shelter said. "We know how difficult this must be for you and the whole community."

Given Wurtz's warning about Rachel's distress, he was again struck by how calm she appeared compared with the other two women. Beside her, Emily had a distraught look in her eyes, and tears streamed down her cheeks. Mary had a hand over her mouth and sobbed quietly. By contrast,

Rachel stared out the window toward the dining hall and church.

"We need to ask you some questions to help us find whoever did this to Jacob," Shelter said. He paused for a moment before continuing. "Rachel, your husband went to Winnipeg yesterday morning. Can you walk us through what happened before he left?"

It was important to establish a timeline from the moment Jacob woke to the moment he was killed. But an equally important goal of this question was to get Rachel talking and remembering details that could be important. Seven people in the living room were now looking at the young woman expectantly, but she remained silent. Mary shifted her weight onto one hip and spoke to her daughter-in-law.

"Rachel?" When there was still no response, she leaned in to bring her mouth close to Rachel's ear and whispered something in German.

As if emerging from a dream, Rachel looked at her and then focused on Shelter. With a slight shake of her head, she responded in English in a clear voice with the same light German accent as the others.

"Like any other morning, I got the children ready before going to work in the kitchen. After breakfast, Jacob went to speak to Amos. There was a problem with a combine."

"His brother," Wurtz said.

Rachel sighed, glanced at Shelter, then lowered her eyes to a handkerchief intertwined with her fingers. In a quiet voice, she asked, "Why would someone want to kill Jacob? This makes no sense."

"We will do everything we can to find the person who did it, Rachel," Shelter said. "What happened after he returned from talking to Amos?"

Rachel pursed her lips, looked up at the ceiling, then focused once again on Shelter. "I was cleaning up after breakfast with the other women when he came to the dining hall to say goodbye. He said he would be back in the evening before the children were in bed."

Over the last hour, Shelter had been struck by how traditional the division of roles seemed to be in the colony. The men took care of the heavy farm work and business, while the women were responsible for cooking, cleaning, and child-rearing. It felt like stepping back into the 1950s. From his readings as a student, he was aware of this aspect of Hutterite life, but it was still striking to see it up close. "How was his mood? Anything different from normal?"

"He seemed upset, but he often has been lately. He's not been himself since his grandmother died. The trouble over the land for our new colony has made it worse. There is a man who is trying to stop us. It has weighed on him for months."

"The man you're talking about is Lanny Butler?"

Rachel nodded. The other two women watched her intently.

"Jacob had gone to the farm," Rachel said. "But the man threw him off the property."

"When was this?" Traverse asked.

"A month or so ago, the first time."

"The first time?"

"He went back the day before he went into the city."

"Did he speak to Mr. Butler the second time?"

"I assume so, because he was very upset that evening and wasn't in the mood to talk."

"You must have asked him what was wrong. What did he say?"

"He wouldn't tell me anything. He said he would find out more in Winnipeg."

"Find out more about what?"

She shook her head. "He said he had to be sure before he could tell me."

For the first time, she bowed her head and sobbed. Mary put an arm around her shoulders and whispered to her.

Shelter waited until she'd wiped her eyes and composed herself. "This seems to have been an unscheduled meeting. You have no idea what it was about, specifically?"

She shook her head, and Wurtz interjected, "He told us he needed to see the lawyer. As far as we knew, it was about the land."

Shelter turned back to Rachel. "You say his grandmother died recently?"

"It was very bad. Stomach cancer. She was in so much pain. We did all we could to make her comfortable, but it was terrible. Jacob was very close to her. She was the second elder we've lost this year. It's been a very hard time for the community. And now this."

Her eyes were red-rimmed. She paused to dab at her nose with an embroidered handkerchief, but her voice remained firm.

Mary Waldner, who'd been listening intently to this exchange about her son, cleared her throat before speaking.

"We cannot understand how this could have happened to Jacob. Where was he found?"

Shelter was unsure how to proceed. He became aware of three sets of women's eyes on him, waiting to hear how violence could have taken a son, brother, and husband from them.

"You know Elias Stahl?" he asked Rachel.

Shelter sensed a chill come over the room. "Why are you asking about Elias?" Mary asked in a stern tone.

Shelter's eyes went to Jacob's mother for a moment before returning to Rachel. "You know him?"

"Yes. I met him once when he came to the colony," Rachel said.

Mary interjected again, "Of course, we know him. What has this to do with Elias?"

From behind, Wurtz said, "Officer, you are upsetting the ladies."

Shelter twisted in his chair to address the minister. "I'm sorry, but we have no choice." Turning back to Rachel, he said, "Jacob planned to meet Elias at the house in Winnipeg, where he was killed."

Shelter heard Mary inhale sharply. In his peripheral vision, he saw Emily's eyes grow wide, and the uncle's face contort into a frown. Rachel lowered her eyes to her hands, now folded on her lap.

"Meeting with Elias," Mary said, "in a house?" She looked at Wurtz, standing behind Shelter. "Why would they meet?"

Wurtz spoke to the women in Hutterite dialect. Mary gave a quick shake of her head, and her eyes narrowed. She looked to her left at the other women and the uncle.

When she turned back to the officers, her glare went from Shelter to Traverse, but she remained silent.

Traverse turned to Wurtz. "What did you say, please?"

"I told them that you believe Jacob and Elias were in a homosexual relationship."

Turning back to the women, Traverse said, "We understand this is upsetting, but we need to know whether you have ever had any reason to be concerned about Elias's dealings with Jacob or anyone, including concerns about his temper or any violence?"

Traverse had been looking at Rachel when he asked the question, but it was Mary who answered in a quiet, angry voice. "Rachel does not know Elias. She moved here from a colony in western Manitoba to marry Jacob. It is true that Elias and Jacob were close friends when they were young, and yes, they ran away together. You say they met in Winnipeg. This is possible. But we know Elias and his parents. He could have nothing to do with what has happened to Jacob. And Jacob could have had nothing to do with Elias's—what is the word you use?—lifestyle. This is impossible. It is evil, an abomination."

Mary took Rachel's hand, and Shelter saw her squeeze it. "Rachel is Jacob's wife, and they have three small children together, as God intended families to be."

A silence fell over the room, broken only by Emily's sobs as she covered her face with her hands. Rachel put an arm around her sister-in-law's shoulder and drew her close.

"That's enough," Wurtz said. "I, or Mr. Hofer, can answer any other questions you have."

Again, Shelter turned to the minister. "No. I'm sorry, we're not finished." Without waiting for a reply, he addressed Rachel. "Did Jacob have enemies? Conflicts with anyone here on the colony or elsewhere in the area?"

Rachel hesitated, and before she could answer, Wurtz intervened again, causing Shelter to let out a quiet sigh of exasperation. "We have good relations with our neighbours, and any conflicts in the community are resolved in a spirit of love and forgiveness."

"Rachel?" Shelter said, refusing to be distracted by the minister's comment.

"He was angry that we could not get the land we bought."

"Angry at Lanny Butler?"

She shrugged. "I don't know. Yes."

Shelter made a note. "Jacob had his computer with him when he went to the city?"

Rachel nodded.

"It has disappeared. Do you have access to his email account—the password?"

"No. That was his personal information."

Shelter glanced at Traverse, and the two detectives got to their feet to leave. Shelter reached into his shirt pocket and drew out some business cards. "My cellphone number is on here. Please call if you can think of anything that can help us. Do you have phone numbers I could have in case I have other questions?"

He reached out to Rachel with a card, but Wurtz stepped forward and took it from him. "I am sorry. They cannot give you their phone numbers," Wurtz said. "I will give you my cellphone, and if you have to speak to Rachel or Mary, I will arrange it."

Shelter was preparing to argue the point when Rachel slowly recited her cellphone number. Wurtz wheeled around to face her. “Rachel, please!” But she repeated the number, and Traverse took it down in his notebook.

Shelter was impressed by this act of defiance. It shifted his perception of her. The Hutterite leaders were co-operating with the investigation, but maybe Rachel possessed some hidden information about her husband, and that was why she’d insisted on giving her number. Perhaps it was something she preferred not to say in front of the others.

If so, he had to find out what it was.

NINE

ON THE SIDEWALK outside the house, Wurtz asked if they needed anything else. From his curt tone, Shelter could tell he was displeased by the turn the interview with Rachel had taken.

"I have one or two more questions about the Butler farm," Shelter said.

Wurtz took off his glasses and wiped them with a handkerchief. "We can talk on the way to the parking lot."

At that moment, Shelter noticed a woman not dressed like the Hutterite women emerge from one of the houses. She followed the sidewalk toward where it intersected with the one they were on. She wore a green cotton V-neck top, matching close-fitting drawstring pants, and white running shoes. A stethoscope was draped over her shoulders. She appeared deep in thought, her eyes on her phone. As she approached, her slow gait and dark brown hair parted in the middle sparked something in Shelter's memory.

He searched for the connection. Then, with a jolt, he realized it was Julie Klassen. He'd dated Julie during his first year at the University of Winnipeg, and his mind raced to understand what she was doing here.

He recalled that she grew up in the nearby town of Krefeld and had moved up to Winnipeg for nursing school. So, it made sense she'd be here.

As he watched her approach, he struggled to see in her the beautiful woman he'd been so infatuated with two decades earlier—her thick dark hair, high cheekbones, and spray of freckles across her nose. Of course, the decades take their toll on everyone, but now Julie's face was gaunt and creased by lines running across her forehead and around her mouth and eyes. Her hair had streaks of grey. She was tall—only a few inches shorter than his own six-foot-one-inch frame—but much thinner than she'd been, back in the day.

Shelter had lost track of her after they broke up, and he began seeing Christa. He hadn't thought of her in years. Her head was still lowered as she drew close to them, and she was unaware of their presence. Wurtz called out. "Hello, Julie."

Her head jerked up from her phone. "Oh, hello," she said with an embarrassed laugh. Her eyes swept around the group of men before returning to Wurtz's face.

"This is Julie Klassen," Wurtz said with a smile. "Julie is the provincial nurse who comes to help us. We are grateful to have her."

Klassen gave a bashful smile to the men in front of her. She was about to say something when her eyes darted back to meet Shelter's.

"Hello, Julie," he said.

The smile slid from her face to be replaced by tight lips and narrowed eyes. It took her a moment to put the pieces together. "You're here about Jacob."

Shelter had taken a step to shake her hand but was stopped dead in his tracks by her icy tone. "And you're the nurse here."

"You two know each other?" Wurtz asked, his tone now wary at the undercurrent of tension.

Unlocking his eyes from Julie's, Shelter turned to Wurtz. "We were friends at university."

Klassen hadn't taken her eyes from Shelter's face. Finally, she turned to Wurtz and said, "What's happened to Jacob is absolutely horrible. I spoke to Rachel for a few minutes this morning to offer my condolences." Turning to Shelter, she added, "I hope you find whoever did this." Without saying goodbye, she circled the men and headed toward the parking lot. Wurtz glanced at Shelter with a quizzical look before continuing down the sidewalk.

As they walked, Shelter was at a loss to understand Julie's cool reaction to seeing him. "Has Julie been with you long?" he asked Wurtz.

"A few years," the minister said. "We mostly take care of our own people, but she comes if we need her. She's very good with our seniors. She was especially helpful in caring for Jacob's grandmother during her last weeks."

It occurred to him that Julie's role as a nurse to the Hutterites would give her valuable insights into relationships in the colony, a perspective he might not be able to get from anyone else. "You'll have to excuse me for a moment," he said, bringing the group to a stop on the sidewalk once again. He jogged after Julie, catching up to her in the parking lot. He called to her just as she was about to climb into a beat-up red Toyota Corolla. She stood behind the open door as if it were a shield. "What?" she demanded.

Again, he was taken aback. "I might need to talk to you."

"Talk about what?"

"What happened to Jacob. Get your help understanding these people, this place."

"They're not zoo animals, for God's sake. Ask them your questions."

"You have a perspective we can't get from them. Let me give you a call."

"I don't know anything about it," she said in a dismissive tone. "And I don't want to get involved."

She ducked into the car. He stepped back as she hit the gas, throwing up gravel. She accelerated in a wide semicircle onto the driveway and turned onto the road.

Shelter watched the little car for a minute as it moved across a tableau of blue sky and grain fields, followed by a cloud of dust.

Waiting for Wurtz and Traverse to join him in the parking lot, Shelter went over the exchange with Julie. Surely, she couldn't still be angry about their break-up, after all these years.

He searched his memory for the details of how their relationship had ended. What he most remembered from that time was the intensity of his connection with Christa after their first meeting at a social on a hot summer evening in Gimli. It had progressed fast after that weekend. Had he started sleeping with Christa before ending it with Julie? Not sure.

It was true that the breakup hadn't been easy. He'd told Julie the relationship just wasn't working for him anymore, and she'd angrily accused him of dumping her for another woman, even though he was certain she was unaware of Christa. At the time, he'd recognized the pain she was in, but he'd told himself it wasn't anything a few weeks wouldn't heal. With the passage of time and the wisdom of age, though, he realized he should have been more sensitive to her feelings. Still, it was so long ago, and they'd been just kids, barely twenty years old. His thoughts were interrupted by the approach of the other men.

When Traverse was close enough, he whispered, "Who was that woman?"

"An ex. I'll tell you about it later."

Shelter turned to Wurtz and asked where the Butler farm was located. The minister pointed northwest. "In that direction, about forty kilometres."

Shelter recalled that Wurtz had told them the farm was three thousand acres, an impressive size. "What's it worth?"

Wurtz studied him for a moment, apparently deciding whether to reveal what the colony had agreed to pay, and then seemed to decide they would get the information easily enough from a real estate agent. "The prices have been rising in this region," he said. "We agreed to a number in the range of seven thousand dollars an acre. It will stretch us to the limit, but we need it for our future."

Twenty-one million dollars, Shelter thought, a hell of a heavy lift for a community of just one hundred and eighty people. "I had no idea land was so expensive."

"And then we will have to spend millions more to build the new colony," Wurtz said. "We know how we look from the outside when we come in and buy land. But what people don't see is that it takes an average of thirty years to pay off a new colony. Our children will be paying that loan off."

"Your accountant who's been advising you on the purchase," Traverse said, "where can we find him?"

"Mr. Deacon has an office on the main street in Krefeld." They'd reached the detectives' car. "What else is there for us to do?"

"Someone will have to come to Winnipeg today to identify the body," Traverse said.

Wurtz sighed and said, "Yes, we know. I will go with Jacob's brother."

Shelter noticed the minister's shoulders were hunched and his features had a grey cast. What a heavy burden this man must carry. He had to shepherd these families, hewing to five-hundred-year-old beliefs and traditions that kept them apart from what they saw as a sinful outside world. It would be a job made harder with every passing year, he imagined, as the internet and smartphones grew ever-more attractive to members of the community. Now murder had pierced the colony's carefully constructed defences, bringing its people face-to-face with the violence that was Shelter's everyday reality.

As they left the colony property, Shelter noted the media were still on duty. The broadcast reporters would have filed for the noon news, and now they'd be waiting to interview someone from the colony—another difficult task that would fall to Wurtz or Hofer.

From the passenger seat, Traverse said, "It seems like the men keep a pretty tight rein on what goes on in the colony. Can you imagine having to inform someone every time you wanted to go somewhere?"

"I guess it's part of keeping outside influences at bay. How about their take on homosexuality?"

"And women."

Shelter took a sip of cold coffee left over from the morning drive. "The wife may know more than she was willing to say in front of Wurtz and Hofer. And she's got a defiant streak. We need to talk to her again."

Shelter glanced into the rear-view mirror as the colony's buildings grew smaller in the distance. It seemed unthinkable that anyone in this peaceful Christian community could have killed Jacob. But the Hutterites were human, after all, and that meant they weren't immune to the ugly emotions that led to murder. Nothing could be ruled out. A line from an Agatha Christie novel he'd once read came to mind: "There is evil everywhere under the sun."

They'd driven a few kilometres when Traverse said: "How about the Butlers? The father cuts Lanny out of the will, and then the brother turns around and sells the farm out from under him."

"Lanny won't get off the property and threatens Jacob," Shelter said. After a beat, he added, "By the way, where's he getting all that money to make an offer for the farm?"

"With no visible collateral?" Traverse pulled out his laptop and logged into the police database. It took him less than a minute to find Lanny Butler's criminal record. "He got a conviction for a B&E in 2015 and was charged for trafficking coke and weed in 2018. It was knocked down to possession. Both times, he got probation."

Shelter looked over at Traverse with a raised eyebrow. "Let's pay him a visit after lunch. Can you call Jen and see if they've found Martin Garnier?"

Traverse pulled his phone from his jeans pocket and called Jennifer Kane. Listening to Traverse's side of the conversation, Shelter could tell Garnier remained elusive.

Traverse ended the call and put the phone back in his pocket. "He's not at the condo and isn't calling back. Elias says he's gone out but doesn't know where."

Garnier knew the police were looking for him, and he was avoiding them. That behaviour made it a priority to find him.

Pulling into Krefeld, Shelter slowed the car. He judged that not much had changed in the town since his time dating Julie Klassen. With no contours to the land or waterways, it had been laid out on a grid, with a dozen streets running in each direction off a central main drag. The population of maybe five thousand worked mostly in retail, farm supply, and health care. Shelter knew there was also a fairly large printing plant on the south side of town.

There was no shortage of land out here, and the streets were wide, with spacious lots surrounding modest brick and vinyl-sided bungalows. On their way to Main Street, they passed two Mennonite churches. During the months they'd dated, Julie had filled him in on the town's history. It had been founded by Mennonite immigrants from Russia who'd come to Canada in the late 1800s and early 1900s in search of religious freedom and the right to practise pacifism. They didn't share the Hutterites' communal beliefs, and most had assimilated into mainstream society. The surrounding farmland was among the best in the province, and the town had flourished.

He parked on the diagonal in front of a diner on the main street. He'd been to the restaurant before and knew they served simple but good Eastern European food. Shelter had a bowl of borscht with an egg-salad sandwich on black bread. Traverse had perogies with fried onions and a scoop of sour cream.

"You ever been in this town?" Traverse asked when they'd been served.

"Yeah. When I was going out with that nurse we bumped into at the colony."

"Right, the nurse. She was pretty frosty. What happened between you two?"

"Nothing," Shelter blurted a little too quickly. "I have no idea what her problem is, but I'm thinking she might be able to help us."

"If she'll talk to you," Traverse said with a smile. "Your charm seemed to be working about as good as it usually does. How long did you go out with her for?"

"Most of our first year of university."

"You came down here with her?"

"A few times."

"Stayed over at her family's house?"

Shelter looked up from his soup bowl to see whether Traverse was pulling his leg. He shook his head with a smile. "No way. Her Mennonite parents were strict. Nice people but conservative."

"I'd be strict too if you were hanging around my daughter."

Shelter smiled and took a bite of his sandwich. Back when they were seeing each other, Shelter had loved the contrast between this small town and life in the city. He remembered the thrill of driving out of town with Julie into the limitless expanse of the prairies.

Country folks had a laid-back reputation, but Julie's friends liked to party hard. He remembered driving out to a farm one fall evening for a raucous barbeque. The eating, drinking, and dancing had gone on all night, until he'd finally crashed with Julie in a big tent set up outside the farmhouse. It turned out her parents had been up all night waiting for her to come home, and the incident hadn't made him any more popular in the Klassen household.

Now, he thought about how cold Julie had been earlier that day and wondered again what it meant. Their relationship had been intense, but by spring of that year, he'd had serious doubts about it. She'd become possessive and angry, a side he hadn't seen earlier in their relationship. She'd insisted on knowing where he was at all times and complained bitterly when he went out with his buddies.

He remembered gathering his courage before going to her apartment one evening for the break-up talk. She'd cried and angrily accused him of two-timing her. For Shelter, the reality was that the relationship had run its course. He'd tried to soften the blow as best he could, and Julie had calmed down before he left. They'd met a couple of days later for coffee so he could return a sweater and some books. She'd been distant, but they'd managed to get through the meeting, talking about their plans for the fall. When they parted, he was pretty sure they'd shared a hug and wished each other well.

By then, he was spending all his free time with Christa. Within a year, Kelsey was on the way, and a couple of months later, they'd gotten married. But he'd never forgotten how much he loved the small-town atmosphere of this place, the friendly people, and those first sweet months with Julie, his first real romance. Reflecting now on their time together and the break-up, he realized he shouldn't have been surprised that she held a grudge.

TEN

GUIDED BY THE GPS, Shelter pulled the car to the side of the gravel road across from the driveway to the Butler farm. Mature trees on three sides swayed in the early-afternoon wind. Peering down the driveway, Shelter could make out a row of tall metal grain bins with pointed roofs and two large prefab garages with pitched roofs to the left. To the right was an old-fashioned wood-frame house with a wrap-around porch.

He turned into the driveway and approached the yard slowly. As he got out of the car, Shelter spotted a bearded, heavyset man emerging from one of the garages, a large wrench in hand. He recognized Lanny Butler from his mugshot. Butler was dressed in a frayed grey T-shirt, grease-stained jeans, and a Winnipeg Jets baseball cap. As he approached, Shelter noted full-sleeve tattoos on his arms.

"Mr. Butler?"

"Who's asking?"

"Michael Shelter. I'm a homicide detective with the Winnipeg Police Service. This is my partner, Gabriel Traverse."

Butler looked Traverse up and down for a long second before returning his gaze to Shelter. "Who gave you permission to be on my property?"

"Ownership of this land seems to be a matter of contention."

Butler grinned and rocked back on the heels of his scarred work boots. "Matter of contention, eh?" The expression on his face said *city asshole*. He glanced at Traverse. "Never seen an Indian cop before. You're here about that Hutterite."

"That's right. Jacob Waldner," Traverse said, crossing his arms.

"Don't know nothing about it, and I'm too busy to be standing around talking to you."

"We hear he was out here on Wednesday afternoon. What happened?"

The mocking smile again. He lifted his hat and wiped his brow with his hand. "You're wrong. I never seen him."

A screen door slammed behind them, and when Shelter turned, he saw a man walking toward a beat-up pickup. He was younger and slimmer than Butler, but dressed much the same: T-shirt, jeans, and work boots. Under a worn green baseball cap, his brown hair reached his shoulders. He had a wiry build and was one of the few men Shelter had seen in the area without a beard. He held a leash attached to a squat, muscular pit bull. With barely a glance in their direction, he loaded the dog into a cage in the back of a pickup, got in, and drove onto the gravel road.

Turning back to Butler, Shelter said, "Where were you yesterday morning?"

"I'm not answering your questions, but I'll give you a hint." He pointed toward the horizon. "I've got three thousand acres out here, and it's harvest time. That grain's not coming off on its own."

"So, you were working. Can anyone confirm that?"

Butler eyed Shelter as he pulled a crumpled pack of cigarettes from the back pocket of his jeans. He lit one and took a drag. "You know your way back to the city."

Shelter didn't like this guy and decided to rattle his cage. "All the Hutterites have to do is go to court, and you'll be evicted."

His eyes flashed with anger. "Those fucking Hutterites aren't getting my land." Butler coughed, hacked up phlegm, turned his head, and spat into the gravel. "Not going to happen."

"They already got it, as far as I know."

"That's what you know, eh?" He shook his head. "Well, I'm getting it back."

"Is that what you talked to Jacob about when he was out here?"

"I told you. I didn't talk to him, but I grew up with the Hutterites around here. They won't fight. They're going to sell it back to me."

"How can you be so sure?"

Butler grinned and shook his head through the smoke from the cigarette dangling from his lips. "Get off my land."

They didn't move. "Where are you getting all that money from, Lanny?" Traverse asked.

"Get off now. You're trespassing."

Shelter paused a long second before he and Traverse turned and headed back to their car. Butler watched them get into the vehicle before grinding out his cigarette with his boot and sauntering back toward the garage.

"Nasty piece of work," Traverse said, stating the obvious as he climbed into the passenger seat.

"Oh yeah," Shelter said. "But why kill Jacob and go all the way into the city to do it? How would he even know Jacob was going into the city yesterday morning in the first place?"

"Maybe Jacob had something on him, and he wanted to kill him away from this area."

The car had just reached the end of the Butler driveway when Shelter's cellphone buzzed. He pulled to the side of the road to answer. "I just sent you a picture," Jennifer Kane said. "It's a freeze-frame from the doorbell camera at the house where Waldner was killed."

Shelter could tell from Kane's slight breathlessness that she was excited about whatever the photo showed. "Hold on."

He opened his email and clicked the link she'd sent him. The image showed a short, stocky man leaning against the trunk of a large tree in the park across the street. Shelter used his thumb and forefinger to enlarge the photo. "Who am I looking at?"

"Ian enhanced the image. We're pretty sure it's Elias Stahl's husband."

Shelter brought the image closer to his eyes as Kane explained that they'd missed Garnier the first time because he'd been at the very edge of the camera's field of view. Shelter felt his cheeks warm and his heartbeat tick higher. Garnier had been waiting for Jacob.

"Did you find him anywhere else in the video?"

"No. He's watching the Airbnb when Waldner arrives, then he walks out of camera range. That's it."

"You still haven't tracked him down?"

"Nope. He's not answering his phone, and we've been to the condo a couple of times."

"Keep trying. We're heading back to the city now. We should be back by four."

Traverse had pieced together what was happening from the phone conversation. "If they can't find him this afternoon, I know where he might be tonight. Elias has his big opening at the gallery."

"Right," said Shelter, looking over at his partner. "You're big into modern art. You might have been planning to go anyway."

Traverse rolled his eyes. "Janice is going to kill me if I have to work overtime again tonight. I'm supposed to take Luke to hockey practice." Luke, at thirteen, was the eldest of Traverse's three kids. He'd become a superb athlete, playing intercity soccer in the summer and already practising for his Double-A hockey season. Combined with the younger children's activities—practices, games, and play dates—it put a considerable strain on the couple. Janice had her own heavy workload, teaching, and conducting research at the university, on top of Traverse's unpredictable schedule.

"I'll see if Jen can make it," Shelter said. He hit the accelerator, heading northeast. He glanced down at the speedometer as it hit one hundred kilometres an hour, then set the cruise control. He felt excited. This might be the break they needed in the case.

The atmosphere had grown heavy, and a mass of black rain clouds loomed on the horizon ahead. Perhaps it was the drop in atmospheric pressure that brought it on, but Shelter suddenly found himself back in that run-down house in Winnipeg, kneeling beside the dying young woman. He saw her brown eyes locked on his, and the smell of her blood filled his nostrils. His heart hammered, his vision blurred, and he felt dizzy. He experienced a sense of dread and once again feared he might faint. He brought a hand to his temple and let out a groan.

"What's going on?" Traverse demanded.

"I think you'd better take the wheel."

Shelter managed to steer the car to the shoulder and put it in park. The flashback had vanished as quickly as it had appeared, but he was shaken. He handed the key to Traverse and rubbed his face hard with both hands. He rested his hands on his thighs to stop them from shaking. When he looked over at his partner, Traverse was frowning and shaking his head. "Hey, this is getting serious. You'd better book off sick and get some help."

Shelter nodded but remained silent. Once again, his mind turned to the potential consequences of mental or neurological problems for his career. He knew there wasn't the same stigma attached to it now as in decades past, but he still feared it could lead to early retirement and the purgatory of life as a former cop. Doing what? At best, he could teach policing techniques at a community college or work as a security consultant, whatever that entailed. His identity was tied not only to being a cop but also to being a homicide detective—one of the elite few.

They hustled to switch places in the pounding rain. Now in the passenger seat, Shelter knew his catastrophic thinking wasn't helping the situation. He struggled to calm down. Looking out the rain-streaked passenger window, he felt drowsy, and that was the last thing he remembered until he woke with a jolt at a stoplight at the intersection with the Perimeter Highway on the city's southwestern outskirts. He'd been asleep for close to an hour.

They drove back through the city in silence, digesting what had happened. When Traverse parked in the underground garage at headquarters, he turned to Shelter. "You've got to get whatever is going on in your head taken care of, or I'm going to have to report it. No kidding."

Shelter knew it was unlikely Traverse would follow through on the threat, but he couldn't be sure. He believed his partner of twelve years would never turn him in to the bosses for any reason. But he couldn't deny what Traverse was saying. The insomnia, nightmares, flashbacks, and now the dizziness—it was getting worse.

"Okay. I'll call someone. I'll handle it."

ELEVEN

SHELTER WAS RELIEVED to find the bathroom outside the homicide unit vacant. He splashed cold water on his face and examined himself in the mirror. Whatever was happening scared him. He needed help and promised himself he would call his doctor in the morning. It was on him to get help before he hurt himself or someone else. Thankfully, the nap in the car had done him good, and he felt ready to get on with the day.

When he arrived at the detective bullpen, Jennifer Kane was leaning on the corner of Traverse's desk. She looked up and gave Shelter a smile that told him Traverse hadn't mentioned what had happened on the trip back from the country. Traverse watched him closely and gave him a slight nod before turning back to Kane to continue their conversation.

Kane had caught the exchange of looks. "What's up?"

"Nothing," Shelter said. "Where's Martin Garnier?"

Kane squinted, signalling suspicion, then let it go. She led them through a rundown of her fruitless search for Garnier that day. There'd been no answer at the condo he shared with Elias Stahl, where Kane assumed he worked, given that his LinkedIn account listed his profession as a freelance translator. He'd also failed to return her voice and text messages.

She'd had no more luck getting hold of Elias that afternoon. The art gallery was closed for the day to prepare for the opening. An employee said Elias was showing the town to the Berlin visual artist whose exhibition was being launched. But the employee didn't know where Elias was, and he wasn't answering his phone or responding to texts.

"How do you feel about avant-garde art?" Shelter asked Kane. "You want to go to this thing and try to find Garnier? Gabe can't make it."

"Hmm, sounds interesting. Let me call Sherry." Sherry was Kane's wife. They'd been married for over ten years and were the parents of two children in elementary school—another couple whose lives were constantly disrupted by the demands of homicide work.

While she was calling home, Shelter went to his desk, opened his email, and clicked again on the freeze-frame image of Garnier that Kane had sent him. The photo showed the short, muscular man standing in the park, a little way down the street from the house where Jacob was to meet Elias. It moved Garnier to the top of the suspect list.

Still, they had to keep working on the dispute over the Butler farm. Shelter did a Google search for William Cameron, the Hutterites' lawyer, and found his LinkedIn profile. From the man's work history, Shelter saw that Cameron ran his own firm on Broadway Avenue, the city's main downtown business artery.

Shelter phoned his office, and Cameron's assistant put him through right away. After introducing himself, Shelter said, "I hear you represent the Round Rock Hutterite Colony."

"I represent it and several other colonies. I've been expecting your call."

"The Hutterites tell me Jacob was in town to meet you yesterday. About what?"

"I'm not sure, to be honest. He called on Wednesday and said he had some important information and needed my advice on how to proceed. But he didn't want to discuss it over the phone. I assume it had something to do with the Butler farm. You know about that, right?" Cameron spoke with the authoritative voice of someone used to counselling clients.

"Lanny Butler won't get off the property," Shelter said.

"We've been trying for months to find a solution. Jacob was heavily involved in planning the new colony and buying the farm. We've made several attempts to persuade Butler to leave, including a good-faith offer of cash to compensate him for his expenses. The Hutterites were supposed to take possession in May, but he refuses to leave."

Shelter was again struck by how difficult the situation was for the Hutterites. "Can he do that?"

"He can until someone throws him off."

"Why did his father cut him out of the will?"

"Bad blood in the family, obviously, but I don't know the details. Last winter, Lanny told his brother Daniel he was going to contest the will, but that didn't go anywhere. I advised the Hutterites to simply evict him, but they decided against going that route. Jacob was pretty upset about it."

"Upset enough to do something about it on his own?"

"Like what?"

"That's what we're trying to figure out."

"Not that I know of, but anything's possible, I guess. He did tell me he had to go to another meeting after ours, but he didn't say who it was with."

Shelter's eyebrows shot up. "You asked him who he was meeting?"

"Yeah, but he wouldn't say."

Shelter made a note. "They tell me Lanny Butler made the Hutterites an offer for the property. Any idea where he's getting the cash?"

Cameron paused for a moment. "That might be a good question for the brother. You should give him a call."

Cameron found Daniel Butler's number and gave it to Shelter. "I gotta run. Let me know if I can help."

When he'd hung up, Shelter checked his email and then called over to Kane's desk. "Did we hear from the ME yet?"

"Oh yeah. Frayne wants you to phone him."

"Thanks for mentioning that," Shelter said with a smile.

Kane returned the smile and silently mouthed, "fuck off."

Jonathan Frayne was the provincial medical examiner. He would've been performing the autopsy on Jacob Waldner's body for much of the day. It was Shelter's practice to get the big-picture findings from the ME over the phone and any finer details from reading his report once it was ready. He'd attended his fair share of autopsies and learned that there were better, less distressing ways to spend his time than observing the long, painstaking, and grisly work of the ME.

Frayne was nearing retirement age and old-school enough to answer his phone if he happened to be at his desk. Although he'd been in Manitoba for nearly forty years, he still had the remnants of an upper-crust British accent that reminded Shelter of his grandfather. Besides a dry sense of humour, the two men also shared many physical traits—tall, thin, and balding.

Frayne's first observation from the autopsy was unsurprising. "From the length and direction of the wound, I believe his throat was cut from behind with the right hand. The blade was very sharp. Massive blood loss. Death would have been quite quick." Frayne paused. "One moment, please. Yes. From the orientation of the cut to the throat, it was someone shorter than the victim. So, shorter than six feet, if that's any help to you."

"It is. Thanks. Time of death?"

"Somewhere between 10:30 and 12:30."

This confirmed Shelter's reading of the crime scene. The hand used in the attack wasn't much help. A left-handed person could use their right hand. Although, for what it was worth, he'd been checking, and the suspects so far had all either been confirmed as right-handed or appeared to be so, in the case of Lanny Butler.

"Any other signs of a struggle?"

"Nothing. The hands and body were clean."

"Toxicology?"

"No drugs of any kind, including alcohol, in his system."

"Thanks, Jonathan. I'll wait for the report for the rest."

Shelter found a corner table in the cafeteria and punched Penny's number into his cellphone. He was still shaken by his near loss of control in the car and wanted to talk to her about it. In the little over a year they'd been together, he'd found her to be a steady, reassuring presence in times of trouble.

He'd first learned this when Kelsey unexpectedly returned from university in Montreal the previous fall. She'd become gripped by anxiety as she entered her second year. She'd broken up with a boyfriend, missed her friends in Manitoba, and worried she'd made the wrong choice of program.

Shelter had been deeply worried about her and the possibility that her education would be derailed if she lost a year. Even though Penny hadn't known Kelsey for long, she was able to help quickly. By speaking with father and daughter separately, she helped them take a more objective view of the consequences of taking a break from university. What's the worst that could happen? Kelsey dropped her courses and decided to do something else with her life. Was that so terrible?

Although Shelter didn't like the situation, Penny helped him see that his stress was only making it worse. He made a conscious effort to cool it. Kelsey calmed down, too, after getting some decent sleep and enjoying the delicious, healthy food Penny and Shelter took turns making for her. Within a couple of weeks, she was back in Montreal, seeing a psychologist, and on track in her courses, with no damage to her academic standing.

Penny answered her phone on the second ring.

"You at home?"

"No. I'm at my mom's place. I'm going to stay here for a while."

Shelter was taken aback. He'd been hoping she'd decide they could figure this out after some time to reflect. But now, as both went silent on their respective ends of the line, he realized his hopes had been based on her capitulating to his position. He was unsure how or what to say that wouldn't push her further away. Finally, he said, "I'm sorry about how it went the other night. I didn't get how strongly you feel about this."

"I'm just sad. I don't see how this can work right now."

It suddenly felt as if the whole relationship were hanging in the balance. "We can work it out. Come home, and we'll talk about it."

"No. I've got to get clear on where I'm heading. I feel like there's so much weight on me, and it's just really hard."

He could tell from her voice that she was on the verge of tears. He bowed his head and rubbed his forehead, searching for what to say. Finally, in a low voice, he said, "I don't want to lose you."

"I don't want it either, but sometimes we have to make hard decisions." She fell silent again. He listened to her breathing and wished they were together in that moment. Finally, she said, "I need time to think, okay? I'll call you when I'm ready."

"Okay. All right. I love you."

"I know."

TWELVE

GERHARD FISCHER was the Berlin artist whose work would be on display for a month-long run at the Reservoir gallery. Shelter scanned the website during a quick trip home to grab a sandwich and change into a suit. The gallery billed the exhibition *Gerhard Fischer: Declarations and Confessions* as "an exploration of the renowned visual artist's career, including new works in which Fischer uses powerful imagery to portray the current context of global upheaval and dislocation."

"It looks like we'll be crashing the party," Shelter said to Jennifer Kane when he picked her up at her house off Jubilee Avenue, south of downtown.

"That will be fun," she said with a smile as she fastened her seat belt. Kane had chosen a knee-length floral skirt and a cream-coloured blazer over her white blouse. Shelter and Kane were close friends, and he knew she wouldn't mind his comment on her appearance. "Looks like you got dressed up for the occasion."

"Not so much," she said, looking down at the skirt falling across her knees. "Okay, I don't get out much, and I had this in the closet." She eyed without comment his navy-blue suit, which he wore with a white shirt and no tie. Her eyes went to his face. "Hey, you're not looking so good. What's up?"

Shelter had been expecting a compliment on his attire and was surprised she could detect his disheartened mood. He didn't answer immediately. He wanted to talk to her about Penny's desire for a baby, but he judged that this wasn't the time or place for a deep discussion. "I could be better, but it's okay."

"What could be better?"

"Ah, you know with Penny, it's not easy."

"What's going on?"

"No. Let's talk when there's more time."

Crossing the Osborne Street Bridge, Shelter glanced toward the east. The sun, now low in the sky, illuminated the trees lining the banks of the Assiniboine River and glinted off the water, where a boat was ploughing westward.

"When we get there, we'll take a quick look around for Garnier," he said. "If he's not there, we'll try the condo again."

"I pulled his picture off Google Images." She reached into the inside pocket of her jacket and handed him a photocopy while they waited at a red light at Portage Avenue. From the headshot, Shelter could tell Garnier was quite a bit older than Elias Stahl, probably in his mid-forties. He was clean-shaven, with thinning black hair that had begun to grey at the temples.

After parking and walking a short distance to the Reservoir, Shelter was impressed by the gallery's transformation for the opening. Elias Stahl had clearly done his best to make it a glamourous event. It was dusk, and two spotlights illuminated the building's façade. White lettering on a scarlet banner above the door read: *Gerhard Fischer: Declarations and Confessions.*

A knot of fashionably dressed attendees was smoking and chatting on the street, and as they approached, Shelter saw through the windows a large crowd already schmoozing inside the gallery.

He expected they'd be there only long enough to track down Garnier, if he was inside, but his little joke about crashing the party didn't seem so funny anymore. He felt anxiety creeping into his gut as they got closer to entering the place. Shelter didn't like crowds at the best of times, but the gnawing tension he felt now was different. He took a deep breath and steeled himself. Garnier might not even be here, but they had to find him, and this was worth a try.

They edged past the smokers and entered the gallery. Jazz flowed from speakers strategically placed around the large room, adding to the din of people chatting and laughing. The overhead lighting was low, and the dimness lent the room a mysterious cast, drawing the eye to the paintings, dramatically displayed under track lighting. Most people held wine glasses, and servers circulated with canapés.

He followed Kane as she weaved her way to a corner from where they could survey the crowd, though it wasn't easy to make out faces in the low lighting. Shelter nodded at a bald man in a white linen suit with his back to them. He cupped a hand over his mouth and leaned toward Kane. "That's the chairman of the gallery's board, Leonard Diamond. He was here last night with Elias after the body was found."

"Did he know Jacob Waldner?"

"He says not." Shelter turned to examine a large canvas on the wall to his left. It showed a collage of abstract renderings of military hardware—a tank, a cannon, and an attack helicopter—against a background of multi-coloured slashes of paint. The next painting along the wall depicted the decrepit entrance to a tenement on a trash-strewn street, rendered in drab mustard and olive tones. In the middle of the gallery, a projector played a continuous loop of disturbing images on the wall, including a child screaming and a man throwing a can of red paint at a naked woman.

Shelter turned his attention back to the crowd and spotted Elias Stahl standing beside a burly man with a long white beard, wearing a black T-shirt and jeans. From a photo on the Reservoir's website, he recognized the man as Gerhard Fischer. A woman in the group surrounding the two men said something, and they both laughed heartily. As Fischer replied to the woman, a smiling Stahl scanned the room, clearly satisfied with how the evening was progressing, until his eyes came to rest on Shelter. The smile fell from his face, replaced by a tense expression. He excused himself and headed toward Shelter and Kane.

Shelter half-turned to Kane and whispered, "incoming." Stahl made slow progress toward them, nodding, smiling, and excusing himself as he slipped past guests. When he finally stood before the two detectives, he struck an aggressive pose, fists on his hips. "What the hell are you doing here?" he hissed in a low voice. "I've answered all your questions."

"Hello, Elias," Shelter said. "It's a nice evening you're putting on here. If you'd returned our calls this afternoon, we might not be here."

Stahl scoffed. "What do you want? I'm too busy for this."

"It's actually your husband we're looking for."

The look of irritation on Stahl's face turned to confusion. He scanned the immediate area to see if anyone was eavesdropping on their conversation. "Martin? I'm sorry, but ..."

Kane grasped Shelter's arm. "There he is," she said, pointing toward the door. "He's taking off."

By the time Shelter and Kane could break through the crowd and reach the street, Martin Garnier was halfway down the block, speedwalking toward the river.

"Mr. Garnier, wait up," Shelter shouted. Garnier kept going, apparently pretending he hadn't heard. "Hey! Stop now."

Garnier halted and turned to face Shelter and Kane. He was no more than five feet eight. In the glow of a newly lit streetlight, his cable-knit sweater showed off a well-developed chest and arms, the result, no doubt, of hours in the gym. Shelter surmised that if Garnier had been trying to sneak out of Reservoir to avoid them, he must have already known they were police. Perhaps he'd seen Shelter's picture in the paper or looked him up online. "You're leaving the party pretty early there, Mr. Garnier," Shelter said.

"I'm sorry. You are?" It was an unconvincing performance.

"We're detectives investigating the homicide of Jacob Waldner. We have some questions for you."

"No. I'm sorry. I know nothing about that. I'm tired and have a full day ahead of me tomorrow." Shelter detected a French accent and assumed Garnier was Québécois, since Franco-Manitobans usually spoke English without an accent. Garnier turned to leave down the street, where tall trees filtered the light of a full moon.

"Just a minute." Shelter knew he didn't yet have enough evidence to charge this man, but depending on Garnier's answers, they might arrest him, read him his rights, and take him downtown for formal questioning.

"We've spoken quite a bit with Elias, and we want to get your take on this."

Garnier's irritated sigh struck Shelter as theatrical. He could tell Garnier was nervous, as people often were when talking to the police. "I really don't have anything to say about it."

"We've been trying to reach you all day."

"I'm sorry. I was working on a project at a client's office and had my phone off."

Another transparently fake response. "Did you know Jacob Waldner?"

Garnier crossed his arms tightly across his chest. "Do I have to answer your questions?"

"No," Kane said quietly. "But I'm sure you want to help us get to the bottom of this, don't you, Martin?"

Shelter was always impressed by Kane's ability to use a disarming tone to win over a reluctant witness or suspect. Garnier studied her face for a moment. "All right," he said. "I met Jacob just once when he came to our place for a drink."

He addressed his answer to Kane, and as he spoke, he let his arms drop and seemed to relax ever so slightly. Shelter was happy to let Kane take the lead while he scrutinized Garnier's body language and listened to his tone.

"Do you have any idea who could have killed him?" she asked.

"No. Of course not. It's just horrible. Elias is suffering terribly, and he's had to soldier on with this stupid show.

There was no way to cancel it with that man coming to town. It's been in the works for months."

"Especially awful for him to have seen the body," Kane said. "Where were you yesterday morning?"

"I'm a translator. I was at home working in the morning and then went to visit a client in the afternoon."

"Who's that?"

"He works for the provincial government. He was briefing me on a project we're beginning in September." Garnier gave her the client's name and promised to provide his contact details.

"So, you didn't go anywhere else?" she asked.

"Well, I was out for dinner in the evening, but no, that's it."

Kane's tone became firmer. "That's odd, because we have you on video from yesterday morning in the park in front of the house where Jacob was killed," she said, pointing toward Saint Boniface. "How do you explain that?"

Garnier's eyes grew wide. He shook his head. "No. You're mistaken." It came out breathless, panicky.

"We're not mistaken. Now, explain what you were doing there."

Garnier lowered his eyes to the sidewalk and was silent for several seconds as he considered his options. Finally, he exhaled and said, "I'm not proud of it, okay?" He paused again before adding, "I wanted to talk to Jacob. To tell him to stop sleeping with my husband. I couldn't take it anymore."

"Elias told us you were aware of the relationship and were okay with it," Shelter said. "Was that a lie?"

"That's Elias's take on it. It's convenient for him to think I'm perfectly fine with him fucking his ex-boyfriend, yeah? I agreed to it because I didn't want to lose him. But it's been eating me alive. I needed it to stop, and I knew Elias would never agree to it. Even after we got together, he never stopped loving Jacob."

"How did you know where Jacob would be?"

Garnier gave a shake of his head as he looked skyward. Almost in a whisper, he said, "I know the password to Elias's phone. I saw from their texts that Jacob was coming to town and that they'd be meeting at that house." He looked from Shelter to Kane. "That's when I had the idea to wait for him to arrive."

"Why not just phone him?" Kane asked.

"I needed to talk to him face-to-face. I know it was crazy. I lost control. But that morning, I couldn't make myself go through with it. I'm such a fucking coward." His voice had grown husky, and his eyes were teary. "I just walked away."

"You never spoke to him?"

"No. I decided to have it out with Elias instead." He shook his head and wiped his eyes. "But I ended up comforting him over the death of his lover. Can you believe that?"

"Where did you go when you decided not to confront Jacob?" Shelter asked.

"It's like I said. I went home and worked until my appointment with my client. Then I went for dinner. When I got home, Elias was out."

"Can someone vouch that you were at home when you say you were yesterday morning?"

"I phoned and texted Elias a bunch of times, but he didn't answer. I was also emailing and texting with a couple of clients."

"Did you see anyone else entering the house in Saint Boniface or watching it?" Kane asked.

Garnier shook his head. "I was only there for a short time. I didn't see anyone, other than Jacob."

Kane glanced at Shelter. Her expression was neutral, but Shelter knew from long experience working with her that she wasn't seeing enough here to arrest Garnier. He'd admitted to being overcome by jealousy and waiting for Jacob, but there were no witnesses, video, or physical evidence placing him in the house where the murder occurred. A lot of work would be needed on Garnier, including checking his alibi, phone records, and other CCTV evidence. For now, they needed a videotaped statement. "We'd like you to come downtown to answer a few more questions and give us a DNA sample and your fingerprints," Shelter said.

Garnier recoiled as if Shelter had shoved him in the chest, his eyes wide with alarm. "I've told you everything I know."

"We'll need to go through it again and tie up any loose ends."

Garnier shook his head. "I have to talk to Elias. I don't want to get involved in this."

"Oh, you're involved, Martin."

It had been a long day, and Shelter decided the videotaped interview could wait until the next morning. He reached into his jacket pocket and drew out a business card. "All right, be at police headquarters on Graham at 9:00 a.m. tomorrow. If you think of anything in the meantime, call me."

Once Garnier had left, Shelter checked his watch and saw it was still early evening. "You want to grab a drink?"

"Yeah, sure. What did you have in mind?"

"If you're hungry, we could do the Beijing."

Kane smiled at the suggestion. The Beijing Garden was one of Shelter's favourite hangouts and only a short drive from where they were in the Exchange District. He'd been deprived of his regular lunchtime visits to his Chinatown haunt since they moved out of the old Public Safety Building. But she wasn't as enamoured of the restaurant as he was—and definitely not for a nightcap.

"Let's go to a bar," she said. They agreed on Sally's, a cozy cocktail lounge on South Osborne, a strip of stores and restaurants on the way home for Kane. It would be busy on a Friday night, but they'd take a chance on finding seats.

"What'd you think of that guy?" Kane asked in the car.

"I'm not seeing him as a great fit."

"Yeah, but he said it himself, 'I lost control.'"

Shelter shrugged. He was having trouble imagining this timid man with his carefully curated physique planning and executing a murder in the middle of the day by clinically drawing a knife across the throat of his husband's lover. "I've got the same issue with this guy as with Elias. This murder doesn't look to me like an impulsive act. It took planning and nerve."

THIRTEEN

THE SEATS AT THE BAR were full, but two men were getting up from a corner table. Shelter ordered a light beer because he was driving, and Kane opted for a Manhattan. They talked shop for a few minutes before Kane took a sip of her drink, ate a maraschino cherry, and asked, "So, what's up with you and Penny?"

Kane had first met Penny last winter. She and her wife had joined Penny and Shelter for dinner at a cozy restaurant in Fort Garry. They'd shared laughs over wine and Thai food, and on Monday, Kane pulled Shelter aside in the coffee room to give his girlfriend her seal of approval.

Shelter knew that both Kane and Traverse had quietly hoped he would find a relationship that would fill the void that Christa's death had left in his life. Now, he'd finally found someone.

Shelter wasn't crazy about answering questions about his relationship, but he knew there was no point in going with anything but total honesty with Kane. Resistance was futile. She knew him too well and was good at quickly piercing his defences and getting to whatever he was trying to hide. In police work, he was a master interrogator, even giving a much sought-after course on the subject once a year to other officers. When it came to matters of the heart, though, he was no match for Jennifer Kane.

He didn't try to sugarcoat it. "She really wants to have a baby, and I'm not sure."

"Not sure? Why?"

Here we go, thought Shelter. Kane was a black-and-white kind of person and not afraid to challenge Shelter. "I just don't want to go there at this stage in my life."

"You love kids. This is a chance to be a dad again."

Shelter raised an eyebrow. "Okay. Let's not get carried away. You know the first year is pure sleep-deprived hell that takes you right into the terrible twos." They both laughed, and Shelter continued. "I will admit that three to twelve are glorious. Kelsey was so amazing." His smile faded. "But thirteen to seventeen, oh my God."

During those years, he and Kelsey had both been dealing with Christa's death, and she'd been going through it as a teenager. "I think I was a terrible father back then. I didn't know how to talk to her. She used to make me so damn angry. I don't know if I can go through that again, especially in my mid-fifties."

"That's a long way down the road. It'll be different. I'm not saying it'll be easier. It isn't easy for Sherry and me. Life isn't easy. But you and Christa loved being parents, and you had always wanted more kids." She took a sip of her drink. "Is there something else going on between you and Penny?"

"No. It's good," he said. He looked Kane in the eyes for a moment before deciding it was better to be upfront. "Actually, it's not okay. We've been fighting more over the past few weeks, and now she's staying at her mom's place and talking about not coming back."

"Oh, wow, I'm sorry."

He looked around the bar before bringing his eyes back to Kane. "I'll think about what you said. I know it's on me to decide one way or another." He considered telling her about his insomnia, nightmares, and dizziness, all of which were no doubt making it harder with Penny. But he couldn't take any more deep discussion. He knew he had to see a doctor and promised himself he would make the call soon. "Thanks for listening."

"You did a fair bit of listening," Kane said with a smile.

Shelter laughed. "Well, thanks for making me listen, then."

The next morning, riding the elevator to the office, Shelter sipped a double shot of espresso from a paper cup. He hoped the extra caffeine would help him get through the morning. The same nightmare had woken him at 2:30 a.m., as it had the night before. He'd tossed and turned the rest of the night, his thoughts ricocheting from one worry to another—from the tangled Waldner investigation to his mental health to Penny.

When he finally dragged himself out of bed, his eyes burned, and his brain felt foggy. Pouring himself a bowl of cereal, he was set on edge by his chubby cat Norman's innocent meowing. He reminded himself to keep a tight rein on his mood today. If not, he'd end up apologizing for lashing out at someone, and the day would spiral downward. He yawned and stretched in the elevator, dreading a verbal joust with Martin Garnier.

Garnier arrived on time. Ushering him into an interview room, Shelter suppressed a smile at the formal outfit Garnier had chosen for this Saturday morning trip to the police station—a chocolate-brown suit with a pocket kerchief, a striped, white-and-gold tie, and brogues. The get-up contrasted with Shelter's casual weekend outfit of a plaid button shirt and chinos.

Garnier proved more cooperative than the night before. He repeated his story, admitting once again to spying on his husband's communications, waiting for Jacob to arrive at the Saint Boniface Airbnb, then abandoning his plan to confront him. Shelter saved questions about Elias Stahl until the end of the interview, when he judged that Garnier's guard would be down. "How is Elias doing?"

"Terribly. He broke down when he got home from the opening last night. He puts on a brave front, but this has been so painful for him. He's lost his best friend in the worst possible way."

"What did you think when you heard Jacob had been murdered?"

"God. Nothing. Shock. I still don't know what to think."

"Has Elias offered any thoughts about who could have done it?"

The question drew the first rise from Garnier. His head jerked forward, and his face contorted in irritation. "Didn't he already tell you he has no idea? Why won't you believe him?"

"It's not a question of believing or not believing. It's about looking at it from every angle and finding evidence. From what Elias told me, there was tension in his relationship with Jacob. If you have any concerns that Elias may be involved in this, now is the time to share them with me."

"No. Stop," Garnier said, his voice rising. "It's impossible. No one's gentler than Elias. Please leave him alone to grieve."

Shelter didn't respond but waited a moment before asking Garnier to provide access to his digital communications and contact details for the clients he'd interacted with on the day of the murder. Still shaken, Garnier hesitated before finally agreeing.

Rising to leave, he asked, "Will I have to come back?"

"We'll let you know."

Besides the DNA sample and fingerprints they'd taken, Garnier's statement was now on videotape. That could prove important if new evidence came to light that pointed the investigation toward him.

Shelter had left Daniel Butler a voicemail and a text message earlier, asking for a meeting. It took an hour before a terse text came back, telling him to come at eleven. It included an address that turned out to be a garage on Saint Anne's Road in the south end.

When Shelter asked the teenager working the cash register for Daniel Butler, he pointed to the service bays. From the doorway, Shelter spotted a bald, husky man working under a rusty Dodge minivan on a lift.

"Daniel?" he called out.

Butler emerged from under the vehicle, glancing at his watch. He dropped a wrench on the workbench that ran along the far wall and squirted soap from a dispenser onto his hands. He spent a long minute scrubbing grease from his hands before wiping them with a cloth already stained with oil and grime. He grabbed a large lunch box from the bench. "We can talk out back," he said without smiling or offering his hand to shake.

Butler slid into a scarred picnic table on a patch of asphalt. He wore a grey polo shirt stretched over his enormous belly. It had *St. Vital Auto Service* stitched into the chest pocket. Butler's hands were rough and cracked, the nails black from years spent under cars. The sour odour of tobacco came off him.

Without a word to Shelter, he unpacked sandwiches, a bag of salt-and-vinegar chips, and a Coke from his lunch box. He unwrapped one of the sandwiches, which looked to be ham and cheese, and took a large bite.

Finally, he eyed Shelter and said, "Got some ID there, bud?"

Shelter showed his identification. "I'm investigating the murder of Jacob Waldner of the Red Rock Hutterite Colony."

"I know that," Daniel Butler grunted. "I've been following it on the news. What can I do for you?"

"I'm interested in the farm you sold to the Hutterites. I'm told your brother won't get off it."

"He's a fucking bastard," Butler said in a low growl. Shelter waited to see if he'd anything else to add to this outburst, but he'd gone silent again.

"Be that as it may, I'm trying to understand the background here. If Lanny was living there, why did your father leave the farm to you?"

"It was payback," Butler said. "My father lived in fear of my brother and his buddies every day of his life. But he cut Lanny out of the will without telling him, eh?" Butler's face broke into a smile that showed a tangle of teeth yellowed by tobacco. "Not a fucking cent."

"I understand Lanny wants to buy the farm from the Hutterites."

"If it were up to me, there's no way he'd get it. I'd rather it went to weeds than let him have it."

He slipped into another brooding silence as he finished his sandwich. Shelter was about to ask him another question when Butler banged a fist on the table, making Shelter jump. "Lanny killed your man. No doubt about it."

Shelter looked at him in shock. "What do you know about it?"

"The Hutterite must have had something on my brother," he said, pointing a stubby index finger at Shelter. "Something to get him off the land."

Butler was consumed by a fit of congested coughing, and when it stopped, he was gasping. He looked as if he wanted to spit but swallowed instead.

"What evidence do you have for what you're saying?"

"Evidence? Just look at what an asshole he is, what he's done before. That's all you need to know. It had to be him."

Another coughing fit. This one made him bend at the waist beside the table, resting his arms on his knees.

Shelter waited for his breathing to calm before asking, "What has he done before?"

Butler raised his head and looked at Shelter through watery eyes. "I ain't doing your work for you."

Shelter decided to take another tack. "Where's Lanny getting the cash he's offering the Hutterites?"

Butler let out a derisive laugh. He pulled a pack of cigarettes from his breast pocket and lit one. "Money's not a problem for that bunch."

"What do you mean?"

"You'll have to figure that one out for yourself, too. It shouldn't be hard." The meaning was clear: the money was coming from whatever criminal activity Lanny Butler was involved in.

"So, there's just the two of you then? No other siblings."

"We had another brother. Gerry. He's gone."

"Gone where?"

"Dead."

"Dead how?"

Holding the cigarette between two fingers, Butler rubbed the back of the hand with his thumb. "He got shot. They called it a hunting accident, but that was murder, too."

"Who shot him?"

"Lanny's buddy, Mitch Grimes. He got off on it."

"But you don't believe it was an accident?"

Butler gave a grim chuckle and shook his head. "Yeah, right."

"When was this?"

"Twenty-eighteen."

Shelter suspected the brother's death was at the origin of both Butler's hatred of his other brother and his accusation that he'd murdered Jacob Waldner. "Was Lanny on this hunting trip?"

Butler shook his head. "Just Mitch and Gerry. No witnesses."

"Why would Grimes kill your brother?"

"I heard some stuff, but I don't know what's true."

"What did you hear?"

Butler shook his head. "All I'm saying is it wasn't no fucking accident, and Lanny was in on it."

"Where can we find Grimes?"

"You'll find him wherever Lanny is. If they're not at the farm, they're drinking at the hotel."

Shelter considered how Gerry Butler's death might be linked to the Jacob Waldner murder. Had Jacob stumbled across some piece of evidence related to that killing? Could he have threatened to use it to get Lanny Butler off the farm? Or did he have some other information that threatened Lanny Butler and Mitchell Grimes? It was definitely a path to investigate.

"Who's the eldest among you three?" Shelter asked.

"Me, then Lanny, then Gerry. I'm four-and-a-half years older than Lanny and seven older than Gerry."

"And how old does that make you?"

"Forty-three."

Shelter would have guessed Butler was at least a decade older.

"How often do you see Lanny?"

Butler eyed Shelter for a moment before shaking his head and giving him the same grim chuckle.

"Is what happened to Gerry why you dislike Lanny so much?"

"Nah. I've hated Lanny for as long as I can remember."

FOURTEEN

DRIVING BACK to the office, Shelter reviewed in his mind all the different strands of the case that had emerged. Normally, there was little mystery about the broad outlines of a homicide. Although it could take time to establish the facts and gather enough evidence for a prosecution, it almost always turned out to be a depressingly banal scenario—an enraged husband, a bar brawl, a drug deal gone bad—that ended in an extinguished life and a shattered family. The Winnipeg police solved between eighty and ninety percent of murders, but this was one of the most challenging cases he'd ever come up against. It was going to take every bit of skill, experience, and guile to solve it.

The relationship between Jacob and Elias Stahl. Martin Garnier's jealous rage. The sale of the Butler farm. And the shooting of Gerry Butler years earlier. Had one of these forces pierced the peaceful world of the Hutterite colony and led to Jacob Waldner's murder?

Or was it none of them? Shelter shook his head and sighed as he pulled into the underground garage.

In the detectives' bullpen, Shelter found Himmat Sharma going through Jacob Waldner's cellphone records. Shelter leaned on the detective's cubicle divider. He was grateful for a brief distraction before the dreary but unavoidable job of writing up notes from the interviews with Garnier and Daniel Butler.

"Anything of use in there?"

"It doesn't look like it," Sharma said. "Pretty routine. He spoke to their lawyer a few times and to the accountant, James Deacon, once, but other than that, it's only other colony members or routine business, like a call to the nurse, Julie Klassen."

The content of each call would have to be verified with the other parties. He knew Jacob kept the colony's books, so it made sense that he'd talk with the accountant. His grandmother had died recently, so the call to Julie might have been about that, or about some other sick or injured member of the colony.

Shelter returned to his desk and slouched in his chair, legs outstretched. He checked his coffee mug, but it was empty. The last thing he felt like doing was paperwork. His thoughts turned to his visit to the Hutterite colony the day before.

That world and Jacob's place in it remained too much of a mystery. He understood the broad outlines of how the colony worked—the sharing of everything and each person working in their role to support the community. The minister and general manager seemed to wield a lot of power over the people, but what were the deeper power dynamics? What had Elias said? *"Many rules, many secrets."*

He was finally getting to his reports when Traverse came over.

"You talk to Ian yet?" Traverse asked.

Shelter recalled that Ian Sim had been looking into Elias Stahl's whereabouts on the day Jacob was killed.

"Did he get anything on Elias?"

"He found video of him at the Vietnamese restaurant yesterday around noon. And his assistant confirms she was with him throughout the morning. It looks like his alibi checks out."

"That's good, but we still need to talk to him again to get more background on the colony and Jacob."

Ruling Stahl out as the killer was progress of a kind. It allowed them to stop pouring resources into finding evidence placing him at the murder scene and freed them to use him as a source on other lines of investigation.

But Stahl wasn't out of the woods yet. There was still the possibility he'd been involved in planning the murder. As Shelter dialled Stahl's number, he reminded himself to proceed with caution.

Elias Stahl agreed to meet Shelter for coffee at the Red River Wagon, a diner halfway between police headquarters and the art gallery. The meeting was set for 2:30 p.m.

Realizing he hadn't eaten all day, Shelter decided to grab a quick lunch at the Wagon—as it was known by one and all—before Stahl arrived.

With its neon sign in the window depicting an old-time horse-drawn wagon, the Formica counter running the length of the room, and four booths against the other wall, the Wagon had been a downtown institution for decades. The greasy spoon menu offered burgers, hot dogs, and a few local favourites, including perogies and pan-fried pickerel, but almost everyone ordered the Wagon's specialty, a giant clubhouse sandwich stacked high with chunks of turkey, bacon, tomatoes, pickle slices, and lettuce. Shelter's father had first brought him there as a boy, and he couldn't get his mouth around the clubhouse. It was still a challenge.

"Hey, Mike," Harry Artino called out as Shelter came through the glass door.

Shelter exchanged a fist bump with a smiling Artino. He manned the cash register at the entrance and kept a benevolent eye on the lunchtime rush. He was the son of the Greek immigrant who'd opened the restaurant in the 1960s. Harry's charm was a big part of the Wagon's appeal, but he was nearing retirement age. Harry's kids had no interest in carrying on, and closure was a clear and present danger for Shelter and the Wagon's many other devoted patrons. For now, the lunchtime crowd had mostly cleared out, and he found a booth toward the back of the restaurant.

Thirty minutes later, Shelter put both hands on his full belly. This wasn't health food, but he loved it too much to give it up. His concession to heart health had been to cut back on his visits to the restaurant. He pulled out his cellphone and composed a text to Penny.

Can we get together tonight? I miss you.

While he waited for an answer, he checked his watch. Elias would be arriving soon if he was on time.

Not ready yet. I will contact you in a couple of days.

Shelter was disappointed. He'd hoped she'd come over to the house for a talk. He felt as if Penny had put their relationship on trial and was passing judgment without giving him a chance to plead his case. If he could talk to her, he hoped they could find a way to stay together, even though he still wasn't ready to agree to become a father again.

A few minutes later, Elias Stahl came through the door. He was wearing a tan sweatshirt, jeans, and red Nike running shoes. When he took off his square tortoise-shell sunglasses, Shelter noticed dark circles under his eyes. Once Stahl had ordered coffee, Shelter asked, "Have you recovered from your show?"

"It's been a hellish few days. I'm completely wiped out, but despite everything, I feel like it was the right decision to go ahead, and it seems the board and staff are happy with how the evening went."

Shelter kept a close watch on him, gauging his emotional state and looking for signs of deception. He detected a new tone in Stahl's speech, more low-key and reflective. It felt like he was, unsurprisingly, suffering an emotional letdown after the frenzy of the past few days.

"What have you found out about Jacob?" Stahl asked.

"We're investigating a bunch of different angles. That's why I asked for this meeting. Have you thought of anything that could help us?"

Stahl shook his head, his face tight with concern. "I can't imagine anyone wanting to hurt him."

"Tell me more about your relationship with him."

Stahl played with his coffee spoon before raising his eyes to meet Shelter's. "I loved that boy, and I hated him."

"Hated him. Why?"

"We depended on the colony for everything. Food, shelter, work, community—everything. When we left, it was literally with the shirts on our backs. We'd talked about it for so long, but when we actually did it, it was scary and hard."

Elias dropped his eyes to the spoon again and shook his head at the memory. "We ended up in minimum-wage jobs. Me, washing dishes in a restaurant. Him, working in this dirty cardboard factory. We had a one-bedroom suite, and we were always right on the edge."

He took a sip of coffee. "Jacob couldn't take it. One night, he told me he needed to go back. I guess I should've expected it. Many runaways end up going back, but he left me alone, abandoned with nothing. It was just a huge fucking betrayal."

Shelter thought about the two young men alone in a strange city and an alien culture. Jacob chose to go back to the colony's safety and security, while Elias kept going and made a new life for himself. A farm boy from a closed religious community who turned himself into the director of a major gallery. It was a remarkable achievement. He wondered how it had made Jacob feel to see Elias succeed in the outside world. "You went on seeing each other?"

"No. Not for years. But a couple of years ago, he contacted me. I was still so angry at him."

"You knew he'd gotten married and had kids?"

"Of course. My parents are still there, and my brothers and sisters."

"You agreed to see him?"

"I didn't want to, but I'd seen him on my visits to the colony, and I missed him. It was bigger than me. That's how it started."

"You go back to the colony?"

Again, the grim smile. "The minister lets me back a couple of times a year, but not for the holidays. That's not allowed for 'the lost,'—that's what they call us."

He sighed and glanced around the restaurant before returning his gaze to Shelter. "It's always painful. They think being gay is evil, the work of the devil. And I ran away, so it's a double X against me in their eyes. They think I'm a bad influence on the others."

Shelter thought about how terrible it must be to be cut off from family and community because of who you are. He'd been friends with a gay man in university who'd been rejected by his family, and it had taken a heavy toll on him. "Are attitudes toward gay people changing?"

He shrugged. "Among some of the young, maybe. They see what's going on in the world. But the older generation? No way. Their line is that it's a choice. As if you can choose not to be gay or just be celibate for your entire life." He paused again, deep in thought. He murmured, "Like I didn't pray every night when I was a teenager to be like my friends."

"What about Jacob getting married? Was he living a double life?"

"I feel like in his case, it was more about him and me than about him being gay. I guess you could say he was bisexual, but, as far as I know, there was only ever me. So, I don't think he was living a lie being married, if that's what you're asking."

"If someone in the colony found out about your relationship, could they have used it against him? Blackmailed him in some way?"

"It's possible, but you have to remember that money isn't really a factor because the colony controls all the money and provides for everyone's needs. What's more important is your position in the colony. Your job, reputation, and the respect people have for you. There's a lot of gossip and surveillance among neighbours."

Shelter was intrigued. "Surveillance?"

"It's a Hutterite's duty to keep an eye on his neighbours to stop sin and worldly influences from creeping in. If you see something, you're supposed to report it. But if the secret was known to someone and was being used against Jacob, it doesn't explain why he would be killed. I just don't believe a Hutterite would ever be involved in violence."

Shelter decided to take the conversation in another direction. "Your husband wasn't as laid back about your relationship with Jacob as you told us. He was watching him the morning he was killed."

Elias rolled his eyes. "We talked about it last night. He gets emotional and doesn't think straight sometimes. It doesn't mean anything."

"Doesn't mean anything?" Shelter didn't like how lightly Elias was taking Martin Garnier's actions the morning of the murder. "He was following your lover just before he was murdered, and you misled us about how he felt about Jacob."

Elias's face flushed. "I didn't mislead you about anything. I had no idea he was so upset, but he had nothing to do with what happened to Jacob."

"Why so sure?"

"Oh, come on!" Stahl's raised voice drew the attention of a man at the counter, who glanced over his shoulder to see what was going on before returning to his meal. Elias lowered his voice, but the tone was no less angry. "Martin could never hurt anyone."

He made a show of checking his watch, signalling he was ready to leave.

Shelter still wasn't ready to rule Garnier out as a suspect, but he needed to ask Stahl about the deal for the Butler farm.

"What about Lanny Butler? We know he was preventing the Hutterites from taking possession of his father's farm. What do you know about that?"

Stahl, now sullen, took a moment before dismissing the question. "Like I told you the last time, I knew it was an issue, but I kept my nose out of it."

He got up to leave. He pulled his wallet from the back pocket of his jeans and tossed a five-dollar bill on the table.

Shelter picked it up and held it out to him. "I've got it."

"No, you don't. I don't want anything from you except to catch whoever did this to Jacob. And to leave Martin and me alone."

FIFTEEN

BACK AT THE OFFICE, Shelter found Traverse stuffing a sweater and a Thermos into his backpack. Shelter checked his watch and frowned. It was only mid-afternoon. "Heading home already?"

Traverse looked up, and Shelter saw his face was tense with worry. "What's up?"

Traverse went back to gathering his things. "Luke was at hockey camp this morning and took a slapshot to the head. He's at the hospital. No fracture, but it looks like a bad concussion."

"Oh, no. I'm sorry."

Traverse slung his backpack over his shoulder and gave a shake of his head. "He lost consciousness for a while and was vomiting. I'm meeting Janice at the hospital."

"Holy shit. Let me know if I can do anything."

He headed out. "I'll keep you posted."

Shelter was digesting the news of the injury when the telephone on his desk rang. It showed an unidentified internal number. He was tempted to let it ring through to voicemail, but at the last second, he picked up the receiver.

"Michael Shelter."

It was the receptionist who handled calls to the department's general enquiries line. "Hi, Michael. I've got someone on hold who says her name is Rachel Waldner. She says you know her and needs to talk to you."

"Put her through."

"This is Rachel Waldner. Jacob's wife."

Shelter had been meaning to call her. He hadn't expected her to reach out to him first.

"I have information that may help you," she said, her voice low and tight with tension.

"What information?"

"No. I can't speak now. I have work, and the others will already be looking for me. Can you come?"

"When?"

"Tonight at seven. After dinner, I will take a walk and meet you. I'm not supposed to talk to you, but I need to."

Shelter glanced at his watch and quickly calculated how long it would take him to reach the colony. "I can make it. Where?"

"You drive past the colony. On the same road, after a few minutes, you will come to a bridge over a creek. I will wait for you below, near the bridge. Goodbye."

He considered his options for getting to the meeting. He was still wary of highway driving, and now Traverse was unavailable for the trip. He didn't know if Rachel could get away from her work at another time, and he needed to know what she had for him. It had to be today. He looked over to where Jennifer Kane was working at her desk.

Approaching her, he asked, "You wanna take a drive in the country?"

She pursed her lips and arched an eyebrow, inspecting Shelter. "Not so much. Where's Gabe?"

"His son's been badly hurt playing hockey."

"Oh my God. Which one?"

"Luke," Shelter said. He relayed what he knew about the boy's concussion. "I've got to get out to the Hutterite colony to talk to the victim's wife. Can you make it?"

She sighed. "We're coming back tonight?"

"I think so, but I'm not sure. We may have to stay over."

She picked up the phone. "I'll let you know."

Five minutes later, she came to Shelter's desk with her purse. "Let's go."

In the garage, Shelter threw her the car key. "You drive, okay?"

She caught the key and scrutinized Shelter. He usually drove when they were together. "What's going on?"

"I'll tell you on the way," he said, circling to the passenger side of the car.

Kane tossed her blazer into the back seat and got behind the wheel. She wore a sleeveless cream-coloured blouse that showed off her toned arms. He didn't understand how she fit exercising in with the craziness of detective work and a couple of kids at home. She'd put it down to what she called her "before seven after seven" routine. She rose early enough to get workouts in before 7:00 a.m., when the kids got up, and did more in the evening after dinner, when the kids were doing their homework or watching TV.

Shelter had shaken his head in disbelief and laughed when she described this torture to him. He'd never have that kind of self-discipline, even if he somehow convinced himself the commitment was worth it. He might not be among the dysfunctional, booze-soaked fuck-ups you found on the police force, but he wasn't part of the new breed of fitness-obsessed jocks with their bulging pecs, Apple watches, Ziploc bags of veggies, and omnipresent water bottles, either. He took his sleep when he could get it and stuck to his activities—a softball league in the summer, curling in the winter, and irregular visits to the YMCA. On weekends, he'd have a few too many beers, an occasional rye and soda, and more pizza and barbecued meat than was good for him.

She waited in the car outside his house while he grabbed a change of clothes. Then they stopped at her place to pick up her things. It was just after four by the time Kane could bring the car up to speed on the open highway heading southwest. "Okay. Why am I driving?"

"I've been having trouble sleeping lately, and a few other weird things have been happening."

"Like?"

"Nightmares."

"You've always been a terrible sleeper."

"No. It's worse."

In that moment, Shelter decided to leave out the most disturbing symptoms—the flashbacks, the racing heart, dizziness, and the out-of-body experience at the Saint Boniface house. He didn't want to raise Kane's concern or face more pressure to take time off. He had to keep working. It was the only thing keeping him grounded. "Gabe wants me to see a doctor."

Kane's head swivelled like a tank turret, taking aim at him before bringing her eyes back to the highway. "I feel as though you're not being upfront with me. What else is going on?" She evidently hadn't made the connection between the symptoms and his shooting the young woman. He decided not to make the link for her.

"There's the Penny thing," he said. "But that's different. No. That's it."

Her quick shake of the head and pursed lips said, *I don't believe you*. "So, you're going to see a doctor, right?"

"I'll call in the morning." He knew he'd made the same commitment to Traverse the night before. He'd been sincere when he said it, but he'd been busy all day and let it slide. Now he resolved to get on it as soon as they were back in the city.

It was 5:30 p.m. by the time they reached Krefeld, and they decided to grab a quick bite before heading out to the colony. After downing burgers at a roadside stand at the north end of town, Shelter called the Krefeld Hotel to check on room availability in case they needed to stay the night. A young woman assured him there would be no problem.

As they headed north out of town, Shelter noticed a combine harvesting wheat, a cloud of chaff and straw blowing from its rear. It looked like some great mechanical locust eating its way across the landscape. The drought had worsened the wildfires in the forests to the north. The smoke drifting south made the air hazy and turned the sun into an orange ball hanging above the western horizon. Farmers would be working into the night, taking meals in the cabs of their machines, until the crops were off the fields. They worked far harder than anyone in a city job, and for their efforts, they got crushing debt loads, constant worry about the weather, pests eating their crops, and mechanical breakdowns.

Shelter found the creek on a map on his phone. It was a thin finger of water intersected by a secondary road, a little way from the colony. After a twenty-minute drive from Krefeld, they passed the access road to the Hutterite community. Shelter craned to see if he could spot any activity, but his view was blocked by trees and buildings. A minute later, the bridge Rachel had described came into view. Kane parked where the car would be partially hidden by scrubby trees and bushes. When Shelter got out, he glanced at his watch. They were five minutes early. At that moment, Rachel stood up from where she'd been sitting below the bridge, hidden by tall reeds.

After Shelter introduced Kane, Rachel led them down a footpath until they were out of sight of the road. Shelter surveyed the creek bed, where the flow had now dwindled to a trickle. A little way to the right, he spotted an enormous grey rock in the shape of a mooring buoy. It seemed likely it was the round rock from which the Hutterites had taken the name of their colony.

When Rachel turned to face them, Shelter was once again struck by how lovely she was, with rosy cheeks, wide brown eyes, and dark hair beneath her kerchief. "I don't have much time," she said, glancing toward the bridge.

Shelter swatted at a mosquito drawing blood from his neck. This close to a waterway near dusk, he feared the blood-thirsty insects would soon start to swarm. "You said you had some information for us," he said.

She reached into the pocket of the light jacket she was wearing over her dress and handed Shelter two pieces of paper. One looked torn from a notebook, and the other was a folded eight-by-ten sheet.

"I found these in the pocket of the shirt Jacob was wearing the day before he went into the city. I thought they could be important."

Scrawled on the page torn from a notebook was: *180 T x 8 DIL. MARS.*

"Do you know what it means?" Shelter asked, passing the paper to Kane for her to examine.

Rachel shook her head. "I've never seen it before, but it's Jacob's writing."

Shelter unfolded the larger sheet and found a hand-drawn diagram in pencil. It showed two rectangles on the left, another on the right, and a row of triangles between them. Surrounding these shapes were squiggly lines that resembled a child's drawing of a cloud. One of the rectangles on the left was circled.

"Do you know what this is a drawing of?"

Rachel shook her head.

"No, but I don't think these papers are about colony business. They seemed important. I thought about giving them to the minister to pass along to you, but I wanted to speak to you in person. Is there any news about who did this to Jacob?"

"Not that we can share with you right now. I'm sorry. But we are working hard on it. You can be sure of that. We'll let you and the rest of the community know as soon as we have something concrete." Shelter paused to let her take in this information. "You were right to call me. Can we keep these?" he asked, holding up the papers.

She nodded and stepped back. "I must go now."

"Before you go," Kane said, "I wanted to ask you a question."

Rachel glanced toward the road, her brow pinched with concern but waited for Kane to continue.

"Are there tensions in the community? Someone who resented Jacob for some reason?"

She thought for a moment. "We strive for harmony, but we are human, and we have to live together," she said. "So, of course, there will always be certain conflicts."

"What sort of conflicts was Jacob involved in?"

"His uncle is the general manager and decides who does what in the colony. Not everyone is happy with their jobs, or with the job Jacob had. He could go to Winnipeg regularly. He also had time to use his drone. But these things could have nothing to do with what happened to him."

"A drone?" Shelter asked.

"The colony bought a commercial model, and he learned to fly it long distances to check on the crops. It was his passion."

Shelter heard a vehicle slowing on the road. He stepped forward a few feet as a black pickup truck pulled up behind their car. He heard Rachel draw in her breath and, turning, saw that she'd moved to where she could see the road. Her eyes were wide, and she'd brought a hand to her lips. Shelter quickly pocketed the papers she'd given him.

A young Hutterite man jumped out of the truck and climbed down to the footpath. Ignoring Shelter and Kane, he spoke sharply to Rachel in German.

"Amos, I am trying to help them," she replied in English. Turning to the detectives, she said, "This is Amos, Jacob's brother."

Amos had been out in the fields harvesting when Shelter and Traverse visited the colony the day before, and they hadn't had a chance to speak to him. This was an opportunity to learn what he knew about Jacob's trip to Winnipeg and any other light he could shed on the investigation. "Hello," Shelter said. "I wanted to ask you about Jacob's reasons for going to Winnipeg this week."

Looking at Shelter for the first time, Amos said, "We want to cooperate with you in any way we can, but you must go through the minister." He reached out to grasp Rachel's forearm. "Come on."

She jerked her arm away from her brother-in-law and silently followed him to the pickup. Amos pulled a U-turn and sped away.

By the time the Hutterites had left, Shelter and Kane were hustling to the car to escape the mosquitos. Especially with the drought, the insects weren't as numerous as in the spring and early summer, but they'd still sustained several bites.

In the driver's seat, Kane scratched welts on her arms. Shelter, who was wearing long sleeves, had a couple of bites on his neck. From long experience, he knew scratching would only worsen the discomfort and make it last longer. So, he clamped his hands on his knees and waited for the first excruciating minute to pass. Finally, when the familiar burning itch became tolerable, he held up the sheet of paper Rachel had given him. "I think I know what this diagram is."

"What?"

"The Butler farm, but I want to take another look to make sure."

SIXTEEN

Shelter directed Kane to drive north, away from the colony. He took out his cellphone and opened a map of the area, tracing their route from memory. The sun was setting, and the air had grown cooler. Shelter rolled down his window and glanced at his watch. It was another thirty-five kilometres to the Butler farm. He calculated they'd have plenty of time—half an hour at least—to take a look at the property before dark.

"What did you think of what Rachel said about tensions in the colony?" Kane asked.

"I'm sure there are conflicts, but enough to kill someone?" He glanced doubtfully at Kane.

"It must be so hard to be bossed around by men like that."

"You wouldn't like it, eh?" Shelter said with a smile.

"No, I wouldn't."

"The men make all the decisions. It's the way they've lived for hundreds of years." Shelter thought about the Hutterites' roles, routines, and shared faith. "It must be comforting for them to be part of such a tight-knit community where you know your place and that you'll always be taken care of."

Kane glanced at him, shaking her head. "Oh, come off it. Your patriarchy's showing there, Mike." After a beat, she added, "It must be stifling. What about their dreams?"

"They're not asking for anyone's approval. It's how they choose to live."

"What choice do the women have?"

Shelter thought it over. He had no idea about the joys and sorrows of Hutterite women, men, or anyone else, for that matter. "I don't judge," he said finally. "I imagine the hardest part must have been for Rachel to come from another colony and find her place in this one."

"She's not from Round Rock?"

"She's from a colony in the western part of the province. From what I understand, women marry into other colonies, so they have to move away from their homes."

"Hmm. How do the men and women get to know each other?"

"I know they visit other colonies for special occasions like weddings and funerals. I'm guessing they meet then." He considered what it would be like for brides to move from one tight-knit colony to another, often travelling long distances to their new homes. "I imagine it can't be easy for the women," he said. "I wonder how they're made to feel accepted and comfortable." He spotted the highway he'd been looking for. "We're turning here."

Kane pulled the car onto another provincial highway and picked up speed again. The setting sun and smoke in the air had turned the clouds on the horizon into shades of pink and purple. The fields on either side of the road were covered in stubble of a deep golden hue where the wheat had already been harvested.

After ten minutes, Shelter pointed to a shelter belt of trees in the distance. "That's the farm. We'll take a first pass to have a look, then circle back." Kane turned off the paved provincial highway and onto a gravel road. The farm was a couple of minutes from the intersection. As they passed the driveway, Shelter twisted in his seat and glimpsed lights in the farmhouse windows on the right, but he couldn't see anyone in the yard. "Let's go back slowly."

Kane made a U-turn. The tires crunched over the gravel as they crawled toward the driveway into the farmyard. It was impossible to get a clear, head-on view without exposing themselves to the buildings, but the trees offered some cover from which to see. The sun was dipping below the horizon, and daylight was slipping away. They had a good view of the house on the right side of the lot, but the outbuildings on the left were now hidden.

"You saw the two large buildings on the other side of the yard from the house?" Shelter asked. The ugly structures with their pitched roofs had replaced the cavernous wooden barns that had once dotted the prairies and were now mostly torn down, burned, or collapsing. These buildings had large sliding doors for storing machinery. "They're these rectangles," Shelter said, pointing to Jacob's diagram on his lap. "The triangles are the storage bins."

"And these are the trees," Kane said, pointing to the squiggly lines surrounding the boxes on the diagram.

"Jacob circled this building for a reason," Shelter said, pointing to the farthest storage building, where he'd seen light shining from a window as they'd passed the yard. He reached into the glove compartment and pulled out binoculars. He peered at the farmyard for a minute, weighing his options. Without a warrant, going on the property was trespassing, but he wanted to know what was happening in that building. Finally, he turned to Kane and said, "I'm going to get a better look."

"What? No. It's too dangerous."

"Let's back up until we're covered better by the trees."

Kane gave him a long look and shook her head but started the engine and threw the car into reverse. She backed down the road until the car was hidden from the farmyard by trees. It was almost completely dark now. Shelter opened the door and turned to Kane. "Stay here. I'll be back in a couple of minutes."

"Mike. This is crazy."

He was already out of the car. He descended into the dry ditch and then climbed into the field, crushing wheat stubble as he broke into a slow jog. Hugging the tree line, he caught glimpses of the storage buildings through the foliage and stopped when he was parallel to the far end of the second structure.

He advanced into the trees, pushing back branches with his arms, aware of every rustle of the underbrush and every snap of a twig as he crept toward the building. Light shone from a window midway down the structure. He edged forward. Craning his neck, he peeked inside and saw two men and a woman chatting in what looked like a makeshift lounge. One man sat in an armchair, his profile visible. The other man and the woman sat on a couch, their backs to Shelter.

He couldn't get a good look at them through the grimy window, but he recognized the one in the armchair as Lanny Butler. The other man stood, stretched, took a pull from a beer bottle, and said something. Dressed in denim overalls, he was tall, overweight, and balding, with a long black beard.

Shelter shifted to get a look at the rest of the building's interior. As he expected, there were various pieces of farm machinery, but in one corner, he spied a squat steel machine with a hand crank and a small hopper sitting on a portable table. Beside the machine, he could make out a scale and a blender. It looked like an improvised operation for making something. Pills?

"Hey!"

Shelter snapped his head to the left. The long-haired man he'd seen with a pit bull jumped off the farmhouse porch and ran toward him. Shelter pivoted and crashed into the trees, branches clawing at his face and arms. His foot hit a root, and he fell hard. Regaining his feet, he felt a sharp pain in his ankle. It made every step agony.

He heard a dog barking in the distance, and his heart jumped into his throat. He tried to run faster, but his ankle slowed him to an awkward trot. He broke into the field and made for the car. He was within twenty metres when he heard a dog barking and growling behind him. He glanced over his shoulder. The pit bull. Gaining on him.

He waved frantically to Kane. The car's back door swung open. Shelter dove into the back seat and slammed the door just in time. The dog hurled itself against the door. Claws scratched at the window, and spittle flew from its bared teeth. Shelter looked up and saw the man emerge from the tree line, raise a rifle to his shoulder, and aim. "Get down!" he shouted at Kane.

But no crack of rifle fire came. No impact.

Gravel sprayed from the rear tires. The car jolted forward, throwing Shelter against the seat. The rear wheels fishtailed before Kane brought the car under control. She accelerated toward the intersection with the provincial highway. Their headlights lit up the stop sign.

Shelter's ankle screamed with pain. He twisted to look back just in time to see a black SUV swing onto the road and accelerate.

"We're being followed," he shouted.

The SUV was gaining on them fast. Kane barely slowed to make a wide right turn onto the highway. She hit the accelerator, and Shelter felt himself pushed back into his seat by the gain in velocity.

He turned again and saw the black SUV turn onto the highway. The vehicle had plenty of power and once again began to cut the distance between them. Shelter had only seen pickup trucks in the farmyard. "Where the hell did that come from?" he demanded. Headlights flashed in their rear-view mirror.

"It just appeared," Kane said.

"What do you want to do?"

"See who it is and what the fuck they want."

Kane slowed the car, and as she did so, Shelter touched the service pistol in his hip holster. At the same moment, a red emergency light flashed from the dash of the SUV, and the driver activated strobing lights.

"Oh, for chrissake. It's police," Kane said, her eyes darting between the rear-view mirror and the highway.

She steered the car to the shoulder. The SUV pulled in behind them. Shelter turned and saw a pair of men in street clothes exit the vehicle and approach on either side of their car. "They've got their guns out."

The one on the passenger side of the car was wearing jeans and a blue polo shirt. Shelter watched as he stopped behind the car, an automatic pistol at his thigh. He was tall, with dark hair and a close-cropped beard, and moved in a slight crouch. Turning, he saw the other, older man positioned behind the driver's side. Kane rolled down her window, and from behind, the man on her side called out, "RCMP. Let's see your hands. Both of you."

"We're Winnipeg police," Kane called out, turning her head to be heard.

"Your hands."

Kane put both hands on the top of the steering wheel, and Shelter raised his in the back seat.

"Okay. Outta the car. Both of you. Slowly."

Shelter felt searing pain from his sprained right ankle. He pushed open the back driver's-side door and tried to put weight on the injured leg. Pain shot through him, and he fell back onto the car seat with a groan. He tried again, using the door frame to lever himself to his feet.

The RCMP officer glowered at him, showing no concern for his injury. "Let's see some ID."

Leaning against the car door, Shelter dug out his ID and handed it over. The Mountie was wearing khaki pants and a short-sleeved plaid shirt, over a paunch. He was bald and looked to be in his late forties, at least a decade older than his partner, who remained behind the car.

Once he'd checked Shelter's ID, he gave Kane's a cursory glance before turning off the flashlight and nodding to his partner to come forward. In the SUV's headlights, the older man glared from Kane to Shelter, then, with a quick, sharp shake of his head, said, "Okay.

I'm RCMP Sergeant Alex Peterson, and that's Corporal Bill Korchinski." He eyed the Winnipeg cops for another moment. "What the fuck do you think you're doing?"

Shelter was in pain. He didn't like being chased. And he didn't like this guy's tone.

"Hold up there. Let's see *your* ID."

Peterson shook his head in disgust but dug out his ID and passed it to Shelter, who gave it a perfunctory once-over.

The Mountie snatched it back. "Now, what are you two doing out here?"

Peterson would be well aware of the Hutterite's murder and likely already surmised that was why a pair of Winnipeg detectives were in the area.

"We're investigating the Jacob Waldner homicide," Shelter said, his tone as testy as the Mountie's. "What are you guys up to?"

Ignoring his question, Peterson asked, "What's Butler got to do with it?"

Shelter shrugged. "We're following up on a lead."

"You got a warrant to be on that property?"

The Mounties obviously had the farm staked out. Shelter went over in his mind where they could have been parked and concluded the only possibility was behind a line of trees, a couple of hundred metres down the road from the Butler place. "I asked what you're doing out here."

"A drug enforcement operation. You just risked fucking up six months of very expensive work involving a half-dozen agencies, including your own."

"How're we supposed to know you're staking out a farm in the middle of nowhere?"

"By checking Butler on CPIC," Peterson said, referring to the national database where police forces across the country shared information.

"Of course, we ran him on CPIC," Shelter said. "There's nothing there about your investigation."

Peterson sighed in exasperation. "It's a silent hit, but we didn't get a notification."

A silent hit meant that an alarm went off at CPIC headquarters in Ottawa when a target of an investigation was searched by someone from another police force. The alarm didn't appear on the searching officer's computer, but the investigating officer would be notified immediately with the searcher's name and the time of the search. It was then up to the investigator to contact the searcher.

The silent hit system was designed to protect investigation security, and it worked well most of the time. But it was run by humans, and that meant errors did occasionally occur. Shelter surmised a CPIC mistake had left him in the dark about Peterson's drug investigation. He and Peterson eyed each other for a second as they each processed what had happened and concluded it wasn't either of their faults.

"All right, someone's screwed up," Peterson said in a more conciliatory tone. "But you need to stay away from Lanny Butler and his crew."

Shelter wanted to de-escalate the confrontation as well, but there was no way he could go along with what the Mountie was asking. "Can't do it," he said. "He's a credible suspect in our case."

Peterson shook his head and glared. "I don't give a fuck. Those guys are the source for dozens of fentanyl ODs."

Shelter remained silent. He wasn't giving ground. After a moment, Peterson dropped his head again and kicked the gravel. When he spoke, his tone suggested he'd resigned himself to dealing with these Winnipeg cops. "We'll sort it out in the morning. Be at the Carman detachment at nine-thirty."

Shelter felt his shoulders tighten and his hands ball into fists in reaction to being ordered around. His throbbing ankle was not helping his mood. But he needed to know what the Mounties had on Butler and his buddies. A morning meeting meant staying the night in Krefeld, but Shelter had already decided there was more work to do in town the next day. "We'll be there."

Without another word, Peterson turned and stalked back to the SUV with Korchinski in tow. Shelter and Kane stood side by side, watching their rear lights disappear into the darkness. "Asshole," Kane said.

Shelter nodded, but he knew he'd been wrong to go onto the Butler property, and he'd pay for it in the morning. He hobbled back to the car.

"What's with your leg?" Kane asked.

"I twisted it at the farm. It'll be okay, but we're going to have to stay the night. It's not just meeting the Mounties—I want to take another run at Butler."

SEVENTEEN

BY THE TIME they'd checked into the hotel, the adrenaline had worn off, and exhaustion hit Shelter deep in his bones. He got into bed, but sleep wouldn't come. His mind was racing. If a murder investigation were a jigsaw puzzle, none of the pieces of this one would fit together.

Lanny Butler's refusal to get off the Hutterites' land felt central to the murder. But how? Jacob had gone to the Butler place the day before he was killed. What happened out there? Had Jacob discovered proof that Butler was running a drug operation and tried to use it as leverage? Was that what his drawing of the farm indicated?

Shelter considered other possibilities. He'd already decided that a killer from the Hutterite community was a long shot. Even if someone nursed a secret hatred of Jacob, it seemed implausible they'd turn to violence, given the Hutterites' religious convictions and commitment to pacifism. That left Elias Stahl and Martin Garnier in the city. Stahl's alibi had checked out, but Garnier's was shaky. Nevertheless, the way Waldner was killed didn't fit with a crime of passion.

He groaned and rolled onto the side of the bed. It was no use. It was still only eleven, and at this rate, he was going to be up all night. He had to find a distraction. He got out of bed and gingerly pulled on a pair of jeans over his painful ankle. He dug a T-shirt out of his overnight bag and threw it on, along with a light sweater. His plan was to go for a short walk to clear his mind, but when the elevator doors opened onto the lobby, he heard country music pumping from the bar. His ankle was too sore for a walk. A drink was a better option.

The room was dimly lit and smelled of stale beer. It was Saturday night, and the place was busy. Most of the tables and seats at the bar were occupied. Shelter wasn't a country music fan, but he knew the tune playing over the speakers was by Luke Combs. A few couples in jeans and cowboy boots moved slow and close on a small dance floor. The crack of pool balls came from a table in front of the bar. Along the wall to his right, a row of patrons sat mesmerized in front of video lottery terminals.

Shelter found a vacant table in a corner and scanned the room. It was the kind of small-town joint where everyone would know each other's business, both mundane—jobs, family connections, couplings, and break-ups—and exceptional—accidents, bereavements, run-ins with the law. Then there would be the secrets, shared by some, withheld from others.

A pool player righted himself after a shot, and Shelter saw it was Lanny Butler, in from the farm for late-night drinks. He was carrying on a running commentary with a group of men and women seated around two tables pushed together. The table was strewn with beer bottles and glasses. Shelter could see the drinkers were in high spirits, laughing and calling back to Butler. Shelter noticed the long-haired man from the farm was Butler's pool opponent.

Now that Shelter got a closer look at him, he recognized him as Mitchell Grimes, Lanny's right-hand man. After meeting with Daniel Butler, Shelter had done a search of Grimes's record. It turned up an acquittal on a manslaughter charge in the death of Gerry Butler, as well as a conviction for trafficking, and another for aggravated assault with a weapon. He'd used a baseball bat to put a man in the hospital. It landed him in Headingly jail for two years less a day.

Shelter wondered whether Grimes would recognize him from earlier that evening—or had it been too dark at the farm? He studied the others at Butler's table. He recognized an overweight, black-bearded fellow as the man he'd seen earlier in the garage. The others were strangers to him, except for one of the women who held his attention. She lifted a hand to whisper a comment to the woman beside her. There was a time when she'd whispered secrets in Shelter's ear in just this way. It usually wasn't a secret at all, but Julie Klassen loved the shared intimacy, and to hell with you if you thought she was being rude. It'd been years since he'd seen her do that, but it was a gesture he'd never forget.

Lanny Butler finished his pool game and returned to take the empty seat beside Julie. She made a comment to him and laughed, but he ignored her, taking a long swig from his beer bottle. She got up and made her way to an exit on the opposite side of the bar. Shelter glanced back at the table and saw that Butler was now joking with his buddies. Keeping his eyes on Butler's table, Shelter skirted the dance floor and pushed the release bar on the exit that opened onto the parking lot.

The familiar aroma of marijuana hit him as he stepped into the light of an overhead lamp. For a moment, he thought Julie had already left, but then, from the corner of his eye, he saw the glow of an ember. Leaning against the building, she'd been observing him from outside the cone of light.

"Hello, Julie."

"What're you doing here?"

"Having a drink." He stepped out of the light, and his eyes adjusted to the darkness. "How's it going?"

She was dressed in a long-sleeved checked flannel shirt and jeans, despite the warm evening. When she shifted so the light hit her face, he noticed her pupils were contracted to pinpoints and wondered if she was on something stronger than weed. She appraised him with a half-smile before giving a quick shake of her head. "Still in town?"

He hadn't expected a hug, but there was that icy tone again. "I'm back and forth."

She'd smoked the joint to the end. She threw it on the ground and crushed it under a beaten-up sandal. She pulled a vape pen from her back pocket. "Any progress?"

She'd have been following the investigation in the media. The homicide had been the top news story in the province all week, but the reporters had little to go on and turned to interviewing people in Krefeld who were just as clueless about the crime. Shelter had seen a TV crew interviewing people on the main street and knew the *Free Press* had a reporter in town.

"Did you know Jacob?"

She eyed him suspiciously before answering. "More his wife. She's a good woman, and I liked him too." Julie went silent, chewing her lip, her head bowed.

"Any idea who'd want to hurt him?"

She lifted her chin and gave a harsh chuckle that turned into a wet cough. "Get the fuck out of here. What would I know about it?" The obscenity was another uncomfortable marker of how much she'd changed in the twenty or so years since he'd last seen her. Back then, she wouldn't have been caught dead with someone like Lanny Butler. He felt his concern for her deepen.

"How're your parents?"

"No way. You don't roll up here and start asking me about my life." She paused a beat, glaring at him. "You dumped me hard. You were a real asshole."

He was unprepared for the vehemence of her feelings. Again, he searched his memory for what had happened between them way back then. In his foggy memory, he quickly reached the same conclusion as he had when they'd met at the colony. The break-up had been unpleasant—they always were—but not traumatic.

He raised his head and met Julie's accusing eyes. "I'm sorry if I hurt you. I have good memories of our time together."

"Yeah, whatever." She took a drag on the e-cigarette. "I held a grudge for quite a while. You did damage. But I let it go, eventually." Another drag. "You still with that blond babe?"

"She died of brain cancer seven years ago."

It was Julie's turn to be shocked. Her features softened. "Oh, shit. I'm sorry."

For the first time, Shelter caught a glimpse of the sweet young woman he'd been close to all those years before.

Back then, she'd been light, fun, and adventurous. They'd taken a couple of gruelling canoe trips and driven to the Rockies in his old Honda to learn to ski on real mountains. Now he wondered what journey had brought her to this dark parking lot. What could he do for her? He suppressed an urge to reach out and touch her shoulder.

"Kids?" she asked.

"A daughter," he said. "She's twenty."

"Twenty? You're too young to have a twenty-year-old kid."

"Let's say it wasn't super planned. But we decided we wanted kids young and then travel when they grew up. It didn't work out that way." Shelter paused and held Julie's gaze. "You?"

She looked away. "No. I never found the right guy. And now, it's too late."

The statement seemed premature to Shelter. She was in her early forties. Lots of women had kids at that age, but she'd apparently ruled out the possibility. "I'm here tomorrow. Let me buy you a coffee."

Her lips and brow tightened, and her eyes darted toward the door. She stuffed the vape pen into her back pocket and grabbed for the door handle. "I'll think about it."

"You're hanging out with Lanny?" Shelter said.

She recoiled at the mention of Butler's name. "Those guys didn't see you come out here, did they?" She asked it in an urgent, breathless whisper, her eyes wide with anxiety.

Shelter remembered watching Butler's table as he exited the bar. He shook his head. "No way."

He recalled what he knew about Butler and his crew—the suspicious killing of Gerry Butler, the drug investigation, and the refusal to get off the farm. He felt fear for

Julie growing in the pit of his stomach. "Are you seeing Lanny?"

She exhaled, and her shoulders dropped. When she spoke, her voice was calmer. "I'm not seeing anyone." She studied his face before glancing at the door again. "I've been gone too long."

Shelter lightly placed a hand on her arm. "Take this." He offered her his card. "It's got my cell number on it."

"I can't take that."

"Just my number then."

She considered for a moment, then drew a cellphone from her back pocket. He recited the number, and she punched it in. She put the phone back in her pocket and grasped the door handle. She was trembling under the light of the overhead lamp.

"Call me tomorrow, okay?" he said.

She pulled the door open and was gone.

Shelter hobbled through the parking lot, his ankle throbbing, and entered the hotel lobby from the street. Julie was right to worry about being seen with him. If his instincts were right, the danger was real.

EIGHTEEN

SHELTER'S BACON AND EGGS arrived just as Kane entered the hotel restaurant. When she'd ordered her breakfast, he told her about his late-night visit to the bar and his conversation with Julie Klassen.

"She was your first girlfriend?" Kane asked after taking the first sip of her coffee.

"Before I met Christa," he said. "She was pretty harsh last night. Apparently, I was an asshole when I broke up with her."

"Imagine that. A young man being insensitive to a woman's feelings."

Shelter grimaced. He was still processing how carelessly he'd broken up with Julie. Showering and dressing, he'd replayed the scene of their final meeting and how little thought he'd given to her feelings at the time. It translated now into a desire to help her get her life back on track if he could. "She doesn't look good," he said. "I think she's got a drug problem."

Kane's breakfast arrived, and as she spread jam on a piece of toast, Shelter's cellphone buzzed where he'd left it on the table. He picked it up and rolled his eyes. "MacIsaac. This is going to be about our run-in with the Mounties." He let the phone ring a couple more times, preparing himself for the wave of stress about to hit him.

As usual, Neil MacIsaac didn't bother with a greeting or small talk. "I just had an irate RCMP inspector on the line. He tells me you were trespassing last night on the property of a target of a drug task force."

To Shelter's surprise, MacIsaac's voice was unusually subdued. His tone suggested resignation to his fate as a middle manager, forced to endure an endless stream of problems. "He also says you led his people on a high-speed chase. Please tell me this is not an accurate portrayal of events."

Shelter had his eyes on Kane as he listened to MacIsaac. It was damage control time. "I wouldn't call it a chase. They followed us at high speed, and we stopped to find out who they were. That's it."

"Okay. Let's leave the chase aside. You went onto the Butler property without a warrant?"

"Um. I can't say for sure whether I actually crossed the property line," he lied. "It was dark, and there were trees."

MacIsaac let out a long, soulful sigh that said, *please stop bullshitting me*. "This Mountie is a nasty piece of work, and he wants your head. You get that, right? I calmed him down, but we agreed we need to coordinate our investigations." He paused for a moment, and Shelter could hear him shuffling papers on his desk.

Shelter said, "We've already got a meeting set up with them for 9:30 this morning."

"That's good. Be on time. And, Mike, be nice." After a beat, MacIsaac asked, "What did you see at Butler's farm?"

"Looks like he could be running some kind of drug operation out of there."

"Any link to the Waldner murder?"

"Not sure, but Waldner was there the day before he was killed."

"What else?"

"We've got a few other leads. How about I put it in an email?"

"Get it here before the end of the day."

Shelter shook his head and set the phone on the table.

"I've got to be back in the city by the end of the day," Kane said. "We're going out for dinner with friends, and the babysitter is lined up. It's the first time we've been out in months. Sherry's going to kill me if I'm late."

"I'd like to talk to the Hutterites' accountant before we go, if possible. Either way, we should be back in lots of time."

He picked up the phone and dialled the number Simon Wurtz had given him for the accountant, James Deacon.

"What can I do for you?" Deacon said after Shelter had introduced himself.

"I know it's short notice, but can my partner and I drop by for a chat?"

"Sounds ominous," Deacon said with a chuckle. "What do you want to know?"

"Let's talk about it when we get together. When can you do it?"

"I'm at home this morning. How does 11:30 sound? I'll text you the address."

"Perfect. Thanks."

For the first time in days, Shelter felt well-rested and relieved that the pain in his ankle had eased up. When he told Kane he was good to drive, she looked at him skeptically for a moment but didn't object, handing him the key.

He kept the car at a comfortable ten kilometres per hour over the speed limit, heading northeast along a mostly deserted stretch of two-lane highway.

Carman was a small town on the way back to the city. It was a beautiful day. Wisps of high-altitude cloud turned the sky a pastel blue as they drove through grain fields broken only by farmsteads, power lines, and, for a stretch, towering wind turbines turning lazily in the sunshine.

While going through his email over coffee before breakfast arrived, Shelter had seen that the homicide team in Winnipeg had little to show for their efforts over the past day. They'd picked up images of Jacob's truck from cameras on commercial streets near the Saint Boniface house but not of a vehicle obviously following him. Detectives had checked tips from the public sparked by the heavy news coverage, but none had led to anything.

They drove toward Carman in silence for fifteen minutes before Kane said, "You've got a family doctor, right? Get her to check your ankle and, at the same time, give you a referral for your head problems."

Shelter hadn't forgotten his promise to get help. "I'll give her a call when I get back to town."

"Don't wait, okay?"

He nodded, but now that it was becoming a reality, he felt resistance building inside him at the idea of going to the doctor. He expected it would lead to a referral to a psychologist. He knew there was no longer a stigma attached to getting therapy, and he didn't see it as a sign of weakness. Still, he was troubled by the idea of revealing his innermost feelings to a stranger, of exploring buried memories, and of what he might discover about himself. He knew it would be easy to let the first call to the doctor slide. He was tempted to do just that.

Kane interrupted his thoughts. "Have you called Penny?"

Shelter kept his eyes trained on the highway and quietly drew deep breaths to tamp down his irritation. "She asked me for time, and I'm respecting that."

"I feel like she's going to want you to make a move."

Shelter would have told anyone else to butt out of his business, but they'd shared so much over the years about their relationships and raising kids that it wasn't surprising for her to offer her opinion. It never got easier to open up about what was going on in his life, but he knew it was necessary and good for him to get it out.

With Gabriel Traverse, it was different. He'd been a huge source of quiet support when Christa was ill, and afterward, as Shelter struggled to raise Kelsey. They trusted each other with their lives, but like most men, they didn't share intimate feelings. For that, he turned to Kane. He knew she would always be caring yet totally honest with him. It was what he needed, especially since he'd lost Christa as a confidante.

"I did make a move," he said. "She told me she doesn't want to talk right now."

Kane was quiet for a moment. "What's holding you back? Are you worried the relationship isn't solid enough to have a baby?"

"No, it's not that. I guess I felt stampeded. It's a big decision." He paused to gather his thoughts about becoming a father again. "At first, I thought it was the age thing—having a baby in my mid-forties. But the more I think about it, the more I realize it has to do with what happened with Christa. We wanted another kid so badly, and the miscarriages were really hard on both of us. And then she was gone. I guess I might be afraid of going down that road again."

He'd never expressed these emotions before, even to himself. It was strange, and even as he said it, he wasn't sure this was how he truly felt about the situation. "It's just really confusing," he said, looking over at Kane.

"I can see that," she said in a quiet, concerned voice. "But you can't just give up on her."

"I know that, but I can't make her come back if she doesn't want to."

"You can keep trying."

Now Shelter *was* starting to get annoyed, but that was normal when he talked to Kane about this kind of thing. When he calmed down, he invariably found she was right.

"I'll think about it."

"Don't think too long. You're going to lose her."

At the RCMP detachment, they were met at the front desk by Brendan Korchinski, Alex Peterson's sidekick from the night before. He was friendly this morning, chatting about the fair weather as he led them to a conference room. It was Sunday, and the office was empty except for a uniformed officer working at a desk. Shelter's twisted ankle still hurt, but he was barely limping. He told himself he'd be back to normal in a day or two.

Peterson rose from his seat at the head of the conference table and shook hands with the Winnipeg detectives. Once they were all seated, he said, "Our bosses agree it makes sense to coordinate our investigations. I'll start by describing the operation you stumbled into last night."

Shelter's jaw tightened at the word "stumble." Peterson apparently hadn't got the memo that this was supposed to be a fence-mending session.

"Two months ago, our guys in Vancouver made a major bust," he said. "A couple of kilos of fentanyl, twelve of meth, and five of coke." He paused to take a sip of coffee. "We think it was supposed to be shipped out here."

"Based on what?" Shelter asked.

"We've got cellphone traffic between dealers in Vancouver and Mitchell Grimes, and we've got a source here. As you probably know, both Grimes and Butler have priors for dealing smaller quantities of coke and weed. We think they've moved into the big leagues with this Vancouver connection and have become the major source of fentanyl and other drugs into Winnipeg. They've been lying low since the Vancouver bust to see what happens, and we've detected a severe supply shortage in the city in recent weeks. Butler and Grimes are urgently looking for an alternative source."

Shelter thought of the rash of fentanyl ODs in Winnipeg and southern Manitoba this year. "That's why you've got his place staked out?"

Peterson nodded. The isolated location and large farming operation would have made excellent cover for dealing in quantity, at least until the Mounties discovered what Butler and Grimes were up to. This was a good reason why Butler was determined to stay on the property, regardless of what the Hutterites said or did.

"We've got intel they're talking to the Hells Angels in Toronto," Peterson said. "We're hearing a meet is set for some time this week at the farm."

"Who's this source of yours?"

"I can't tell you that."

Shelter's brow furrowed. "If you guys have a source in the Butler organization, they could have information on the Waldner murder."

Peterson raised his hands in a gesture of apology. "Look. We want to help you clear your homicide, believe me. We've asked our source about it, but we've got nothing for you."

Shelter wasn't giving up on getting access to their informant. It could be the break they needed. An idea popped into his head. He recalled Daniel Butler hinting that the money Lanny wanted to use to buy the farm came from illegal activity. "Is Daniel Butler your CI?"

Peterson smiled and shook his head. "Danny? We've talked to him, but he's not going to roll over on anyone."

"Who are you dealing with on the Winnipeg police?"

"Paul Stevens. We've already discussed it with him, and he agreed that we can't share our contact with you for now. It's just too sensitive. Now, what's happening on your side?"

Shelter let out a long breath. He hated being stonewalled, but there was no way to force Peterson to reveal more. He knew Stevens, the head of the Winnipeg drug squad, from their time together in uniform and from a couple of cases where drug dealers got popped. He wasn't a bad guy. Maybe Shelter could get more out of him. If not, he'd have to go up the chain of command to squeeze more information out of the Mounties, and that would take time.

He pulled his notebook from his jacket pocket, where he'd listed some bullet points to guide him in bringing the RCMP officers up to speed on the Waldner investigation. He reviewed Jacob's relationship with Elias Stahl. Then he moved on to the sale of the Butler farm to the Hutterites and Lanny's refusal to vacate the property. "Jacob's wife gave us what we believe is a drawing he made of the Butler farm with a circle around one of the outbuildings," Shelter said. "That's what we were checking out last night."

Peterson opened the file folder in front of him and took out a professionally produced diagram of the farm. "This building," Shelter said, pointing to a rectangle.

"What did you see?"

"Not much. I only had a few seconds. A couple of guys and a woman were hanging out in there. I saw some equipment that looked like it could be drug-related."

"We've seized fentanyl pills in Winnipeg that we think are being made at the farm. Did you get a good look at the folks in that building?"

"They were facing away from me, and there wasn't much time. I recognized Lanny, and there was another guy, bald and fat, close to three hundred pounds, with a dark beard." Peterson nodded, a gesture Shelter took to mean he knew the man he was describing. "I did get a look at the dude who came out of the main house and sent his dog after me. I'm pretty sure it was Mitchell Grimes."

Peterson removed a photocopied photo from his file folder and slid it across the table.

"That's him," Shelter said. "Besides letting his dog loose on me, he pointed a rifle at our car. What's his story?"

"Officially, he works as a hired hand on the farm," Peterson said. "But he's been Lanny's buddy and right-hand man since they were boys. Besides the trafficking bust, he's got a couple of other convictions. He also got off on a manslaughter rap. He shot Lanny's brother Gerry during a deer-hunting trip. It was ruled an accident, but people around town don't believe that story."

"That's what Danny Butler told us. What do you know about it?"

Peterson shrugged. "Gerry was an addict. Our assumption was he was killed over a debt, for stealing product, or because Grimes was worried Gerry was talking to us."

"Was he?"

Peterson locked eyes with Shelter for a moment before shaking his head. "No, but Grimes is one paranoid dude."

Shelter pushed the photo of Grimes back to Peterson. "Jacob Waldner went out to the farm the day before he was killed," Shelter said. "Did you guys see him out there?"

Peterson shook his head. "We don't have the budget for 24/7 surveillance." He looked from Shelter to Kane. "We've discussed it, and we can't see a motive for Butler or Grimes to kill your guy. Obviously, the Hutterites aren't in the drug trade, and the land issue feels pretty routine." He paused. "We've got a lot of experience with Hutterites out here. They're good people who keep to themselves. If I were you, I'd look at the gay relationship angle in the city."

Shelter bristled at this unsolicited advice on his case. "Don't worry. We're looking at it."

Peterson smiled at Shelter's frosty tone and shrugged. "Just trying to help."

"I saw Butler at the Krefeld Hotel last night with Grimes and a bunch of other people. It seemed like his home away from home."

Peterson glanced at Korchinski, sitting beside him, before saying, "You need to stay away from that bar and the Butler farm."

Shelter felt another surge of annoyance. He wasn't going to be bullied. "We're always careful. We've got a homicide investigation going here."

"Listen, you have no idea what you're getting into, and you're going to fuck it up. You're risking hundreds of hours of investigative work right as this meeting with the Hells Angels is about to happen. You're putting people in danger."

Shelter stood up, and Kane followed suit. "We'll keep you informed of anything we come up with. We'd appreciate the same from you."

Peterson frowned at them as they gathered their notebooks. Shelter turned to Korchinski, who'd risen to escort them to the door.

"We'll find our own way out."

NINETEEN

JAMES DEACON'S HOUSE could fairly be described as a McMansion. With its central turret, multiple roof peaks, and three-car garage, it wouldn't have been out of place in a cookie-cutter subdivision outside Phoenix or Atlanta. Here, the house had been plopped down on the flat prairie with a half-acre of well-watered sod and a dozen struggling saplings to heighten the contrast with the surrounding landscape.

Coming up the long driveway, Shelter noticed to his right a pair of horses grazing in a corral and what looked like a stable behind the house. He parked beside a white pickup and a two-seat Audi sports car. The sun reflected off the Audi's Mediterranean-blue paint, and Shelter judged it was no more than a year old.

Before he could ring the bell, one of the enormous double doors swung open. Shelter found himself face-to-face with a woman in her early thirties, decked out in a white sleeveless top, a lemon-coloured skirt that reached mid-thigh, and matching sneakers. She wore a visor over hair cropped to the shoulders, expertly dyed blond. A tennis bag hung from her arm. "Oh, hello?"

"We're here to see Mr. Deacon," Shelter said.

She called over her shoulder, "Jimmy, some people for you." Turning back to Shelter, she smiled and said, "Your name?"

"Michael Shelter. And this is Jennifer Kane."

"Hmm." She looked him up and down with unabashed interest but didn't bother to introduce herself. "Well, you'll have to excuse me, Mr. Michael Shelter." She said it in a gently mocking tone, then turned to bid Kane goodbye with a perfunctory nod. "I'm late for a match." She skipped down the front steps and hurried to the Audi. Shelter and Kane watched as she threw her tennis bag behind the seats and jumped into the car.

"I see you've met my wife," Deacon said from behind them. Turning to greet the accountant, Shelter was surprised to see him cradling a chubby infant. A nursing blanket was draped over his shoulder to protect his shirt.

Shelter's first thought on seeing James Deacon was of a laid-back golf pro he'd known at his father's private club. Tanned and dapper in a blue Oxford shirt and jeans, Deacon was in his early fifties with salt-and-pepper hair.

Stepping back to let them into the foyer, Deacon glanced down at the gurgling, wide-eyed baby. "This is Oliver. I hope you don't mind if he joins us. He's just had a snack and isn't due to go down for his nap for a while." He shifted the baby and laughed. "He weighs a ton."

Shelter and Kane smiled at the child and made the usual noises about how cute he was. In this case, no lies were required. He was a curious, smiling little fellow with a shock of black hair. Despite his resistance to having another child of his own, Shelter loved kids and was unperturbed by this unexpected guest at the meeting.

"Come this way. We can talk in my office."

A few inches under six feet, Deacon had a beer belly and walked with the confident gait of a jock. He led them through the air-conditioned central hall with a floor of black-and-white tiles. Shelter appraised the expensive fixtures and furnishings and made a quick mental judgment that he'd take his old, two-storey clapboard house with its cracked foundation anytime over this nouveau-riche monstrosity. "Nice house," he said.

"Oh God. Don't get me started," Deacon said with a chuckle. The baby was squirming, and he transferred him from one arm to the other as he walked. "I would have been happy staying in our house in town. I was actually more comfortable there. But Cheryl wanted more space and her horses nearby. So, one thing led to another, and here we are. We moved in last year."

Deacon led them to an office that ran along the north side of the house. A heavy wooden desk dominated the back of the room. "I was just finishing up some work. I'll be with you in a moment." He went to the desk and began shuffling through a stack of papers with one hand, bouncing the baby on his hip. "Oh, for God's sake," Deacon said, dropping a few papers on his desk. He took the baby in both hands, turned, and thrust him into Kane's arms. "Here, take him for a sec, will ya?"

Before she could object, Kane was holding the kid in outstretched arms as if he were radioactive. It took a moment for her to arrange him in the crook of her arm. Looking up into her unfamiliar face, the baby's little body stiffened, and he began to wail. "Shhh. You're okay, little guy," Kane said, but the crying became louder and the squirming more energetic.

"Here, give him to me," Shelter said. Kane shook her head and tried to turn away, but Shelter had already gotten his hands on the baby. She was forced to let go.

She rolled her eyes as Shelter cooed and rocked the child in his arms. The baby's movements calmed, and his crying lessened then stopped altogether. He seemed fascinated by Shelter's face, gurgling and breaking into a toothless grin. Shelter gave Kane a victory smile. She raised her eyebrows and shook her head in mock disgust. He couldn't help but laugh at this confirmation of his effect on babies.

Deacon looked from Kane to Shelter. In response to his unasked question, Shelter said, "It's nothing. A private joke."

"Looks like you've got the magic touch there, detective," Deacon said, taking Oliver back from him. "We can sit over here," he said, pointing to a couch and two armchairs at the other end of the room. "Can I get you some iced tea?"

"I'm good," Shelter said, and Kane shook her head. "Other kids?" she asked.

"Two teenagers from my first marriage, one in elementary school from Cheryl's, and little Oliver here. We had him in the early spring. It's quite a mixed bag," Deacon said, taking the armchair to the left of Shelter. "But we manage to make it work."

Shelter had balked at raising a child with Penny, and he was only in his early forties. What would it be like starting again at this man's age?

"You have children?" Deacon asked.

"A daughter. She's twenty."

"We have two in elementary," Kane said.

Deacon gave them a polite smile before getting down to business. "I've been following your case in the news. Any progress?"

Shelter repeated his stock answer to this question. "We're working on it."

Deacon was bouncing the baby on his knee. "What can I do for you?"

"I wanted to get more details about the sale of the Butler farm to the Hutterites. I'm told Jacob went to the farm the day before he was killed. Do you know why?"

"I don't, but he was upset," Deacon said, leaning back in his chair. "As you probably know, I've been advising the Hutterites on buying the farm. Lanny Butler's refusal to get off the property has become a huge problem for them, especially for Jacob. He was leading the project."

"The sale closed. So, Butler's a squatter," Shelter said. "Why not just get him kicked off the property?"

"Not so easy. First, they'd have to get an order evicting him. Then there'd be an appeal process, of course. But the Hutterites are loath to use the courts and have been in a quandary about what to do. In the end, I advised the elders to wait to see what Butler does, and that's what they've decided to do."

"But it seems quite important for the colony to find land."

"It was a difficult decision. They've put so much time into planning this and making sure the money for the purchase was saved. It was natural for Jacob to be disappointed."

"The money for the down payment?" Kane asked.

Deacon smiled and glanced down at the baby, who'd fallen asleep in his arms. "I shouldn't really be discussing their private financial information, but that's accurate. They're frugal and have the resources to buy land and the best equipment for top dollar. It can make people very unhappy around here."

"Why?" Shelter asked.

"When the Hutterites buy a farm like the Butler place, they're going to want more land in the surrounding area to give them a large enough base to support the colony. People know that, and prices go up. That makes it hard for established farmers to expand and for young people to get a start."

Shelter hadn't considered the impact a new Hutterite colony could have in a region like this one, the resentments it could stir up. "If the decision was made not to evict Butler, why did Jacob go there?"

"He was angry and confused about what to do next. Maybe he was still holding out hope he could convince Butler to leave."

Shelter's attention was momentarily drawn to a large black cat crossing the room. "So, you advised them to wait?"

"We agreed it was the best course. I told them Lanny might decide to leave the farm on his own and assured them that if he didn't, they could always sell the property in the future. That's probably what Jacob was going to discuss with the lawyer in Winnipeg."

"I understand Lanny Butler has made them an offer for the land," Shelter said. "Any idea where the money's coming from?"

Deacon shrugged. "No idea. I don't have anything to do with Lanny Butler or his buddies."

"You don't know them?"

"Everyone knows everyone around here, but I stay well clear of them."

"Maybe Jacob saw something he wasn't supposed to see and threatened to go to the police."

Deacon's lips curled into a shrewd smile, and he shook his head. "You're wondering if that's what got him killed? I'm sorry, but I think you misunderstand the Hutterites. They don't make threats, and they don't get involved with the authorities unless they absolutely have to."

"Who would have wanted to kill him?"

"I really have no idea, detective."

"What are they saying in the colony?"

"That's not something they would discuss with an outsider." He lowered his eyes to the baby in his arms. "I have to get this little fellow down for his nap."

Walking to the door, Deacon said, "I take it you know that Jacob's funeral is this week?"

Shelter knew Waldner's body would soon be returned to the colony but was unsure of the funeral's timing. "Are you going?"

"No, I'm leaving that to the Hutterites, but it'll be quite a crowd. They're coming in from all over the province and even from colonies in the States. It could be over a thousand."

TWENTY

FROM DEACON'S HOUSE, they got on the highway and were back in the city by mid-afternoon. After dropping Kane off at her house, Shelter picked up some groceries and a case of beer. It was Sunday after a long, hectic week, and he was looking forward to getting his mind off work by putting his feet up and watching a football game in the cool of the basement rec room.

He parked beneath the boughs of elm trees that came together to form a canopy over his street in the Wolseley district. Tragically, more and more of the mighty trees were being cut down across the city, despite a decades-long battle to stop the spread of Dutch elm disease. As he walked from his car, he noticed the sun was lower in the sky for the time of the day, a reminder that fall was just around the corner, with the long months of harsh winter to follow. The prairie summer was just too short.

Shelter threw his keys on the entrance hall table and strode into the gloomy kitchen. He was back to coming home to an empty house. He was hungry, but the prospect of making a proper meal and eating it alone was unappealing. Instead, he put a frozen pizza in the oven and cracked a beer. While the pizza cooked, he reflected on the coming months. Kelsey would soon be returning from her grandparents' place in Gimli and packing up to head back to university in Montreal. He already missed her, and that deepened the pain of Penny's absence. He was looking at living the lonely life of a bachelor in this big house.

"Oh, man," he whispered to himself. He needed to talk to Penny. He knew he shouldn't contact her in this dark mood, but he couldn't help himself. His call went to her voicemail, and he left a message asking her to get back to him as soon as she could. He was just finishing the pizza when his phone buzzed.

"Hey. I got your message."

"What are you doing?"

"I'm working a shift."

"I want to see you."

"I don't think so."

"I know you're upset, and I am too. I think if we could talk, it might get us somewhere."

Penny sighed and went silent for a couple of seconds. "I'll meet you at Sid's at five."

Sid's was a hipster joint on Corydon Avenue serving vegetarian sandwiches and fair-trade coffee. It was one of Penny's favourite spots, and while Shelter preferred greasy spoons, he didn't have a problem with the vibe at Sid's.

"See you there."

Shelter waited for Penny on the street in front of the restaurant. She arrived a couple of minutes past five, and they embraced briefly before getting coffee at the counter. At that hour on a Sunday, only one student was studying on a laptop, and a couple were working on a dinner of sandwiches and salad. Penny pointed to a table at the front of the restaurant where they'd have privacy.

When they were seated, Shelter broke the ice by asking how her day at the café had gone. Penny told him about a fight she'd had with a cook she'd often had trouble with in the past. He asked her a few questions about it, but the conversation felt strained. Shelter noticed she was avoiding his eyes. When she paused, he reached out and touched her hand. "I'm sorry about the other night."

She withdrew her hand and ran her fingers through her hair. "It's not your fault. You feel how you feel. That's it."

Maybe the insomnia and flashbacks from the shooting had kept him from thinking straight about what he wanted. But since talking to Kane, he'd realized she was right. He loved kids and he loved Penny. If he didn't take this leap now, he could regret it for the rest of his life.

He met Penny's eyes. "I've been thinking about what you said. A baby is scary, but I'm ready to start trying."

Penny shook her head and looked away, scanning the restaurant. She turned back to him. "Having a baby isn't supposed to be a trial. I don't feel like I can trust you now."

Shelter could hear her breathing. He put a hand on hers again and whispered, "We can do this."

"It's not just the baby, Mike. It's what's going on with you. You don't sleep. You're pissed off all the time. I feel like I don't know you anymore."

Shelter looked away, thinking about what she'd just said and how he'd been with her over the past weeks. He couldn't deny it. He constantly felt numb and angry. He couldn't stand being around himself. Why would she want to bring a child into the world with him?

Her head was bowed, and she whispered, "The place we're at is too different." She moved her hand from under his and slowly lifted her chin. "Remember this," she said, spreading her fingers on the table. "Look at my hand and remember this exact moment with me."

"What?" he asked, lowering his eyes to her hand. "Remember what?"

"Just look at my hand, and we'll remember it together. Forever. Like one of those random moments from when you're a kid, the ones you never forget. Licking candy floss off your fingers or lying on your back watching big clouds float by."

A tear fell onto her hand. "All we do is forget," she said, turning her head to look out at the street, where cars flowed past. "Making love, nights out on the town, trips. It all just fades away. But if we want to, we can remember this one little moment together."

"What are you talking about?" Shelter asked, his voice rising in alarm. "I just told you. I want to have a baby with you."

"If we go ahead with this, one day we're going to end up at a table just like this one. Only we'll be older, and there'll be a child involved." She was quiet for a moment. "Just look at my hand and promise you won't forget."

Their eyes met. Another tear escaped and rolled down her cheek before she wiped it away with the back of her other hand. Shelter looked down at her hand on the table. The veins and tendons stood out as she pressed it down hard.

"We can share this moment for the rest of our lives. We'll have that."

"Stop right now," he said. "This is bullshit. I love you. Do you love me?"

"It's too late."

"Why? If I'd said I was ready to start trying for a baby a couple of days ago, you would have been happy and excited."

"But that's not what you said, is it?"

"I've thought about it. I love you, and I'm ready. It will work. Just give it a chance." He looked deep into her eyes. "Let's go home."

She shook her head. "No. I don't believe you want this, and I don't want to force you to do it. The stakes are too high."

He lowered his head and studied her hand again. The slender fingers. The close-cropped nails. The tiny mountains of her knuckles and the silver bracelet he'd given her on their first anniversary.

When he looked up, she was assessing his reaction. Did he get it now? Did he understand this was the end? He stood up and left the restaurant.

He hurried to his car, parked a short distance away on a side street. He'd gone to the meeting assuming he could mend the relationship with his words, only to find that she was the one who held the power. He silently cursed his arrogance.

He squeezed his eyes shut and gripped the steering wheel. Suddenly, images of the woman in the North End hallway returned. They flashed in his mind like slides projected in a darkened theatre. The shotgun barrel pointed at him. Squeezing the trigger on his pistol. The woman lying face-up on the dirty carpet. Her pleading eyes. A pink bubble of saliva in her mouth. Blood pumping from her chest. The sound of Traverse rushing into the room. Her eyes rolling back in her head. The sour odour of her last breath.

Shelter let out a groan and shook his head. His breath came in gasps. His heart pounded in his chest. He had to calm down. He forced himself to take long, deep breaths. He let go of the steering wheel and dropped his hands to his lap. He made an effort to release the tension in his shoulders.

The images stopped, and the waves of panic began to subside. He opened his eyes and struggled to focus on his breathing. Slow in, slow out. Memories of the shooting tried to force their way into his mind, but he pushed them away.

His cellphone buzzed. He'd carried it in his hand from the restaurant and tossed it onto the passenger seat. He picked it up, hoping it was Penny. Instead, it was an unknown number. Could she be using a new phone? He hesitated, his finger hovering over the green answer button on the phone's screen. He touched it.

"Penny?"

Silence. Then a woman's voice. "Penny?"

Shelter struggled to identify the caller. "Who is this?"

"You don't remember my voice?" The tone was nervous, edgy.

"Julie."

"You said I could call if I needed you. I need you."

Shelter felt his jaw tighten and his molars grind. He had to get her off the phone. He just wanted to go home, have a drink, and get into bed.

"It's not a good time. I'll call you tomorrow."

"I'm in trouble. And there's no one else who can help me."

"What kind of trouble?"

"Come here, to my place." She was jumpy, on the edge of hysteria—blasted on something.

"I'm in the city, and I'm tired. We can talk tomorrow."

"No!" she shouted. "They're going to get me killed."

"Who?"

"The fucking Mounties."

At the mention of the RCMP, Shelter became fully focused on Julie's voice.

"What about the Mounties?"

"They want me to wear a wire," she said. "I can't do it. I'm so scared."

Shelter made the connection to Peterson in an instant. A wire meant Julie was the RCMP's informant, the source Peterson had refused to identify earlier that day.

"Julie, start from the beginning. How did you get involved with them?"

"I got busted in the city."

"Carrying drugs?"

"They said I'd get off if I helped them."

"Help them get Lanny."

She let out a short, derisive laugh. "You think Lanny's got the brains for this shit? He does what Mitch tells him."

Shelter knew how important it was for the RCMP to make their case against Grimes and Butler and to cut off the new supply from entering the province. If the Toronto connection was made, it would nullify all the work they'd done on the West Coast. Julie was the key. They wouldn't let up on her at any price.

"Tell me about Mitchell Grimes."

He could hear her breathing grow ragged. She began to sob. "He's a bastard. He'll kill me if he finds out. He's already done it."

"You're talking about Gerry Butler."

"Blew him away with a hunting rifle for fuck's sake."

"You know that for sure?"

She began to cry again. "Everyone knows it."

Listening to Julie, Shelter's eyes locked on a young mother pushing a stroller across the intersection in front of him. His eyes burned. The pain behind them was red-hot. "I don't know what to tell you, Julie. I can't interfere in an RCMP investigation."

For a minute, all he could hear was Julie's breathing. Then she said, "I know what happened to the Hutterite."

Shelter felt his pulse quicken, but he had to be careful. Julie might say anything if she thought it could get her out from under Peterson.

"What do you know?"

"The whole story."

"Tell me."

"Uh-uh. I'm not saying anything until you come here and see me."

"Julie, I can't help you with the Grimes thing."

"You'll think of something."

Shelter sighed in exasperation, but he needed to find out what Julie knew. He looked at his watch. "I'll come now."

"No. It's too late. I'll see you after work tomorrow. At five. Call me when you get here."

TWENTY-ONE

OVER BREAKFAST the next morning, Shelter decided to head back to Krefeld alone later in the day. He didn't want to drag another detective out to the country for what could be a waste of time. Before leaving for work, he called Traverse to fill him in on his conversation with Julie and found his partner was also dubious about the chances it would lead to a break in the case.

"She just wants to use you to get the Mounties off her back," Traverse said. "I doubt she's got anything."

"You never know. How's your boy?"

"He's better. Thank God. He's back home, and we think he's going to be okay."

As he spoke, Shelter put his coffee cup in the kitchen sink and walked to the living room window. The street was bathed in early-morning sunshine. The positive medical report made him hopeful that Traverse would soon be back at work. "I'm happy for you, man. That was scary."

"He can't take bright lights or loud noise. He's on limited screen time."

"Uh-oh. That's not going to be easy."

"Yeah, well. The chances of a full recovery are excellent, and Janice said there's no point in me sitting around the house."

"Driving her crazy, eh?"

"Yup. I'll be back at work tomorrow. Why don't you wait? We'll go to the country together. Going alone is a really bad idea, the way your head is."

"Nah. I'm okay."

"I'm against it, but you're the boss. If you need me, call."

"I'll let Jen know what's happening."

He was anxious to hear what Julie wanted to tell him and had trouble concentrating on the paperwork he'd let pile up. He left for the country after a late lunch. It was just before five in the afternoon when he pulled into Krefeld. He parked on a side street and called Julie. It rang through to her message. He sent a text, then called again a couple of minutes later. No response.

Shelter cursed under his breath. He'd driven for an hour and a half and was now stuck waiting for her. It took another fifteen minutes before his phone buzzed with a new text. She'd sent him a pin—Google Map coordinates. When he clicked the link, the location showed as the intersection of two rural roads about ten kilometres out of town.

When he pulled up to the location, Julie was leaning on the hood of her red Toyota, drawing on her vape pen. It was a sunny but cool evening. She was dressed for work in baby-blue nurse scrubs and white running shoes. Her hair was pulled back and held by a scrunchie. The intersection she'd chosen was half a kilometre from the nearest farmhouse.

In response to his greeting, Julie gave a sardonic smile and pushed herself away from the car, sliding the pen into her back pocket. He was unprepared when she took a couple of steps toward him and embraced him in a tight hug, murmuring her gratitude.

The fruity scent of her shampoo filled in his nose as he disengaged from her embrace and stepped back. He forced himself to smile to hide his discomfort with the hug. He noticed her eyes were glassy, and the pupils were once again pinpoints. "Isn't this close to your dad's farm?" he asked.

Julie's response was a nod to the north. The land was perfectly flat, and Shelter could make out the farm in the distance. He remembered visiting it when they were dating. It had been in their family for a couple of generations. Years earlier, her grandfather had sold the surrounding land but held on to a few acres around the house. Julie and her brothers had spent their summers there, swimming in a pond dug for the purpose and roaming the countryside.

"You still go there?" he asked.

She shook her head. "Nobody goes much anymore. It's falling apart, and Dad's talking about selling it."

"That's too bad. It's a beautiful spot."

She shrugged and looked him in the eye for a second. He sensed her mood darkening and suspected she was thinking about their time together. He looked away toward the farmhouse. Memories of that time flooded into his mind. Soon after they'd started dating, they'd driven from Winnipeg to the farm. They'd skipped classes on an unusually warm Wednesday in late September and taken off in his mother's car. After a tour of the town, she'd taken him for a swim in the pond. They'd skinny-dipped in the cool water and made love on a blanket by the tall reeds and bulrushes that had grown up around the swimming hole. She was tall and sun-tanned. Shelter had been so far down in the pecking order at his high school that he couldn't see the top. He'd been surprised and flattered that such a beautiful girl would be interested in him. It made his infatuation all the more intense.

Glancing at her now, he saw that her eyes were closed. She rubbed them with her knuckles, as a small child would. When she finally opened them, she studied his face. She reached out and touched his cheek with the back of her hand. "You know, I thought I'd never get over you. It hurt so damn much."

"I'm sorry."

"I couldn't get over the idea that we'd never do the things we did together again. The little things. Talking on the phone. Cooking together. Touching in bed. That's what it feels like to have your heart broken. But that's not something you'd know about."

He struggled to keep his face impassive. But he saw from the small, ironic smile on her face that she knew she'd stung him.

"You're just not a loving person, Mike. I finally figured that out."

It was meant to hurt him, but he was determined not to let that happen. He wasn't going to argue with her about his alleged emotional shortcomings. They regarded each other in a silent standoff. The wind whistled in his ears, and he smelled a sweet, earthy aroma from the fields.

Despite his resolve not to get involved in Julie's drama, an image of Christa flashed into his mind, followed by a scalding thought: Could he have loved her more deeply?

Just as quickly, his mind went to Penny. Had she seen it too? Finally, he grunted under his breath and turned his eyes away, annoyed at being led down this mental rabbit hole against his will. "I'm sorry, Julie, but you don't know me," he said.

She shrugged. "You found someone you liked better. That's it. But it was hard." She turned and began walking up the road.

Shelter inhaled deeply, let the breath out in a long stream. He made an effort to drive the painful thoughts from his mind and think rationally. It was true that she knew nothing about his life, and her attempts to wound him said more about her own misery than about who he was then or now. He wouldn't play her game any longer. Following her, he said to her back, "You said on the phone you know something about who killed Jacob. What is it?"

She stopped and raised an elbow to her mouth to cover a bout of coughing. When it ended, she pulled a tissue from the pocket of her uniform top and blew her nose. She reached for her vape pen. After exhaling a cloud of vapour, she said, "I need you to get the Mounties off my back. Snitches get two bullets in the head."

"It's like I told you. There's nothing I can do. What are they offering?"

"They say I'll do probation at most if I wear a wire and testify. Otherwise, I'm getting three years, and that means a federal pen. I can't take that. No way."

"Sounds like a lot of time for a first offence on a drug charge. You can tell them you're not playing ball and see what happens in court. It's better than being dead."

Her nose was running again. She wiped it with the tissue. "I'm fucked either way."

Shelter shrugged. "You have a choice to make." He waited a moment before asking, "Do the drugs have anything to do with Jacob Waldner's murder?"

"Nah."

"Then what?"

She slid a hand into the pocket of her pants and shifted her weight so she was resting on one hip.

"I'm not telling you anything until you promise to get the Mounties to back off."

He shook his head and pursed his lips. "I'll talk to Peterson about the wire, but it's their show. Most likely, he'll tell me to go to hell."

"They'll listen to you. Tell them I'm helping you with your thing."

"We'll see. What have you got?"

"When I go out to the colony, part of the job is taking care of the women. Answering their questions about sex, helping them through their pregnancies—that kind of thing. It's an uptight place, and the young women don't know anything. Anyway, I got to know Rachel pretty well."

Shelter focused on her face, following every word.

"She calls me sometimes when she needs something." She glanced down the road and nudged the gravel with a toe. "Last month, she called and asked me to get her a pregnancy test."

"They don't have them at the colony?"

"They do, but she didn't want anyone out there to know her business."

"What's this got to do with Jacob's murder?"

"I hear he's not the father."

Shelter took him a moment to digest the news. "She told you that?"

"No, but people tell me things. And Rachel was really nervous and kept insisting I keep the pregnancy a secret."

"If Jacob wasn't the father, then who?"

"I don't know. I didn't ask."

"Who told you this?"

She shook her head. "I can't betray a confidence."

Shelter sighed and shook his head. The person who told Julie about the other man would know his identity. "Come on, Julie. You already betrayed Rachel's confidence by telling me she's pregnant. I need to know who told you about the affair."

She glared at him and snapped, "I can't tell you. So, back off."

Shelter studied her face for a moment. "Even if she was pregnant by another man, I don't see how Jacob gets killed over it."

She let out a derisive laugh. "Adultery's not some little thing for the Hutterites. If Jacob found out, he could have forced whoever it was out of the colony without a cent to his name."

Shelter remembered that Jacob was upset the night before he left for Winnipeg. Could he have discovered that someone in the colony was having an affair with his wife and that she was carrying that man's baby? Could he have threatened to expose the relationship? He wondered how he'd investigate this. Even if the Hutterites had suspicions about a secret affair, would they share the man's identity with him? And that wasn't all. Asking about an affair at the colony could tip off the killer.

"Let me look into it," he said. "Anything else?"

She gazed at her father's farm. In a quiet, distracted voice, she said, "No. That's it." She turned and stepped toward him. Reaching for his hand, she looked into his eyes and said softly, "We were good together."

Shelter was again taken off guard. Was she under the illusion that they could somehow get back together after all these years, or that by seducing him, she'd be more likely to get his help with the RCMP? He fought a sense of revulsion and the urge to snatch his hand away from her. Instead, he touched her shoulder with his other hand. Despite her harsh words only a few minutes earlier, he felt sadness and concern for her. He had lots of experience with addicts and saw the signs in her. She seemed to be sinking. "I can get you help."

Her brow furrowed, and her shoulders tensed. She jerked her hand away. "The only help I need from you is to get those fucking Mounties off my back. Can you do that for me?"

He shook his head. "I told you. I can talk to them, but it won't make any difference."

"I helped you. Now you help me."

Shelter shook his head again.

"Fucking useless," she shouted. She pulled her keys from her pocket and marched to her car.

As she climbed in, he called, "Get some rest and stay off the streets. I'll be in touch."

She glared at him as she pulled away, leaving a cloud of dust behind her Toyota. He would try to get her help for what looked like a serious drug problem, but for now, he was focused on Rachel's pregnancy and on learning more about it.

Driving back to Krefeld, Shelter checked the dashboard clock. He wanted to visit the colony to talk to Rachel, but he needed time to prepare. He was tired and decided a visit would have to wait until the next day, even though it meant barging into the colony as they prepared for Jacob's funeral.

He went over in his mind what Julie had told him about Rachel Waldner's pregnancy and the possibility that the father was someone other than Jacob. If it was another Hutterite, and Jacob had discovered the affair, it could have been a motive for murder. But how could the killer have travelled from the colony to Winnipeg and back in the middle of a workday without being detected?

He recalled asking Wurtz for that day's records to see who besides Jacob had signed out a vehicle. Now, he realized he hadn't followed up on that request. It was a mistake, one that needed to be corrected immediately. Of course, a killer could have gained access to a vehicle from outside the colony, but that seemed like a difficult challenge. And he still would've had to account for being away for at least half a day during the hectic harvest season.

How else could he establish whether she was involved with another man? A round of interviews would be necessary. His mind turned to Rachel. The young woman would surely deny an affair.

He was used to discussing these kinds of issues with Traverse, and now Shelter felt as if he had the full weight of the investigation on his shoulders. His partner had a cool intelligence, and Shelter needed him on the job. He was relieved he'd be back at work the next day.

He decided to stay overnight and checked back into the Krefeld Hotel. By the time he got to his room, he could barely keep his eyes open, but he made a brief call to Simon Wurtz. The minister sounded unhappy to be contacted, especially because the colony was busy preparing for the arrival of the funeral mourners.

"I'm sorry, but I need to sit down with Rachel Waldner again," Shelter said.

Wurtz reluctantly agreed and promised to prepare the vehicle records. He said the mourning rituals for Jacob would begin the next evening with what he called a wake, no doubt translating from the German word. It sounded to Shelter like what Catholics call the visitation. It would be followed by the funeral itself the following day. Wurtz didn't offer details of these ceremonies, but it was clear that the next two days would require much organization and hard work to transport, house, and feed all the mourners.

After finishing the call, Shelter kicked off his shoes, lay on the bed fully clothed, and was out within seconds. When he woke, he glanced at his watch. He'd slept for nearly an hour and felt groggy. He swung his feet off the bed and got up slowly. He stretched and shuffled to the bathroom to splash cold water on his face and brush his teeth.

It was after 7:00 p.m., and he hadn't eaten since breakfast. He wondered where he could get something decent on a Sunday evening in this town when his phone buzzed again. The screen showed the name Gabriel Traverse.

"Hey. What's up."

"I thought I'd check in and make sure you're surviving without me."

"Just barely."

Traverse laughed. "What's going on down there?"

"Julie Klassen tells me our victim's wife is pregnant and might have been having an affair."

"Who was she supposed to be having an affair with?"

"Not sure. I'm heading out there to talk to the wife and the Hutterite minister in the morning."

"How does Julie know this?"

"She says she hears things when she's nursing out there." He paused for a beat. "I could use some help."

Traverse chuckled. "You're lonely without me? That's what I'm calling about. I just got off the phone with MacIsaac. We agreed I'd stay here for now and hold down the fort while you're there. We just landed a murder-suicide in Transcona, and the workload is getting a little crazy. I also want to stay close to Luke."

Shelter was disappointed but couldn't argue with the decision. Earlier, he'd seen email traffic about the Transcona homicide, a domestic dispute that had ended with the husband shooting his wife with a rifle before turning the gun on himself. Winnipeg averaged around forty murders a year, far fewer than you'd see in an American city of the same size, but enough to keep their unit busy year-round. He was careful to keep his voice steady so as not to betray his feelings. "No problem. I'll keep you posted on what's going on. I should be back tomorrow or the day after."

He was on his own on this one.

TWENTY-TWO

PULLING INTO THE PARKING LOT at the Round Rock Hutterite Colony the next morning, Shelter saw Elias Stahl engaged in a heated discussion with Simon Wurtz. The young director of the Reservoir Art Gallery was jabbing his finger at the minister's chest and barking something. Wurtz shook his head but appeared calm.

The physical contrast between the two men was striking. As usual, Wurtz was dressed in the traditional Hutterite outfit of a buttoned shirt and suspenders. Elias stood several inches taller and looked ready for a fashion shoot, with salon-cropped blond hair, a new pair of jeans, a white long-sleeve shirt, and shiny cowboy boots.

The argument between the two abruptly stopped when they caught sight of Shelter. As he got out of the car, Wurtz said something urgently to Elias in German, no doubt a warning not to air their disagreement in front of the police. Elias's chin went up in disdain. He muttered a few words in response before stepping away from the minister.

"Good morning, gentlemen," Shelter said. "Elias, I'm surprised to see you here."

"It's the wake today, and he won't let me pay my respects to Jacob's family," he said, glancing at the minister, his face flushed with anger. "I've got every right to be here."

Wurtz responded to him, speaking quietly in German.

Stahl wheeled on him and, in English, said, "Is it Christian to keep me away from my friend's wake?"

"This is the decision," Wurtz replied in English.

"It's because of who I am."

"You have made your choices."

"Oh my God. It's not a choice. It's how I was born."

"Your ..." Wurtz searched for a word, "lifestyle is not what I am talking about. You chose to leave our community. Now you must accept the consequences."

Elias bowed his head. When he looked up at Wurtz, his tone had changed. Now he pleaded, "At least let me see my parents." It was as if he'd suddenly recalled the power this man held to deny him visits with his family.

Wurtz glanced at Shelter and back at Elias, considering what to do. "Go to the office, and I will arrange it for you."

Elias got into his car and pulled away to the parking lot. Shelter could see many more pickups, vans, and buses parked in the lot than on his previous visits. He watched as Elias got out of his car and headed for the colony office. Shelter turned back to Wurtz. "Where can I find Rachel?"

"Rachel is under a great strain, and we still have the funeral to go through. We have considered your request to speak with her. I must ask once again that you allow me to answer your questions on her behalf. I am sure I can provide the information you need or get it for you."

He said it in a quiet, earnest way. Shelter understood he was walking a tightrope between cooperating with the investigation and protecting his flock in these difficult days. But Shelter had no choice but to press ahead.

"I'm sorry, but I have to talk to Rachel in person," he said, matching the minister's respectful tone. "Finding who killed Jacob must take priority. That means I have to speak with anyone I think can help us. I understand this is a difficult time for Rachel and your whole community. But I must speak with her this morning."

Wurtz studied his face before nodding his acceptance. "She is ready to see you. Please follow me." Shelter understood that Wurtz hadn't expected him to agree to speak on Rachel's behalf, but he'd obviously felt the need to give it a try.

As they walked side by side toward the central quadrangle, they had to stop twice to make way for groups of adults to pass. Looking toward the dining hall and church, he saw a circle of men in conversation. The colony was filling up with visitors. "Where will you put all these people?" Shelter asked.

"Many will come only tomorrow for the funeral and then return to their colony. For the rest, we have places here or at other colonies. Don't worry." The tone was patient, with no trace of resentment over the disagreement they'd had over interviewing Rachel.

"Can you tell me a bit more about your tradition for the funeral?"

"It starts this evening with the wake. Jacob's coffin will be brought into the dining hall, where everyone will be gathered. Another minister and I will lead, and the evening consists basically of remembrances of Jacob, words of comfort for the family, and singing. After refreshments, the coffin will be carried to the family home for the night."

Shelter was struck by how different the Hutterite traditions were from those of the Protestant church he'd grown up in. "The coffin stays at the house?"

Wurtz nodded.

"And what happens tomorrow?" Shelter asked.

"All morning, people will come to the family home to pay their respects to Jacob's family."

"In the presence of the coffin?"

"Yes, it will be in the living room."

"An open coffin?"

"Yes."

Shelter tried to imagine the scene, the family receiving visitors in the presence of Jacob's body, displayed in an open coffin. An open coffin wasn't a part of Shelter's liberal denomination's tradition. Of course, he'd seen many dead bodies at crime scenes and in the morgue, but only once in an open coffin.

He'd been around twelve years old when he accompanied his parents to a visitation at a funeral home for a Catholic neighbour. Entering the reception room, he'd been led to the casket by his mother and father to pay their respects. He'd been fascinated by the sight of the man he'd known all his life lying still on the casket's white satin lining, wearing a suit and tie. The scent of orchids had filled his nose, and he could feel his mother fidgeting beside him. She'd complained bitterly on the way home about "morbid Catholics."

Wurtz continued, "And then around 2:00 p.m. is the funeral service followed by the burial."

"It's very sad," Shelter said. "Such a young man."

"Yes, we grieve deeply for the loss of Jacob, but for us, grief is infused with the hope of resurrection as taught by the scriptures. In our language, we always say *auf Wiedersehen*, which means 'until we meet again.' We believe that death does not have the final answer and that life ultimately triumphs over death. This belief is a significant focus of our funeral liturgy."

They'd reached Jacob and Rachel's home when Shelter was struck by a thought. "We still haven't received those records you promised about who used vehicles on the day Jacob was killed."

"Oh, yes. I'm sorry. I will get them for you when you leave."

Once again, the minister let himself into the house without knocking. The door opened into the living room. Rachel was seated alone on the couch, and a hardback chair had been positioned in front of her.

Shelter noticed a box of children's toys against one wall, and under a side table next to the couch, a small black machine with four propellers. It took him a moment to recognize it as a drone. He recalled that Rachel had told him flying the device was Jacob's hobby. A very modern pastime, he thought. Another example of technology inserting itself into the life of the colony.

"Hello, Rachel," he said.

She gave him a brief, timid smile. As Shelter took his seat, Wurtz gestured to Rachel. "Come with me for a moment," he said.

He led her down the hallway, where he whispered to her, a hand on her arm. She watched him intently as he spoke. After a few moments, Wurtz led her back into the living room. Rachel wore a long black dress. She wasn't obviously pregnant, but perhaps those who spent all day with her could detect it. She arranged herself again on the couch. Wurtz went to sit in an easy chair to the left of the couch, but Shelter lifted a hand. "I need to speak to Rachel alone."

"I am afraid that's not possible. I need to hear what is said, and she needs my support."

Shelter shook his head and deliberately hardened his tone. "I'm sorry, but we have our way of doing things, just as you do. I have to speak to Rachel alone." Wurtz considered his options. Finally, he backed away from the chair. "I will be in the kitchen if you need me, Rachel."

When he'd left the room, the young woman turned back to face Shelter.

"Rachel, I know it's a hard time for you, but I have to ask a few more questions. How are you?" He aimed for an even, reassuring tone.

"I am fine," she said, pronouncing each word distinctly. Her face was composed. It was clear she'd steeled herself to get through one more episode in an ordeal that had turned her world upside down.

Her husband had been killed, and her community had just learned that he'd been involved in a forbidden sexual relationship. What had the people's reaction been? How had they treated her? Rachel faced a life of caring for young children, and the person who had killed her husband was still out there.

"Are you getting the support you need?" Shelter asked.

"Yes. Everyone has been very good to me. Our faith in God and in each other sees us through, even in the worst of times."

There was no way to soften the blow of what he had to ask. He had to plunge in. "We have been told you're pregnant. Is this true?"

Her brow pinched in surprise, then her eyes dropped to the coffee table. She reached into her pocket and brought out a cloth handkerchief with trembling fingers. She shielded her lower face with a hand, the handkerchief intertwined with her fingers. Finally, she dropped her hand and said, "It is true. I am expecting in February."

Shelter inhaled and prepared to ask the next question. "I'm sorry, but there's no easy way to ask you this. We've heard you might be involved in an affair with another man. Is this true?"

Rachel's head jerked, and her mouth dropped open. "An affair?" The handkerchief fell to the floor. She glared at Shelter. "Of course not."

She grabbed the handkerchief in one savage motion. Her reaction confirmed what he'd thought when he met Rachel at the creek a few days earlier. This woman was no shrinking violet. She had a mind of her own and was now well and truly angry.

"It's the devil that puts those kinds of thoughts into people's minds," she said. "I loved Jacob, and he loved me. Of this, I have no doubt."

Beyond denying an affair, Shelter sensed she wanted him to understand something else without saying it: she and Jacob had been having sex, and the baby was his. Still, he had to make the implication explicit. "The baby is Jacob's?"

"Yes, of course it is," she said, her voice rising and her eyes flashing with anger. She paused, then spoke again in a calmer tone. "Anything else people are saying is sinful. They should be ashamed of themselves. Who told you these things?"

It was a good question. He wondered who on the colony could have whispered malicious rumours in Julie Klassen's ear and why. It was understandable that she knew about the pregnancy, but it seemed surprising that a Hutterite would share gossip about an extra-marital affair with an outsider. It occurred to him that Julie might have overheard women talking about it. It was possible she understood Low German, having been raised as a Mennonite in southern Manitoba, but even so, would the Hutterite dialect be intelligible to her? He should have pushed harder for her source and resolved to question her about it as soon as he could. In the meantime, he was vague about where he'd gotten his information.

"We're told it's a rumour in the colony."

She shook her head in disgust but didn't insist on knowing who'd passed the rumour on to him. Shelter watched her closely, trying to gauge whether her denial of an affair was truthful. On balance, he thought it was, but he knew from experience that impressions could be dead wrong.

He'd have to decide how far to push this line of investigation. He glanced around the room as he formulated his next question. He again noticed Jacob's drone under the side table. In that instant, an idea came to him.

He recalled Rachel telling him that flying the drone was Jacob's passion and that the day before he was killed, he'd taken it to the Butler farm to survey the land. What if the drone's camera had captured something Jacob hadn't expected? What if it were those images and not a confrontation with Lanny Butler or Mitchell Grimes that had upset him so much?

"Jacob's drone," he said.

"Yes," Rachel said.

"I'd like to look at what's recorded on it. Is there someone who can help me with that?"

"I've watched Jacob operate it. It's not complicated." Her anger had been replaced by a cool but courteous tone. She called to Wurtz in the kitchen. When he returned to the living room, Shelter explained that he needed to look at whatever video had been recorded on the drone.

Wurtz nodded his consent to Rachel, who went upstairs and returned with a laptop. She opened it on the coffee table and picked up the drone from the floor. Its body was only a little larger than her hand, and its propellers were attached to the four legs that extended from the body. Wurtz examined it with a look of distaste.

After a few clicks of the mouse, Rachel said, "The video is downloading now."

Shelter and Wurtz took positions on either side of her on the couch, where they could see the laptop screen. A series of separate images appeared on the screen, each a video clip. Rachel positioned the cursor over the first one.

"Just a second," Shelter said. "Why was Jacob shooting video at the Butler farm?"

"The sale had closed, and we were the owners," Wurtz said. "He wanted a closer look at the quality of the crops and at features of the property like the fences, ditches, and a large gully."

"But you had decided not to evict Lanny Butler."

It was Rachel who answered. "Jacob was having a hard time accepting the community's decision. He was holding out hope that we would somehow still get the land."

She clicked on the first video clip. The screen filled with an overhead shot of a yellowish-green field that

Shelter knew to be mature canola. The image was sharp and high-definition. The farmhouse and outbuildings were nowhere to be seen. Shelter assumed Jacob had been flying the drone from one of the roads that bordered the Butler property. If no one was out on the land, he could get a close look at the farm without worrying about provoking a run-in with Butler.

The house and buildings were a different matter. He would have had to risk detection to get close to them with the drone. They watched the video for a few minutes. Jacob flew the drone along a fence line and then traced the path of a gully, a natural trench cutting across a field that was a common feature on the prairies.

"Can you find any footage of the buildings?" Shelter asked.

"I can try." Rachel clicked on another video. As she fast-forwarded through images of the fields, it was clear that Jacob had shot video from different locations around the farm. It was the last clip that contained video of the farmhouse and outbuildings. These images appeared to have been shot from a much higher altitude than those of the fields, presumably because Jacob wanted the drone to remain undetected. The buildings, farm equipment, and vehicles looked like toys from this height.

The drone had been hovering over the farmyard for a minute when two men emerged from one of the storage buildings and walked toward the house. Shelter recognized Lanny Butler and Mitchell Grimes. He wondered whether they might have been able to hear the drone. He had his answer when Butler stopped suddenly and looked up. He pointed to the sky and said something to Grimes, who looked skyward, shielding his eyes with a hand.

Butler spun toward the building they'd just exited and cupped his hands around his mouth as if shouting. A warning to someone inside? At the same time, Grimes jogged toward a pickup truck and threw open the door. His head and torso disappeared into the cab. He emerged a moment later with a rifle.

Jacob had apparently seen enough. The drone flew north, and after a minute, the video camera showed Jacob standing beside his pickup, a controller in his hands, before abruptly cutting out.

Shelter let out a frustrated sigh. It added up to exactly nothing. A few images of Lanny Butler and his buddy Mitchell Grimes chatting. Yes, there'd appeared to be someone else in the farm outbuilding that Lanny had hastened to warn about the drone. But they had no way of knowing who it was or why Butler had tried to protect them. "Can you roll it back? Let's have another look."

He studied the segment again, leaning forward to get a closer look at the farmyard. He kept his eyes on the storage building as Lanny turned toward it to yell something. But there was nothing to see. Whoever was there had remained hidden from the drone's camera. Shelter shook his head and bit his lip in frustration. "Let's have one more look, please."

Wurtz glanced at him, his brow furrowed with annoyance. "We have to get back."

"Just one more look."

Rachel hovered the cursor over the video clip and clicked. The sequence played again—the farmyard, the two men emerging from the building, the moment they noticed the drone, Butler shouting toward the building, Grimes getting the gun from his truck. "Hold it there."

Rachel clicked to pause the video. The drone was flying away from the farmyard. "Go back just a couple of seconds," Shelter said.

Rachel slid the time bar at the bottom of the clip back a millimetre, and the video started again.

"Stop." She froze the video. It showed Grimes with the gun at his shoulder, pointed skyward. But it wasn't Grimes who had caught Shelter's attention this time. It was something behind him that made him lean forward for a closer look.

Shelter hadn't noticed it before because of the camera angle. He could only make out the rear end of the car. It was parked beside the same garage he'd peered into a couple of nights earlier. He was no car nut, but he appreciated German design and engineering excellence. Most people in Manitoba who could afford high-end sports cars steered clear of them because they weren't of much use during the long, harsh winters. He'd only seen a couple of Audi two-seat roadsters, and only one with a deep Mediterranean-blue paint job. It had been parked in front of James Deacon's garage.

He stared at the frozen image, trying to work out the implications of the Hutterites' accountant being on the Butler farm. He replayed in his mind the conversation with Deacon two days earlier. He remembered the accountant saying he kept his distance from Butler and his crew. He'd have to match the Audi's licence plate to Deacon, but it appeared he'd been with them the day before Jacob was killed.

Was it Deacon whom Butler warned to remain out of sight while the drone was overhead? Had Jacob nevertheless spotted his distinctive car, just as Shelter had? Was

Deacon's presence on the farm what had made Jacob so upset that evening? Was that why he'd circled that building on the diagram Rachel had given to Shelter?

Shelter felt his heart rate increase as he made the connections. He looked up from the screen to find Rachel and Simon Wurtz staring at him and realized he'd been lost in thought for several seconds.

"Do you have what you need?" Wurtz asked.

"Remind me what services James Deacon provides to the colony."

Wurtz gave him a quizzical look before answering. "He handles our accounting and advises us on business decisions. Why?"

"Advising you on buying the Butler farm?"

"Yes. This was one of the matters we discussed."

"Remind me what he advised you when Butler refused to leave the property?"

"He said we should avoid litigation and wait to see how the situation developed."

"He advised you against evicting Butler?"

"Yes. Why are you asking about James?"

Shelter pointed at the rear end of the Audi on the screen. "I believe this is James Deacon's car. Does it surprise you that he'd be meeting Lanny Butler and Mitchell Grimes? Would it have surprised Jacob?"

Wurtz's brow furrowed with concern. He spoke a few sentences in German to Rachel, his tone low and urgent. She appeared equally disturbed and paused before replying, in German. The minister turned to Shelter. "I can think of no reason why he should be meeting with those men at that time. We didn't ask him to speak to them on our behalf."

Shelter went over the sequence of events in his mind. It seemed there'd been no confrontation between Jacob Waldner and Butler or Grimes that afternoon. He'd apparently never even spoken to them. But Jacob had returned home upset and made a last-minute appointment with the colony's lawyer in Winnipeg, as well as another meeting. He hadn't told Wurtz, his wife, or his lawyer who that second appointment was with, but something important had caused him to change his plans so suddenly. The land, but what about it? The Hutterites had already decided not to evict Butler. What had changed that afternoon?

Shelter brought a knuckle to his lips and closed his eyes. It had to be the Butler farm that held the key. But what about it? He concentrated, searching his mind for the answer. Finally, it came to him in five words: *Not the land, the money.*

He opened his eyes. "Where do you keep your savings?"

Wurtz, who'd stood up and been pacing behind Shelter, stopped and became very still. "It is invested."

"Invested where?"

"In safe things. Jacob handled this with guidance from the colony's general manager. We always insisted that it be kept in safe investments. No risk."

Shelter turned on the couch to face Wurtz. "Who is the money invested with?"

"James Deacon."

TWENTY-THREE

THE FINANCIAL RECORDS were stored in a battered filing cabinet in the colony office. A yellow file containing investment statements was among the records generated by the colony's everyday business—bulk food purchases, utility bills, insurance policies, and bank and credit card statements.

Wurtz handed the file to Shelter, who laid it on a wooden desk wedged into a corner between the filing cabinet and a window. The desk, handcrafted from maple, was where Jacob would have sat to work on the colony's accounts. "Let's see the banking records as well, please," he said. Shelter wanted to get a feel for the colony's expenses and income.

Wurtz passed him another pair of files. The first contained statements for business accounts, and the second contained records for several credit cards in the colony's name. Shelter sensed Wurtz standing a couple of paces away, watching his every move. He ran a finger down the entries on several statements, seeing nothing out of the ordinary.

It was what he found in the yellow file that set off alarm bells in his head. The documents showed the colony's investment holdings. All were conservative, plain-vanilla assets—short-term guaranteed investment certificates and government treasury bills. Again, no problem there. It was exactly what you'd expect to see in an account where the money had to be kept liquid. He found a $4.2 million transfer that he assumed was the down payment on the Butler farm. The latest statement showed a balance of $4,865,310.13 in the remaining investments in the account.

But Shelter noticed the documents hadn't been issued by any financial institution. Instead, the letterhead showed Deacon Inc., Chartered Professional Accountants, with a logo featuring a stylized blue D and a white arrow pointing upward to the right, suggesting growth. Shelter pointed to the stack of papers. "Where are these investments held?"

A puzzled look came over Wurtz's face. "Mr. Deacon takes care of our investments."

"Yes. But which brokerage firm does he deal with? Where are the assets actually held?"

Wurtz frowned and shook his head. "Jacob took care of those details with Mr. Deacon." After a pause, he said, "Is there a problem?"

Shelter kept a neutral expression. "Not necessarily. But normally, there'd also be statements here from the firm that holds the securities. May I look at your other files?" Shelter quickly went through the filing cabinet and shuffled through papers in the desk drawers. No sign of brokerage statements. "Did Jacob or anyone else keep records somewhere else?" Shelter asked. "At his home, maybe?"

"No. I am sure not," Wurtz said. He was wringing his hands, and tension had raised the pitch of his voice.

"Maybe, there were only electronic documents."

"There are always paper copies for the elders to review." The minister ran his eyes over Jacob's desk, his brow furrowed. "I will call James."

"Let me do it," Shelter said.

He was careful to keep the excitement out of his voice, but the pieces were beginning to fall into place. He recalled how close Deacon was to the Hutterites and how he'd managed their financial affairs for years, as his father had before him. It was the kind of trusting relationship that offered fertile ground for fraud. If Jacob had discovered that the accountant was embezzling from the colony, it would have been a powerful motive for murder.

Wurtz, his jaw tense beneath his beard, asked, "Should we be worried about our money?"

"Leave it with me. I'll keep you informed."

In the outer office, Wurtz handed Shelter the vehicle records he'd requested and then walked him to the parking lot. Shaking his hand, he said, "I don't know how all this is connected to Jacob's death. We can only trust in God to lead us through this time. I know you will do what you can to help us."

When Shelter had driven a few kilometres and was safely out of sight of the colony, he pulled to the shoulder to consider his next steps. He felt a lift in his spirits and a low-voltage sense of relief. There were still many questions to be answered, but he finally felt he had a substantial break in the case, or at least the chance of one. He got out of the car and leaned against the hood, surveying a field of deep green soybean plants with the buzz of crickets in his ears. The line that had come to him earlier was now on a continuous loop in his mind. *Not the land, the money.*

He knew Jacob Waldner managed the colony's day-to-day bookkeeping, while James Deacon would have handled the financial heavy lifting—the tax preparation and investing. Without confirmation from a financial institution, there was no way to know if close to $5 million in Hutterite funds was where Deacon said it was.

If Jacob had seen Deacon's car at the Butler farm, it could have raised the same questions in his mind as it had in Shelter's. What was he doing with Lanny Butler and Mitchell Grimes? That would have led him to think about the colony's savings. Deacon's grandiose house, expensive cars, the horses—could he afford all that on what he made as a small-town accountant?

He was reminded of a case he'd worked on when he was assigned to the financial crimes unit in his first year as a detective. It was a small-time Ponzi scheme run by an unlicensed investment advisor. The guy preyed on members of his evangelical church, persuading them to invest their savings with him in an investment fund that turned out to be fictional. He cooked up statements that showed his clients were making impressive, if unspectacular, returns on their money. In reality, he was using the cash to pay off his house, buy cars, and take gambling trips to Vegas with his wife. Whenever someone wanted to withdraw cash, he'd pay them with the savings of other investors. When it all came crashing down, scores of people, many of them senior citizens, found their retirement savings gone. He ended up sentenced to four years in prison but was out in two on good behaviour. It seemed a small price to pay for all those ruined lives. Deacon's do-it-yourself monthly statements looked similar to the ones used in that scam.

Shelter needed to find out more about the money. Traverse answered his call on the third ring. "Hey, what's up?"

"I think I've got something." Shelter described seeing Deacon's car in the drone video and the missing brokerage records from the colony office. When he was finished, he waited for Traverse's congratulations on his breakthrough.

Instead, he got deep skepticism from his partner. "If he was out at the farm, so what? They know each other. There's no link to the murder."

Shelter felt tension knit into his shoulder muscles. Had his need to find Jacob's killer led him to make too much of what he'd seen on the video? No. He couldn't accept that. "Deacon told me he stays clear of Lanny Butler. What's he doing at his farm?"

Traverse let out a sigh. When he spoke, his tone was unyielding. "You didn't find any investment records, but that doesn't mean they don't exist. The Hutterites came up with the money to buy the farm, right? We need more."

"No doubt. Let's get it. We need to dig deep into Deacon—money problems, professional complaints, lawsuits, everything. And we'll need to go through the CCTV again to see if we can pick him up following Waldner's truck. Put Sharma and Sim on it."

"Yup."

"I'm going to bring him in for a chat."

"I'll come down tomorrow morning."

"No. I've got it. I need you working on this up there."

Traverse went silent for a moment. "Keep me posted."

The call ended, and Shelter leaned back against the car and stared toward the horizon, where the sky met the prairie in an almost unbroken line in the far distance. The initial excitement had worn off, but he still felt energized. Traverse was right about the lack of hard evidence, yet there was enough to go after James Deacon.

He thought about who could help. Peterson had never mentioned Deacon, but the RCMP officer liked to play it close to the vest. He could have something on Deacon from his drug investigation into the Butler crew. If he did, it was quite possible he hadn't made a connection between the accountant and Jacob Waldner's murder.

He pulled out his phone and texted Peterson. *Hey Alex. I'm working on something and need to talk to you. Are you around?*

The answer came back within seconds. *I'll be at the Carman detachment at eleven tomorrow.*

When Shelter was back on the highway, the sky opened up, and the force of the downpour made him feel like he was driving through gauze. The wipers slapped across the windshield but couldn't keep up with the volume of rain washing over the car. The spray from a passing semi-trailer's tires momentarily encased the car in water.

Looking to his right through the rain, Shelter could make out a grain combine immobilized in a field. A bolt of lightning cut a jagged white line across the horizon, followed an instant later by a loud crack of thunder. He wondered if the machine and the man on board were in danger of being hit. The farmers' prayers for rain had been answered too late. The deluge would make a bad year worse, turning the fields into mud, delaying the harvest and inflicting more damage on drought-devastated crops.

On Krefeld's main street, Shelter pulled into a parking space and cut the engine. Rain drummed on the roof and danced across the street. He didn't know if it was the stress of driving in the rain or the complexity of the investigation, but his head was throbbing. He rubbed his temples and considered what approach to take with Deacon. Obviously, the accountant was going to have to show where the Hutterites' money was, but, before that, Shelter needed to find out if the RCMP had anything on him.

He booked a room at the hotel, ordered food from the restaurant, and watched TV for the rest of the evening. His headache dissipated, and he was able to let go of thoughts about the case for a few hours.

As he climbed into bed, he sensed he was closing in on the killer. The meeting with Peterson in the morning would take him one step closer.

TWENTY-FOUR

IN THE DARKNESS, the red digital numbers on the clock radio read 4:47 a.m. Once again, he'd had the terrifying nightmare of shooting the woman in that dilapidated house. It had jolted him awake, drenched in sweat, his heart thumping. He'd thrown back the covers and sat on the side of the bed, rubbing his thighs as he slowly calmed down.

He had no hope of getting back to sleep. He dressed in jeans and a flannel shirt, crept downstairs, and passed the vacant front desk. Once outside, he regretted not wearing a sweater. Autumn came early in Manitoba. He thrust his hands into his pockets, pulled his arms close to his ribs, and turned down a side street, not knowing where he was headed.

A couple of the bungalows on the street already had the lights on. He imagined these were farmers who'd moved into town but hadn't lost the habit of rising early to get the day started. As he walked, his thoughts turned to his disastrous talk with Penny. He went over what they'd said at the restaurant and once again rebuked himself for going there believing he had the power to make things right. She'd decided otherwise.

It hurt like hell, but he still wasn't ready to give up. There was too much good between them, and the relationship had been solid until only a few weeks before, when their arguments had become more frequent. And then came the big blow-up about having a baby.

There was no bigger decision than bringing a new life into the world, and it wasn't surprising they'd fought over it. But he needed to persuade her that he was ready to try for a baby and that he'd be there for her for the long run. He told himself their commitment would endure if they could just get over this ordeal.

It took him less than fifteen minutes to walk to the end of town, where the houses gave way to small businesses in prefab buildings and a dealership with tractors, front-end loaders, and combines lined up in the yard. Beyond lay the provincial highway and open prairie. He crossed the highway and the ditch to the edge of a wheat field. Bending at the waist, he broke off the head of a plant and rubbed it between his hands. Only a few wheat kernels came off in his palm.

The severity of the drought had made the news throughout the summer, but it was far from the everyday concerns of city folk like Shelter, who were happy to enjoy the warm, sunny days and make the most of Manitoba's few short months of summer. Here, as the sun crept over the horizon, he could see that the wheat was dry, shrunken, scorched.

He thought again of his mother as a little girl, searching the skies west of her family's farm for rain clouds. What an uncertain life these people led compared with his own secure job in the city. Police work came with a constant threat of violence, but at least he never had to worry about how he was going to pay his mortgage.

As he turned to head back into town for breakfast, he noticed a pickup truck rolling down a driveway from a farmhouse a couple of hundred metres to his left. The truck turned onto the highway in his direction but didn't pick up speed. The driver brought the vehicle to a stop on the shoulder in front of Shelter. The old man at the wheel rolled down the passenger window.

"Can I help you?" he called out. His expression was friendly, his eyes peering at Shelter through steel glasses perched on a jowly face. He was dressed in blue overalls and wore a Case tractor cap over a fringe of white hair.

"Is this your land?" Shelter called out.

"Mostly the bank's." The farmer smiled at this retelling of one of the oldest jokes in the book. He shut off the engine and got out of the truck. He met Shelter on the shoulder, and they shook hands. He waited for Shelter to explain what he was doing in his field.

"I'm visiting from the city and was just taking a look at the crops. Drought's been pretty bad, eh?"

"I've seen worse."

"I can't imagine the stress."

"No use worrying about it," the farmer said, tipping his cap back on his forehead. "Prices are good, so that helps, and we've got crop insurance."

He stepped into the field and plucked the head from a wheat stalk. He rubbed it between his hands, just as Shelter had a few minutes earlier. He held the seeds in his palm. "You see the red colour? That's a sign of excellent quality. The yield's going to be down, but quality will be better. So, you see, a lack of moisture ain't necessarily such a bad thing."

He brushed the wheat seeds from his hand. "Visiting from where?"

"Winnipeg."

"What business are you in?" Shelter was expecting the question, and his guard was up. His first impulse was to give a generic job description like "I work for the city" to avoid questions about the case. Still, this old guy might be able to shed some light on what's been going on in the area. "I'm with the Winnipeg Police Service."

The farmer thought for a moment. "The Hutterite boy?"

Shelter nodded.

"Terrible for those folks. I'm told he had a wife and kids."

"Do you have much interaction with the Hutterites?"

"Some. We do a bit of business with different colonies." He pulled a pack of cigarettes from his breast pocket and lit one.

"What kind of business?"

"There's one colony I bring my combine parts for them to fix. I bought windows and doors from another. And when I go hunting, I bring my deer to another colony, and they process it for me."

"What do you think of them?"

"They work hard and are damn good farmers. On a personal level, they're some of the nicest people you'll ever meet. And they pitch in one hundred percent when there's a disaster like a flood or a fire."

"You heard about the Round Rock Colony buying the Butler farm?"

"You bet." He took a drag of his cigarette. "There's something that doesn't make people too happy around here."

"Why not?

With the smoke between his two fingers, he pointed to the horizon in a sweeping motion. "Look at my situation. Both my boys have left to work in the city. So, for the help I need, I gotta hire men. The Hutterites don't pay their people anything. That's a big advantage. It's why they can afford the best equipment and pay top dollar for land." His light tone had turned rancorous as he warmed to his subject.

Shelter decided to push back a little to see how the farmer would react. "Maybe they don't get paid wages, but they *are* housed, clothed and fed."

The farmer raised a skeptical eyebrow and shrugged.

Shelter said, "I've been told that when people buy land, they know they'll be looking for more in the same area. So, prices go up."

"That's right. And they're already too high." The farmer leaned an elbow against the hood of his truck. "A lot of the older guys like me are selling out. Who's buying?"

Shelter shook his head.

"Hutterites, corporations, and investors. It gets more expensive every year. And when the Hutterites buy, it's off the market forever. At least when a family buys or rents it, you've got some hope the land will come back on the market one day."

"What do you know about the Butler farm?"

"One of the best and biggest properties in this part of the province."

"So you're saying the Hutterites had competition for that land."

"They would have, but they're crafty. When they heard the old man had died and left it to Danny, they went to him and offered above the going price. They had it locked up before anyone else even knew it was for sale."

The farmer dropped his cigarette butt on the gravel and ground it out with his work boot. "I can tell you, no one's getting me off my land. They're going to take me out of here in a box. My kids can do what they want with it after that." He circled the truck and gave Shelter a wave before getting in. "You take care now."

Walking back to the hotel, Shelter reflected on what the old man had said. It was just one man's perspective, but it had given him a deeper appreciation of the role Hutterites played in the rural economy and the complicated feelings it could stir in their neighbours.

Shelter and Peterson were seated in the same airless conference room at the RCMP detachment where Shelter and Kane had visited days before. "What do you know about James Deacon?" Shelter asked.

At the mention of Deacon's name, Peterson's brow knitted with concern. He eyed Shelter before answering. "Why do you ask?"

"We've got a lead on him in the Waldner homicide." He explained that Deacon had claimed to steer clear of Lanny Butler and Mitchell Grimes but had been picked up by Jacob's video at the Butler farm. He then described the suspicious gap in the Hutterites' financial records.

Peterson rubbed his chin as he listened. "Have you got any actual evidence linking him to your homicide?"

"We're working on it. What have you got on him?"

Peterson leaned back in his chair and looked out the window, obviously deciding what to share. After a moment, he returned his eyes to meet Shelter's. "We think he's washing money for Butler and Grimes. The commercial crimes division has had a parallel investigation going on him for a couple of months."

"How's he doing it?"

"It's a bit complicated, but the simple answer is through offshore shell companies."

"How do Butler and Grimes know their money is where it's supposed to be?"

"Good question. They don't, except by creating fear in the heart of our friend Mr. Deacon."

Shelter considered this for a moment before leaning forward in his chair. "What's the surprise here?"

"Excuse me?"

"What happened that no one was expecting?"

Peterson shook his head. "I don't know what you're talking about."

"No one expected that farm to come up for sale. Everyone assumed the old man would leave it to his two sons, and Lanny would stay there. But Lanny gets cut out, and Daniel Butler sells the place to the Hutterites."

Peterson was focused on Shelter now, following his every word.

"Suddenly, everyone needs their money," Shelter continued. "The Hutterites need theirs to buy the farm from Daniel. And just a few months later, Lanny needs his to buy it back. Deacon has to cough up all that cash, but he hasn't got it."

"By stealing from Butler, he manages to put together enough cash for the Hutterites to make a down payment on the farm. But now he knows Butler is going to come for his, and he needs to stall. So, he advises the Hutterites not to evict Butler or sell the farm back to him. Instead, he tells them to wait. It all starts to unravel when Jacob sees Deacon at the farm. He starts to worry about the colony's savings and confronts Deacon. He tells him he wants proof their money is safe, or he's going to the police. That's a pretty good motive for murder, no?"

Peterson made a note and stood up. "It's an interesting theory. Let me make a call."

Shelter watched Peterson through the meeting room's glass wall, talking on his cellphone. He felt a buzzy, euphoric sensation in his chest. Arresting Deacon on a money-laundering charge would allow searches of his house and vehicles. He doubted Deacon was stupid enough to keep the murder weapon, but there would likely be other evidence linking him to the Waldner killing. Shelter struggled to keep his hopes in check.

Peterson returned to the conference room and took his seat across from Shelter. He offered a tight frown and shook his head. "Commercial crimes aren't on board. They're not ready to charge him. They want to help, but they just aren't there yet."

Shelter kept his face impassive. It was a setback, but not an unexpected one. Events never worked out so neatly. The important thing was to keep working on Deacon. What did the Mounties have? Where was he the day Jacob

Waldner was murdered? What did his wife, secretary, and others close to him have to say about his movements? But first and foremost, he had to talk to Deacon to check on the whereabouts of the Hutterites' money and to find out if he had an alibi for the day Waldner was killed. "I'm going to bring him in for an interview. You or someone from commercial crimes is welcome to sit in."

Peterson shook his head. "We want you to wait. Talking to him at this point will jeopardize our investigation."

"No way. We're talking to him, and he might be going under surveillance."

"You've got literally nothing linking him to your homicide."

"I think we do."

"We just need a bit more time."

"We don't have time. If he's our man, we have to get him off the street. I don't mind bringing in all the backup I need from the city. But he's coming in tomorrow."

Back in his hotel room in Krefeld, Shelter called MacIsaac and brought him up to speed on the Deacon lead. A half hour later, MacIsaac called back to say Deputy Chief Jonathan Wilkenson wanted to talk to him. It was unusual to have such a senior officer on the call, but Wilkenson had just gotten an earful from an RCMP boss and sent word down the line that he wanted a briefing on Deacon. MacIsaac said Wilkenson was in meetings all day, so it would have to go to six in the evening. Shelter asked for Traverse to be included, and a Zoom call was scheduled for that time.

Shelter set up his computer on the credenza in his hotel room for the call. He'd met Wilkenson a few times but mostly knew him for his bare-knuckles reputation for dealing with subordinates and pushing his own career ambitions. He was clean-shaven and bald, with a fringe of light brown hair cropped close to his skull. His thin nose, piercing brown eyes, and thin lips gave him the fierce expression of a raptor when he came onto the laptop screen a couple of minutes past six.

After a curt round of greetings, Wilkenson fixed those eyes on Shelter. "I just talked to the senior officer in the RCMP commercial crimes division. He tells me you're about to screw up a drug and money-laundering investigation. He also says this is the second call this week they've had to make about your inter-agency cooperation. He tells me it sucks." Wilkenson flipped open a file folder on the desk in front of him. "All right, let's go through what you've got on this accountant."

Shelter described the drone video that had first put Deacon on his radar as a suspect, and then the problems with the financial records he'd uncovered. "We're going through the street video in the city to see if we can find him following Waldner. I'm going to bring him in for an interview tomorrow, and then we'll see if his alibi checks out."

"Don't bother," Wilkenson said.

Shelter was stunned. He couldn't believe Wilkenson was siding with the RCMP against his own officer. "We've got enough to bring him in."

Wilkenson's face clouded with annoyance. "The Mountie told me this afternoon that they've already checked Deacon's client accounts from top to bottom.

The Hutterites' money is where it's supposed to be, safe and sound in the National Bank. He's not your guy."

Shelter thought he must have misheard. "You're kidding me."

"No. I'm not kidding, okay? Back off. He's not your guy."

Shelter watched in shock as Wilkenson struggled to figure out how to end the Zoom call. When he'd finally disappeared from the screen, MacIsaac mumbled something about Shelter getting back into town to discuss next steps before he too logged off.

That left Traverse to try to soften the blow for his partner. "It was a good idea, Mike. We just have to keep working."

Shelter remained silent for a long minute. He felt utterly defeated and drained. Finally, he shrugged. "I really don't know, Gabe. I'm chasing my tail on this thing. We're back to square one." After a pause, he said, "I'll be back in the morning."

"We'll take it from there, buddy. Get some sleep."

They simultaneously clicked off from the call, and Shelter clamped his eyes shut and leaned back in his chair. Every time he thought he had a viable lead in this case, it turned to dust before his eyes. It was time to face the reality that Peterson had probably been right when he advised him to focus on the gay relationship in Winnipeg as the simplest and therefore most probable line of investigation. A week had disappeared, and he was no closer to catching the killer. The risk of the case going cold was growing. Had his fascination with the Hutterites deluded him into thinking the solution lay at the colony?

"Jesus Christ," he hissed to himself. He leaned his elbows on his knees, made his hands into fists, and brought them to his forehead. He contemplated the depressing prospect of going back to the city and starting over, examining each element of the case and hoping for a different outcome. Maybe he just didn't have the skills to put the pieces together on this one. Maybe it was time to admit he wasn't up to it and hand the lead to another officer. That would be as good as admitting he no longer had what it took for this job.

Could he live with that, or was this how his police career came to an end?

TWENTY-FIVE

SHELTER WAS IN NO MOOD to drive all the way back into Winnipeg on an empty stomach. He had no illusions he was going to kick back, watch some TV, hop into bed, and go to sleep. He was restless and in need of distraction. Where could he get a drink and something decent to eat in this town? He remembered passing a chain steakhouse within walking distance.

The restaurant was surprisingly busy for a weeknight. A hostess told him he could take a seat at the bar. It was a big place with a generic, Western-casual interior with low lighting, booths, and wood panelling. The crowd was on the young side, and the area around the long bar was crowded and noisy. A couple of young men in checked shirts and jeans worked behind the bar while waitresses in white blouses and black slacks ferried drinks and food to the tables. Shelter took a seat at one end of the bar and, within a few minutes, was sipping a double rye and soda and looking over the menu. Given the last few days he'd had, he wasn't going to scrimp. He ordered a salmon tartare appetizer and a rib-eye steak.

The alcohol was having the desired effect. He felt tension release from his shoulders. A warm glow spread through his body, and he sensed his mood lifting. When the bartender brought his appetizer, he ordered a bottle of Cabernet Sauvignon, calculating he would have at least two glasses. The difference in price for a full bottle wasn't going to break the bank.

As he relaxed, he found he could look at losing James Deacon as a suspect in a more rational light. If he was honest, he'd invested too much hope in his theory without enough evidence to back it up. He reviewed the case in his mind. So far, the evidence simply wasn't there for anyone on the suspect list.

And beyond the lack of evidence, none of the suspects felt right as Jacob Waldner's killer. He knew feelings and intuition could steer you dangerously wrong, and he'd take facts and science over them every time. But over the last decade, he'd dealt with a lot of murder suspects trying to save their skins. His feel for when someone was lying had to be worth something.

Elias Stahl had been the obvious first choice as the prime suspect in his lover's murder. His alibi was solid, but maybe they'd missed something, a stratagem that had opened a window of opportunity. Then there was Stahl's husband, Martin Garnier. He'd admitted to being in a jealous rage over Elias's relationship with Jacob, and he'd been caught on video outside the house in Saint Boniface. But the trail of evidence had ended there. The video hadn't shown him following Jacob toward the house but instead leaving in the other direction. There'd been no forensic evidence from the house—fingerprints, fibres, or shoe prints putting either Elias or Martin inside. They were still waiting for DNA, but he wasn't hopeful.

He turned his mind to Lanny Butler, Mitchell Grimes, and the deal to buy the Butler property. Jacob was angry over Butler's refusal to vacate the farm. Was it possible he'd learned they were dealing drugs from there and threatened to go to the police?

From the drone video, it looked like Jacob hadn't even spoken to either man that day. More importantly, it was out of character for a Hutterite to make threats, given their pacifist beliefs and preference for solving their problems without resorting to state authorities.

Finally, there was Rachel's pregnancy and the rumour that she'd been involved in an affair on the colony. He thought back to the painful interview with Rachel. It would take further work to verify her denial of a secret relationship. Only DNA tests on the baby would confirm that someone other than Jacob was the father. But Rachel's horrified reaction to the suggestion that it could be someone other than her husband had felt anything but fake. He sighed and decided to let it all go for the next couple of hours.

He was midway through his steak when a couple vacated the seats beside him, and a group of high-spirited women swooped in to grab them. They were in their mid-thirties and attractive, dressed in a mix of strappy dresses and stylish tops over jeans. They immediately ordered a round of shots, downed them, and whooped. Shelter couldn't help but smile, listening to them tease each other and gossip as more drinks arrived.

There were five of them, two sitting and the other three standing, forming a semicircle. He'd just finished his steak and poured the last full glass of wine when the woman sitting beside him leaned back, laughing at a joke, and bumped his arm. Still laughing, she swivelled in her seat. "Oops. Sorry!"

From her olive complexion and large brown eyes, he guessed her family origins were Mediterranean—Spanish, Italian, Greek, or Lebanese. Her chocolate-brown hair fell to below her bare shoulders, and she had a wide smile. She looked him up and down, apparently noticing him for the first time, and put a serious, appraising look on her face. "Hey, you're not bad."

That drew a roar of laughter from her friends. Shelter shook his head and shot back, "Not so bad yourself," and was rewarded with another smile from her and hoots from the other women.

She said, "Okay. Shots all around. What're you drinking?"

"No. I'm good."

"Get outta here. What's it going to be?"

Shelter looked to the ceiling in mock exasperation, then said, "Make it Jameson's."

"Now we're talking. What's your name?"

"Mike. You?"

"Alice. Nice to meet you." The bartender set up the shots. Nodding to one of her friends, she said, "Shannon just got engaged, so it's ladies' night out."

"Congratulations," Shelter said before joining the others in downing the shots. The other friends began to chat among themselves again, and Shelter expected Alice to rejoin their conversation. But she kept her eyes on him. "So, what's your story, Mike?"

Here we go again, he thought. He was enjoying himself and didn't want to dampen the mood by telling her his real job and why he was in town. He tried to think of a boring job to put a fast end to this line of questioning. "I sell shoes," he blurted.

She raised an eyebrow and pursed her lips in a doubtful expression. Then she pointed at her foot in a sequined sandal. "Size?"

Shelter examined it for a moment. "Looks like a five."

She grinned. "Try seven. Stop bullshitting me."

"Okay. I'm a cop," he said with a shy smile.

"What kinda cop?"

"A Winnipeg cop."

"That explains why I've never seen you around here. I would have noticed."

Shelter returned her smile. He had a buzz on and was enjoying flirting with this woman.

"Hey, we're going dancing after this. Come with us."

Shelter laughed. "Me and five ladies?"

"Sure, why not?" She turned to her friends. "We're taking Mike dancing with us."

The friends giggled, and one of them gave the idea an enthusiastic thumbs-up. "Cool!"

There was no way Shelter was going to continue the evening with this gang. From every angle, he knew it was a bad idea. "That's not happening," he said, signalling to the bartender for his bill. "I'm heading back to the city early tomorrow morning."

Alice pursed her lips in a mock pout. "You sure? It'll be fun."

"I'm sure, but thanks for the offer." He paid and, putting on his coat, he said, "It was nice meeting you, Alice."

Touching his arm, she said, "Maybe I'll see you around."

"Take care of yourself."

He wished the others goodnight and made for the door. The temperature had dropped, and it had begun to drizzle. He concentrated on walking in a straight line. The shot of whisky had pushed him over the line from tipsy to drunk. Back in his hotel room, he downed a large glass of water and a couple of Tylenols in a pre-emptive strike against the hangover that awaited him in the morning. He stripped and fell into bed.

At first, he couldn't identify the noise clawing him from a dream. He finally realized the intermittent buzzing was coming from his cellphone in the pocket of his jeans, which were thrown in a heap on the floor.

He glanced at the clock and groaned: 4:19 a.m. His head pounded despite the painkillers, and his tongue felt like sandpaper. He grabbed his pants and pulled out his phone. He was surprised to see the name on the screen: Julie Klassen. He shook his head and mouthed a silent curse at being woken. He waited for it to go to voicemail, but at the last second decided it might be something important.

"Julie?"

Without preliminaries, she said, "I need you."

Her speech was slurred, and Shelter was certain she was high or drunk or both. He sighed in exasperation. He was never going to get back to sleep. "Where are you?"

"At home. I need to see you. Are you in town?"

Shelter shook his head. He was groggy and in no mood to deal with Julie in the middle of the night. "I'll come in the morning."

"No. I'm not going to make it to the morning. It has to be now. Please."

She sniffed loudly, and he knew she was crying. There was a note of hysteria in her voice. Shelter came fully awake. "What's happening?"

"Just come, for God's sake."

Shelter considered what to do. He recalled her touching him a few days before in what had seemed a clumsy, delusional attempt to rekindle their romance. He knew from years of policing how manipulative an addict could be, but it could be something more serious. She lived in fear of Lanny Butler and Mitchell Grimes, and he felt he owed it to her to make sure she was safe. He was now fully awake. "Where do you live?"

She gave him the address, relief in her voice. "Come right away, okay?"

"Hang tight."

He sat on the edge of the bed, rubbing his eyes. His headache began to ease ever so slightly. He got to his feet, pulled on a T-shirt and jeans, and brushed his teeth. The last thing he wanted was to get involved in Julie's problems if she wasn't in real danger, but he could spare an hour or two.

The address she'd given him was in a row of mobile homes on the last paved street on the southern edge of town. With Peterson's warning to stay clear of her in mind, Shelter cruised past Julie's trailer slowly. The lights were on, and her Toyota was in the driveway. His attention was drawn to a black pickup parked a short way down the street.

Shelter crossed the intersection at the end of the street and pulled into the parking lot of a grain elevator that stood tall in the darkness. He positioned his car so that he had a view of Julie's place and cut the engine.

He didn't like the look of that pickup. It could be the one he'd seen in the yard of the Butler farm. He wanted a better look at Julie's place. He stepped out of the car and walked slowly on the other side of the street. He took a position in the shadows cast by a line of trees and watched her mobile home for a few minutes. The curtains on the front window were pulled back. The lights were on in the living room, but he saw no movement inside.

As he approached the trailer, he noticed it was in bad shape. Paint peeled from its siding, and rust showed around the window frames. The inside door was open, and Shelter peered through the screen-door mesh into the living room. Julie was stretched out on a couch, apparently asleep. He called to her twice but got no response. The aluminum door was unlocked, and the hinges squeaked loudly as he pulled it open.

A hypodermic needle, a spoon, cotton balls, rubber tubing, and a lighter lay on the coffee table, strewn with the remnants of a party—beer bottles, a full ashtray, and a large pizza box. In her sleep, Julie's face was slack and lined. One of the long sleeves of her shirt was pulled up, revealing a red track mark in the crook of her elbow. His reading of the scene was that Julie had become desperate to stop herself from shooting up and turned to him. He'd arrived too late to help her.

"Julie. Wake up." No response. He skirted the table and pushed it back from the couch with his shin. He knelt beside the couch. Her breathing was shallow and laboured. "Julie."

Her eyelids fluttered but stayed closed. Shelter touched her cheek with the back of his hand. Her skin was cool and clammy, and her breathing was a heavy rattle. He raised his voice. "Julie!"

She gave a congested cough.

"Julie, look at me."

Her eyelids opened for a brief moment. Shelter took her hand in both of his. "Try to stay awake. Talk to me."

Her head lolled to the side, and her eyes rolled back into her head. A gurgling sound came from deep inside her chest.

"Julie!" No response. He took both her shoulders in his hands and shook her, repeating her name with increasing volume and urgency. Nothing. He'd seen enough. He pulled his cellphone from his pocket and dialled 911. He told the operator he was with a woman who'd overdosed and gave the address.

As he spoke to the operator, he noticed Julie's breathing had slowed and deepened. It sounded as if she were snoring. Then it stopped.

He lowered his head to her mouth. He couldn't feel or hear her breathing. "Oh, fuck!"

On his knees before Julie's inert body, he heard the operator's faint and muffled voice, as if from a distance. "Do you have Naloxone?"

A kit in the car. He pushed himself to his feet, leaped over the coffee table, and slammed a shoulder into the screen door. He jumped onto the sidewalk and sprinted for the car. He popped the lock, pulled the door open, and dove for the glove compartment. The overdose kit was in a rectangular cardboard box. He grabbed it and jackknifed out of the car.

By the time he'd made it back to the trailer, he was gasping for breath, and sweat was running into his eyes.

He shoved the coffee table across the narrow room and gently lowered Julie onto the floor. Her lips had turned blue. Time was running out.

Shelter tilted her head back, tore open the box, and pulled out one of the blister packs. Tearing it open, he fumbled it onto the filthy carpet. "Come on. Now!" he hissed at himself.

He grabbed the package from the floor and finally managed to open it. The device had a plunger in the middle, attached to a nozzle. He fit it between his forefinger and middle finger and put his thumb on the plunger. He inserted the nozzle's tip into Julie's nostril until his fingers touched her nose, then pressed hard, spraying a shot of Naloxone into her.

He knelt beside her shoulder, placed the heel of his hand over the centre of her chest and the other on top of it. He straightened his arms, ready to push with his full body weight to start CPR, when her loud gasp made him jump. She'd started breathing again.

Shelter turned her on her side into the recovery position and gently tilted her head back so she could breathe fully, just as he'd been trained to do. After a few seconds, her eyes opened, and she turned her head.

She dreamily studied his face.

"Mike. You came."

TWENTY-SIX

SHELTER HEARD an approaching siren. Cradling Julie's head in his hand, he said, "I've got you. Help is coming. Just stay calm."

A panicked look came over her face. "I'll lose my licence." Her speech was slurred and barely audible.

It took Shelter a moment to understand what she meant. A nurse found to have an opioid addiction would have to be reported to the College of Nurses. There'd be an investigation and, at the very least, a suspension. Thinking about it for the first time, he was surprised her drug problem had escaped detection thus far.

He touched her cheek. "Don't worry about that now. Just breathe, okay?" He could see she was alert, and she slowly pulled herself into a sitting position. She'd recovered quickly once the Naloxone was administered. Her head jerked toward the door and then back to Shelter. Her eyes were pleading. "Call them back. Please. Cancel it. I'm okay."

Two paramedics, a man and a woman, barged into the room. Shelter stood back as they put an oxygen mask on her and began taking her vital signs.

Shelter explained that she'd stopped breathing and that he'd administered a dose of Naloxone. The woman nodded, glancing at the drug paraphernalia on the coffee table. Julie kept her eyes on Shelter as the paramedics helped her onto a gurney and pushed her toward the door.

A group of neighbours dressed in pyjamas and housecoats had gathered in front of the mobile home. Following the gurney down the front drive, Shelter became aware of another siren approaching from the south. An RCMP cruiser pulled up, and two male officers got out. After the paramedics loaded Julie into the ambulance, the woman exchanged a few words with one of the cops. She gestured toward Shelter, and one of the uniforms glanced at him and frowned. After the ambulance pulled out, Shelter met the officers on the sidewalk leading to the house. He flashed his Winnipeg police ID and introduced himself.

"What are you doing here?" the lead officer asked.

"I know her, and she called me for help. I found her unconscious, and then her breathing stopped."

Over one of the officers' shoulders, Shelter noticed the neighbours straining to see what was going on in the house. A boy of about nine in pyjamas had detached himself from the group and was sneaking toward a window. "Hey! No. Stay back," Shelter shouted at the kid. Once he'd scurried back to his mother, Shelter turned back to the cops. "We need to keep these people back."

The officer frowned. "You're here from Winnipeg, visiting a junkie in the middle of the night?"

"I'm working a case. That's all I can tell you."

His partner went to the sidewalk to tell the residents to go home, but Shelter knew it would take time to calm the neighbourhood. Shelter turned back to the officer who'd been questioning him.

Still holding his ID, the officer noted his name and asked for his cellphone number before asking him what he'd seen. Shelter described getting a call from Julie and finding her on the couch.

"She's a friend?"

"She's someone I knew years ago. We bumped into each other last week."

Shelter knew Peterson would hear soon enough about Julie's OD and the Winnipeg cop who'd been on the scene. "You know Alex Peterson? He works out of the Carman detachment."

The cop raised an eyebrow and nodded.

"He'll want to know about this incident. He can fill you in."

"What's this case you're working on?"

The question was disingenuous. There weren't a hundred unsolved homicides here that would bring a Winnipeg detective to town. "I think you can guess if you put your mind to it," Shelter said. He paused a beat. "I want to get to the hospital to see how she's doing. You know where to find me," he said, nodding at the officer's notebook.

The emergency room was busier than Shelter had expected for an early Wednesday morning. But then again, given the dysfunctional state of the health care system, an emergency waiting room packed with the sick and injured was no more surprising than seeing kids playing street hockey or a line-up at a Tim Horton's coffee shop.

He flashed his badge and told the triage nurse behind a Plexiglas window that he was there to see Julie Klassen, who'd been brought in by ambulance a little while before. The nurse rolled her eyes and shook her head, a gesture that read as disgust. Her reaction made him wonder whether she'd worked with Julie, or at least knew her, and had harboured suspicions about her drug problem.

The circles under the nurse's eyes said she'd had a long, harried night and was ready to go home. She didn't need to check the computer to confirm Julie's whereabouts in the hospital. She held Shelter's eyes for a moment before saying, "She's under observation. You can take a seat. I'll call you."

He found a place beside a man in ragged jeans holding a piece of gauze to a bearded cheek. On his other side was a young woman in a long, loose-fitting dress, who alternated between texting and keeping a close watch on a sleeping child in a stroller.

Shelter's attention was drawn to a woman hobbling through the sliding doors with the help of a cane. It took him a moment to recognize her. Julie had introduced him to her mother twenty years earlier. He calculated that Sharon Klassen was probably in her mid-sixties, but her deeply lined face and the thirty extra pounds on her diminutive frame made her look much older. Through oval glasses, she squinted under the fluorescent lighting, evidently bewildered by the crowd in the waiting room.

Shelter approached her and introduced himself. "I was friends with Julie many years ago. Maybe you remember me?"

She studied his face before saying in a distracted voice, "Oh, yes. How are you?"

Shelter wasn't sure if she actually recognized him or was simply being polite. He assumed Julie's mother had been notified by the police, though it could have been someone at the hospital who called her. "Julie is in with a doctor. There's a seat over here."

Shelter led her to a pair of seats, where he judged they could talk without being overheard. Sharon Klassen drew a tissue from her purse and used it to cover a dry cough. Finally, she turned to look at Shelter. "Why are you here?"

He turned his shoulders to give them more privacy and said in a low voice, "I'm with the Winnipeg police and working on a case here in town. I went to Julie's place for a visit and found her unconscious."

The old woman gave him a curt nod and turned to look straight in front of her, her face pinched with anxiety. From her reaction, Shelter could tell she wasn't interested in the details of why her daughter was meeting with a police officer. "I was with her. I'm sure she's going to come out of this all right," he said.

Klassen lowered her eyes to the tissue she was kneading with both hands. After a long pause, she looked up at Shelter. Her brown eyes were watery, but she was not weeping. "It's been like this for years. She promises to stay away from it, but she always ends up going back." Klassen glanced at him and must have seen the look of concern on his face. "It's gotten worse since she lost her job in Winnipeg."

She bowed her head again. "She was such a beautiful, happy little girl," she whispered. "Now I can't even let her into the house. My husband doesn't want anything to do with her."

"Addiction is very difficult."

Looking at her, Shelter thought about the heartache she and her husband must have endured. The shock of realizing your child was addicted, and then the dashed hopes as you tried to find some way, any way, to rid her of the monster. He'd seen the devastating impact on so many families. He could only thank his lucky stars the monster hadn't gotten Kelsey. He reached out and touched her shoulder. "Hope is so important. Don't give up on her."

She gave him a weak smile but began working the tissue again. "There's no hope as long as she's with that man."

"What man?"

"Mitch Grimes. He's ruined her life."

"They're a couple?"

Klassen shrugged.

"She gets her drugs from him?"

"I assume so. But he's not the only bad apple in this town."

"Lanny Butler?"

"Him and others." She looked up and scanned the room. "Oh, here she is."

Shelter turned and saw Julie scuttling toward the exit. He jumped to his feet and called out to her, but she was already through the sliding doors. By the time he got outside, she was halfway down the circular drive, where a taxi waited to pick up a fare.

"Julie," he shouted. "Hold up."

She glanced over her shoulder, slowed, then stopped on the sidewalk at the end of the driveway. As Shelter approached, she dug a hand into a pocket of her jeans and pulled out her vape pen.

"Where are you going?"

She exhaled vapour, narrowed her eyes and regarded him with a sneer. Only a few hours earlier, she'd been begging to see him. Now that she'd sobered up, she was back to outright hostility. "None of your business."

"Come on. I'll take you home."

Just then, she noticed something over his shoulder. "Oh, no. Who called my mother?"

"I don't know. Julie, you've had a bad shock. You need to rest."

"I'm fine. Leave me alone."

Shelter felt sure she'd be scoring another fix within the hour.

Leaning on her cane, Sharon Klassen hobbled up to them. "Are you alright?"

"I'm fine, Mom. Please go home."

Sharon shook her head and looked at Shelter with a resigned expression.

"Let me give you a ride," Shelter said to Julie.

"Just leave me alone." She pushed the vape pen into her back pocket and, without looking back, climbed into the back of the taxi. As it pulled away, Shelter turned to her mother, who gave him a sad shrug.

"Can I give you a lift?" Shelter asked.

"No. Thank you. I have my car." After a pause, she added, "I'll try to talk to her later."

She headed toward the parking lot, and Shelter re-entered the hospital to pick up the coat he'd left on the waiting room seat. Walking to his car, he sensed a niggling doubt. He'd missed something, and now it was irritating him like a pebble in his shoe. Shelter knew from experience that it wouldn't stop until he'd tracked down whatever it was in his mind.

He sat on a bench in a grassy area in front of the hospital, crossed his ankles, and hugged himself against the morning chill. He stared at the parking lot, replaying the events of the last few hours, moment by moment, searching for the one thing that had escaped him. It was like the word puzzles he sometimes did online. He just had to put in the time and have faith that the answer would come.

When it did, it was sudden. He held it in his mind, hard and clear as a diamond. As he examined the idea from every angle, he realized it wasn't just one thing but two he had to put together. That's what had made it so elusive.

TWENTY-SEVEN

SHELTER WAS WAITING for the triage nurse when she exited through the sliding doors. She kept her eyes forward, single-mindedly marching toward the parking lot at the end of her shift. He fell in behind her and followed for a few metres until they were well away from the hospital entrance, before calling out to her, "Rough night?"

Her shoulders jerked in surprise. When she wheeled to face him, it took her a moment to place him. When she did, she wasn't pleased. Standing in the weak dawn light with her car key in hand, she pulled the collar of her powder-blue puffer jacket close under her chin. "No more than usual. You came in with Julie."

"Just after. I was the one who found her." He took a closer look at the nurse than he had forty-five minutes earlier. In her mid-forties, she was no more than five feet tall. Her dyed blond hair was cut in a bob, and brown roots were beginning to show. "When we spoke before, it seemed like you knew her."

The corners of the nurse's mouth turned down, and she shrugged. "She was a year behind me in nursing school. She's a friend of yours?"

"We were friends back in the day."

She considered for a moment. "You're Winnipeg police?"

Shelter nodded.

"The murder of that Hutterite man." It was said as a statement of fact. She turned to look toward the parking lot. She was itching to get away from him.

"I noticed you don't seem to be a big fan of Julie's. Why?"

His question brought her eyes back to his face. She looked exhausted, and he sensed she was worried about where this conversation might be leading. "No. It's nothing."

"I saw the way you looked when I mentioned her name. It *is* something."

She sighed and dropped her eyes to examine the key in her hand. "Look, I just want to go home."

"Her mother says she lost her job in Winnipeg. Do you know anything about that?"

The question jolted her. She recovered quickly, glancing at him nervously. Behind them, the doors slid open and closed as patients, workers, and visitors entered and left the hospital. The nurse glanced back and moved farther down the sidewalk under a tall poplar tree. She thrust her hands into her jacket pockets. "I just can't believe she's still allowed to nurse."

"Why?"

"It's a rumour."

"That's okay."

"You didn't hear it from me, but I've got a friend who worked with her at a nursing home in Winnipeg. She got fired from there a couple of years ago."

"Fired for what?"

"She was stealing drugs."

She looked back toward the hospital entrance before going on. "When she was fired, the nursing home said it was because of mistakes she'd made while giving medication to patients, but people found out that story was a cover-up."

Shelter was about to ask about the thefts when he noticed the nurse's brow furrow in distress. He waited for her to gather herself. "What happened?"

She shrugged. "Nothing. Julie was fired, and life went on. Then she started working around here."

Shelter lowered his eyes to the sidewalk and thought about what he'd just heard. Stealing drugs. He now felt a growing certainty that his suspicion was correct. Julie had been treating Jacob's grandmother and had access to her pain medication. Jacob could have somehow discovered that she'd been stealing the drugs. He looked up and met the nurse's eyes. He realized she was thinking the same thing.

"Have you talked with anyone else about this?"

She shook her head. "I can't believe it could be true."

It seemed more likely to Shelter that she'd feared it was true but didn't want to get involved.

The nurse pulled her hands from her pockets and said something that confirmed his suspicion. "I was going to go to the police, but the whole thing seems so crazy. And I was scared. I'm sorry."

"Don't be sorry. You've done the right thing now. What's the name of this nursing home?"

"Oakridge Seniors Residence." Shelter had passed it often—a large building in Fort Garry.

"What's your friend's name?"

The nurse shook her head. "She'd kill me if I got her mixed up in this."

Shelter took the nurse's name and details. When he looked up from his notebook, he saw tears in her eyes. "Get some rest and leave it with me, okay?"

She sniffed and wiped her eyes with the back of her hand. She slung her backpack over her shoulder and was gone.

Sitting in his car, Shelter pulled a file folder from his briefcase containing his case notes. He found a photocopy of the sheet of paper Rachel had given him that evening by the creek. Shelter studied the note scrawled on it: *180 T x 8 DIL. MARS.*

He opened a search engine on his phone and typed in "DIL and opioids". Most of the first-page results were articles about a powerful drug called hydromorphone, brand name Dilaudid. It was a synthetic opioid often used to treat moderate to severe pain and much abused by opioid addicts. He was aware that opioid abuse was an issue for healthcare professionals. But when he did another search, he was shocked by how many stories popped up about nurses and doctors abusing Dilaudid.

He looked at Jacob's paper again with fresh eyes—one hundred and eighty tablets of eight-milligram Dilaudid. Next, he plugged MARS into the search engine and tried a few opioid-related terms. It took some time, but he found a phrase that matched the acronym: Medication Administration Records. MARs were used by health professionals to document and track medications being taken by patients. He found reports that MARs had been falsified by healthcare professionals to cover their theft of opioids.

He felt excitement bubble in his gut. He recalled that the supply of illegal opioids into the province had been suddenly cut off when the RCMP made its bust in Vancouver. Julie suffered from a voracious addiction and had access to a constant supply of powerful opioids at the colony, far from the prying eyes of colleagues in a health facility. She could have easily stolen drugs during her house calls to Jacob's home and falsified MARS documents. It meant depriving his grandmother of medication and condemning her to horrible pain without relief. But there was no limit to how far an addict would go in desperation.

If Jacob had suspected Julie was responsible for his grandmother's suffering, he'd surely have turned her in. Julie would not only have lost her nursing licence and her job but also faced a criminal conviction and jail time. Probably, even more terrifying for her, she would have lost access to drugs.

But if she was stealing drugs, how would have Jacob found out? And once he knew, wouldn't he have confronted her? Or was there some other way that she'd learned he was on to her?

It was terrible for Shelter to suspect that the woman he'd once been so close to could be Jacob's killer, but if she was, he needed to get her into custody right away. He glanced at his watch and saw it was almost 7:00 a.m. He'd need to rouse Gabriel Traverse from his sleep for a second time in a week.

When Traverse picked up on the fourth ring, his partner's voice was a low-pitched, throaty growl. "What is it now?"

"I think Julie Klassen's our killer."

There was a long pause at the other end of the line. When he spoke again, Traverse's voice was clear and alert. "Your ex?"

"She's an addict, and I just met a nurse here who says the word is that she has a history of stealing drugs. Jacob's grandmother had terminal cancer and was on opioids for her pain. Julie was caring for her."

"You want me to come out there?"

"Not right now. I'm going to the colony to check it out. Can you call the College of Nurses when they open and ask about any prior run-ins with her? Then I need you to check out the Oakridge Seniors Residence. The nurse here says that's where she was fired a couple of years back. They might not want to cooperate, so push."

TWENTY-EIGHT

WHEN SHELTER ARRIVED at the colony, the parking lot was filled with more vans and buses, and he remembered that today was Jacob's funeral. It was breakfast time, and in the distance, he saw families trooping toward the dining hall. The women would have been working since the early-morning hours, preparing meals for the hundreds of mourners.

He assumed Wurtz would be at breakfast. He circled the line of Hutterites heading for the dining hall. Several greeted him with a polite nod but otherwise continued chatting among themselves in the sunshine. It was the children who regarded this stranger in a buttoned shirt, blue jeans, and a blazer with unabashed curiosity. Shelter smiled at a little girl, and she hid herself in the folds of her mother's dress.

When he entered the building, it seemed as if the dozens of people seated at the long tables turned as one to regard him—men on one side of the room, women on the other. It took him a moment to realize that everyone was dressed in black for the funeral—dresses for the women and jackets for the men. To his right, a long line of people waited for their turn to serve themselves breakfast from steel pans set up buffet-style just outside the large kitchen. After the initial surprise at seeing Shelter appear at the door, the buzz of conversation quickly resumed, and he spotted Wurtz rise from a table.

"Detective Shelter, we weren't expecting a visit today," Wurtz said, his brow furrowed with concern.

"I'm sorry. I know it's a very busy day," Shelter said. "But there's been a development in the case. I need to ask you some questions."

The minister glanced over his shoulder at the rows of tables. Turning back to Shelter, he said, "Are you hungry? Will you join us for breakfast?"

Shelter was struck by the generosity of the offer on such a difficult day. "No. I'm fine, thank you. I'm afraid it's urgent. Please come now."

"Yes. I just need to ask someone to say grace."

Wurtz said a few words to a grey-haired man at one of the tables, then led Shelter out of the dining hall. They walked in silence to a grassy area. The sun was still low in the cloudless sky, but the temperature was already rising. It would be a hot day.

"How can I help you?" Wurtz's tone was patient and courteous. He seemed resigned to this interruption as just one more trial in a day that would be full of them.

"What can you tell me about Julie Klassen and the care you've been getting from her?"

Wurtz's eyebrows shot up in surprise. "Julie? What does she have to do with this?"

"I'm not sure, but we have to look into every possibility."

Wurtz considered this for a moment before replying. "She is a nice person. Kind to our senior citizens. She's missed appointments from time to time, but other than that, we've had no trouble. Why?"

"She was caring for Jacob's grandmother?"

"We care for our seniors ourselves, but Julie would often come to look in on Carol when her cancer became bad. What is this about, please?"

"I will tell you in a moment. I remember Rachel telling me that Carol was in a lot of pain. Was she taking pain-relief medication?"

"Yes, of course. The doctor told us the cancer had moved into her bones, and there was nothing to be done but keep her comfortable. The doctor increased the strength of her medication, but she was still in terrible pain."

"Where did you get the prescriptions?"

"From a drugstore in Krefeld."

"Where was it kept?"

"In Jacob and Rachel's home. We put it in a locked medicine cabinet, of course, because of the children. To be safe."

Shelter thought back to the small, unidentified key found in Jacob's pocket. Could that have been for the medicine cabinet?

"Julie had a key?"

"Yes. I believe so. Why are you asking these questions?"

"Julie has a drug addiction, and she may have been stealing medication meant for Jacob's grandmother. We're concerned Jacob may have found out about this somehow."

Wurtz studied Shelter's face, working out the implications. When he understood, he inhaled sharply, and his features pinched in shock. "Julie killed Jacob?"

"We don't know, but we need to make sure one way or the other. Can you show me the medicine cabinet?"

"Jacob's coffin is in their home so people can pay their respects before the funeral. This is our tradition."

"I'm sorry, but this can't wait."

"For now, it's just the family there." Wurtz led the way across the quadrangle to Jacob and Rachel's home and tapped on the door before entering.

The open coffin sat in the living room to the right of the front door, supported on wooden sawhorses. It was a simple pine box, no doubt built by the colony's carpenters.

For a grim moment, Shelter studied the body of the young man he'd first seen lying in his blood in the living room of the house in Winnipeg. His hair and beard were neatly trimmed and combed, and he wore a white shirt and a suit jacket. It seemed the colony had employed an undertaker to work on the body. Jacob looked peaceful, his cheeks and lips made to appear healthy, and his shirt collar artfully positioned to hide where his throat had been cut.

Shelter looked up from the body to the Hutterites, who watched him silently from their seats around the room. Rachel, her eyes red and watery, sat on the couch between two older women. All the women were dressed in black.

Shelter recognized Mary, Jacob's mother, and he assumed the other woman was Rachel's mother, visiting from her home colony in western Manitoba for the funeral. They were flanked by two men seated on hard-backed chairs. There was no sign of Jacob and Rachel's children.

"I am sorry, but Detective Shelter needs to check something in the house," Wurtz said. "Rachel, could you help us please?"

Shelter saw the older women on the couch look from Wurtz to the men in the chairs, their faces tense with concern. He said, "There's no need to worry. We won't be long."

Rachel rose and accompanied Wurtz and Shelter into the adjoining kitchen. "I'm very sorry to disturb you at a time like this, but I must ask where you kept Carol's medicine?" Shelter said in a low voice.

Rachel's eyes darted between Shelter and Wurtz. "Why?"

"It may be nothing, but I have to check something."

Wurtz touched her arm to reassure her.

She led them upstairs and down a hallway to a bedroom on the right. The room was unadorned. A double bed in the centre had been stripped. A sliding window overlooked the front of the house. There were no personal items on the side tables or the chest of drawers. The room looked as if it had been thoroughly cleaned and left vacant after Jacob's grandmother's death.

"This is the medicine cabinet," she said, pointing to a white wooden box attached to the wall. Shelter went to it and found it unlocked. Inside were only a bottle of Tylenol, a bottle of stomach antacid, and a bottle of rubbing alcohol.

"What happened to the pain medication?"

Rachel shook her head. "I don't know."

"Who got the prescriptions from the drugstore?"

"I think it was Julie who brought them for Jacob's grandmother."

"Did Jacob speak with Julie the day before he left for Winnipeg?"

Rachel considered the question. "Not that I know of."

Shelter thought for a moment, then turned to Wurtz and asked, "What pharmacy do you use?"

The minister named a chain drugstore and said it was on Krefeld's main street. Shelter glanced at his watch—8:30 a.m. He looked from Wurtz to Rachel. "This may turn out to be nothing. Please don't discuss it with anyone. I'll keep you informed."

When Shelter arrived at the pharmacy, it had just opened. Only a couple of customers were browsing the aisles, and the prescription area was quiet. He showed his badge to the attendant at the intake counter, who relayed the information to a grey-haired man working alone in the raised dispensary. The man, dressed comfortably in a beige sweater over a buttoned shirt, glanced at Shelter and, with a closed-mouth smile, gestured for him to approach. The attendant led him to the dispensary, and the pharmacist shook his hand and introduced himself as Samuel Murphy.

"What can I do for you?"

"I'm investigating the murder of Jacob Waldner, and I need some information about a deceased Hutterite senior citizen named Carol Waldner. She'd been prescribed opioids for cancer pain."

"What does that have to do with what happened to Jacob?"

Shelter didn't want to arouse this fellow's curiosity any more than he already had. "We're just trying to get the full picture of what was happening at the colony around the time of his death."

Murphy looked hard at Shelter before going to the computer. "Here we go. She was on hydromorphone."

"Eight-milligram tablets," Shelter said.

"Why yes. The doctor increased her dose to eight milligrams when a lower dose proved ineffective for her pain."

"Her last prescription was for one hundred and eighty tablets?"

The pharmacist's brow knitted, and he studied Shelter's face again for a moment. "Yes. A month's supply. You found records at the Hutterite colony?"

"No. A handwritten note in Jacob Waldner's pocket. Do you know why he would have made that note?"

"Jacob?" Murphy thought for a moment. "Yes, actually. I called him about it."

"Called him about what?"

"It was routine. To get him to drop off what was left over after his grandmother died. For disposal."

"When was this?"

Murphy thought for a moment. "Sometime last week."

"At the colony, they told me Julie Klassen picks up their prescriptions. Why wouldn't you call her to bring back what was left?"

"We did call her about it, twice. It'd been quite some time, and she hadn't done anything about it. I wanted to get it wrapped up, so I called Jacob directly." He paused. "What does this have to do with his death?"

Shelter ignored the question. "Do you remember which day you phoned Jacob?"

"Just a sec." He tapped away at the keyboard again. "It was last Wednesday afternoon."

The day before Jacob was murdered.

"And you told him you'd been trying to get Julie to bring in the drugs?"

The pharmacist nodded.

"You didn't want to call Julie's supervisor instead?"

"I was going to, but I've known Julie for a long time. I didn't want to get her into trouble over a mistake."

"Has she brought in the drugs since then?"

"She called and said she'd disposed of them at the clinic."

"And you were satisfied with that?"

Murphy's body seemed to tense. His eyes tightened into a glare. From his reaction, Shelter sensed he might have had suspicions about Julie and now regretted not acting on them. "She's a registered nurse. She's licensed to handle drugs."

"That's what I'm worried about."

The pharmacist pursed his lips, lowered his eyes, and shook his head.

"What are the procedures for disposing of opioids?"

"There has to be a witness, and records are kept." Murphy eyed Shelter. "What's going on?"

Shelter struggled to keep his voice calm, though he could feel his heart pounding. "I'm not sure, but I need you to keep this conversation between us."

The two men shook hands.

Leaving the drugstore, Shelter thought about Julie hurrying out of the hospital on her way to get another fix. If he was lucky, she'd be back home by now, dozing on the couch.

If not, it was going to be a very long day.

TWENTY-NINE

SHELTER WAS UNLUCKY. Julie wasn't sleeping off her latest high. When he got to her mobile home, he found the driveway empty and got no answer at the door. She wasn't answering his texts, and his phone calls went to voicemail.

He sat on the steps and rubbed his temples. For the first time in days, he felt unsteady, and pain pulsed behind his eyes. When he stood, his centre of gravity shifted suddenly, and he stumbled, catching himself by grabbing the handrail at the last minute. He shook his head, trying to clear his mind of the sick, woozy feeling.

His phone rang. It was Traverse.

"Julie was fired from the nursing home in 2022," his partner said. "The lady in HR wouldn't say why, and nothing was reported to the College of Nurses."

"They kept it quiet."

"Easier to let someone else deal with her."

"What did the College of Nurses have to say?"

"Jacob made an appointment to meet with them the day he was killed."

"The second meeting, besides the one he was supposed to have with the lawyer."

"Right, and that's not all. Ian went over the video this morning, and we've got her car following Jacob on Main Street and over the Provencher Bridge. It's her, Mike."

There were many things Shelter could have felt in that moment, including a heightened sense of urgency to get Julie off the street. But all he could feel was the pain in his head. It had become a searing, scorching fire at the centre of his brain. Through gritted teeth, he said, "That's great work, Gabe. Now we've got to find her. In the state she's in, she probably wouldn't go to work, but let's call health services anyway and ask if they know where she is."

"Hey, are you okay?" Traverse asked. "You don't sound good."

"I just didn't get much sleep." Shelter paused for a moment before continuing. "She wouldn't go to her parents' house, and the bar is closed."

"She might have made a run for the city."

"Maybe, but from how she looked leaving the hospital, I'm betting she couldn't wait to score. I'm going to try the Butler place."

"Whoa. Wait until I get there before you do anything else. And let the Mounties know you may need backup."

"Nah, she doesn't even know we're looking for her."

"You tried to reach her on her cellphone, right?" Traverse asked.

In his voicemail and text messages, Shelter had urged Julie to get in touch with him. She could have taken it as Shelter simply being concerned for her after the OD. Or it could have tipped her off that she'd become a suspect.

"Mike, seriously, wait for me," Traverse said.

"I'll see you when you get here."

He knew he shouldn't be driving, but he needed to find Julie and get her off the street before she hurt anyone else or herself. His head problems would have to wait.

By now, the route to the Butler farm was familiar. The sun was high in the blue expanse of sky. There were no trees to provide shade, and the sun beat down on the asphalt, turning the provincial highway ahead into a liquid mirage. More fields had been harvested, leaving stubble where golden wheat had wavered in the wind just a few days earlier.

Turning onto the gravel road, his car tires kicked up a cloud of dust. He spotted the windbreak of trees around the Butler farm a few hundred metres ahead. He thought back to the first time he'd been out here with Jennifer Kane, the pit bull chasing him, and Mitchell Grimes aiming a rifle at them. He put his hand on the Glock in its holster on his hip. Going onto the property, he had to be ready for anything.

Pulling into the driveway, he noticed a pair of pickup trucks in the central area between the house to the right and the outbuildings to the left, but no sign of Julie's Toyota. He parked beside the trucks and exited the car cautiously, keeping an eye out for dogs. He wasn't surprised that no one was around in the middle of the day during harvest time. Still, he might find someone in the house.

He'd just started in that direction when he heard a noise behind him. Turning, he saw Mitchell Grimes push open a large sliding door on one of the outbuildings. Dressed in a white T-shirt, grimy jeans, and scuffed cowboy boots, Grimes held what looked like a 30-30 lever-action rifle with a scope. "You were told to stay off this property," he shouted across the yard.

Shelter took a couple of steps toward Grimes but stopped when he shifted the rifle to his left hand. "I need to ask you about Julie Klassen."

"Get the fuck off. Now!"

Rifle or no, Shelter wasn't taking orders from Grimes. He needed to find Julie, and, at this moment, Grimes was his best bet. "Have you seen her?"

"No. I ain't seen that crazy bitch."

"Where would she be?"

"How should I know?"

Shelter didn't feel like playing games, and he was done shouting across the farmyard. He walked up to within five metres of Grimes. "Because you're her supplier, and the last time I saw her, she was looking to score."

Grimes smiled and shook his head. If he was surprised by Shelter's accusation, he wasn't showing it. "Go on, man. You don't know what you're talking about."

"How about I take you to the RCMP detachment and we talk it over there?"

Grimes let out a sigh and looked skyward in a theatrical show of exasperation. "How come you're so hot to find her, anyway?"

"Let me worry about that."

He squinted at Shelter in silence for a moment, putting the pieces together. A homicide cop investigating the Waldner murder was trying to locate Julie. He gave Shelter a Cheshire-cat grin. "She's feeding you a line about who did the Hutterite, right?"

Shelter kept his face impassive, but Grimes's comment suggested he didn't know Julie was the killer. "I just need to ask her some questions. That's it."

Grimes smiled as if to say, *I don't believe you*. "All I know is she's a junkie, and she's broke. She don't come around here no more. Maybe she's gone to the city."

The city was definitely a possibility, but Shelter was struck just then by something in Grimes's voice, a hint of tension that made him suspect he was lying. If she'd gone there in search of what she needed, she could still be close by. Maybe even hiding in that outbuilding behind Grimes. "She's not here, is she?"

Grimes shook his head. "Go now. You're trespassing."

There was nothing else for Shelter to do. He turned and headed for his vehicle. As he crossed the yard, it struck him that if Julie was here, she might have hidden her car. Where would it be? He scanned the trees surrounding the farm buildings. Nowhere to hide a car. Then he peered at the house. For the first time, he spotted a gravel track leading to the rear. Instead of getting into his car, he continued across the yard toward the house.

Behind him, Grimes shouted, "Hey, where're you going? Stop!"

Shelter ignored him and followed the track around the side of the house. And there it was, baking in the sun—Julie's red Toyota Corolla. He heard the crunch of boots on gravel behind him.

"What do you think you're doing?"

Shelter brushed past Grimes and marched back to the central yard, then turned to face him. "Where is she?"

"I told you, she ain't here."

Shelter pulled out his cellphone. "I'm giving you five seconds, and then you're going down for obstructing a police investigation."

"Leave him alone. I'm here."

Shelter swung around to find Julie standing in the doorway of the outbuilding. She had an ironic smile. "You found me. What do you want?" She took a step, leaving the shade of the building, into the brilliant sunshine. She swayed slightly and thrust her hands into the back pockets of her jeans. Her V-neck T-shirt hung off her torso.

"You need to come with me."

"No way. I'm staying here."

Grimes interjected. "No, you ain't," he shouted at Julie. "Get going, the both of ya."

"Fuck you!" she screamed.

Shelter needed to get Julie into custody, but she was becoming increasingly agitated. She paced in front of the outbuilding, her face flushed and her eyes darting from Grimes to Shelter. She wasn't going to make it easy to bring her in.

He glanced at Grimes and said in a low voice, "You stay out of this." Grimes threw up the hand not holding the rifle and took a couple of paces back. Keeping his eyes on Julie, Shelter stepped forward. If he could get close enough to grab her, he'd have no trouble cuffing her.

At that moment, she made a break for it, sprinting to circle Shelter. He lurched to his right to cut her off and grabbed her arm. But she jerked it away and backed away in a crouch, ready to run again.

"Calm down. Let's talk about it," Shelter said, trying to keep his voice even.

Julie straightened and reached behind her back. She drew a semiautomatic pistol from her waistband. She pointed it at Shelter's chest. "*You* calm down, you bastard."

Shelter froze. His vision narrowed to the hand holding the black gun. His heart-rate shot higher, his chest tightened, and his breath came in gasps. As if underwater, he heard Grimes's muffled voice say, "What the fuck. What are you doing?"

In that moment, Shelter felt himself detach from his body. He found himself looking down on the scene as if watching an overhead shot in a movie. The scene showed Shelter and Grimes facing Julie as she slowly backed toward the farmhouse where her car was parked. Shelter felt his knees buckle. The picture became distorted, then went black.

When he opened his eyes, Grimes was standing over him. Shelter shook his head. What had just happened? He felt a sharp pain behind his eyes, but he was back in his body. He blinked and rubbed his eyes.

"You went down hard, man."

"Where is she?"

Grimes pointed to the end of the driveway. The red Toyota was pulling onto the gravel road. It quickly picked up speed, heading north. Shelter realized he'd been unconscious for seconds. He pushed himself to his feet. He felt woozy and staggered a step before steadying himself.

Julie was armed and desperate. He had to go after her. "Where's she heading?"

Grimes shrugged.

"What kind of a gun is that?"

"A Sig 320."

"She knows how to use it?"

"She's fired my Glock a few times."

"Stay here," he commanded. He felt steadier and was able to jog to his car. Pulling out of the farmyard, he saw

Julie's Toyota in the distance, a red shape throwing up a cloud of dust. She was staying off the main road, heading away from town.

At the intersection with the provincial highway, Shelter cut west and floored the gas pedal. He skirted a pickup truck as if it were standing still. He spotted Julie and turned onto the same gravel road she'd taken. The back end of his car swerved as it left the pavement, forcing him to slow momentarily before accelerating again.

He had to cut his speed on the bumpy, rutted road through a tunnel of corn growing high on either side. Emerging from the corn field, he saw that Julie was still far ahead, but the open, flat landscape let him keep her car in sight. Gripping the wheel with one hand, he slotted his cellphone into a holster on the dash, punched 911, and hit the speaker icon. He identified himself to the emergency operator, told her he was pursuing an armed suspect and needed backup. She patched him through to the RCMP communications centre, and he gave the Mountie a description of Julie's car and her approximate location. Next, he called Traverse.

"Hey, I'm following Julie right now," he shouted in his excitement. "She's got a nine-millimetre."

"Following her where?"

"Northwest of Krefeld on a gravel road. She was at the Butler farm, and she ran."

"You called for backup?"

"Yeah, but I don't want to lose her. Where are you?"

"I'm still about a half-hour out."

"I can't figure out where she's going."

"She probably doesn't know herself. Just running. Let her go. The Mounties will pick her up."

Shelter had closed the distance on Julie. He was now less than a half a kilometre behind. He wasn't going to let her go. "I'll keep my distance."

"Mike, listen to me—"

"Hold on, she's turning."

Gravel sprayed from Julie's back tires as she made a hard left onto a paved highway. Approaching the T intersection, Shelter looked up and, with a shock, spotted a billboard by the side of the highway. Over the past week, he'd come to this intersection several times and seen the sign, but always approaching from the east. It read: *You Are A Sinner!*

He leaned forward toward the windshield, his grip on the wheel tightening.

"Jesus. She's going to the Hutterite colony."

THIRTY

JULIE WAS still a couple of hundred metres ahead when she made a high-speed turn onto the access road to the colony. She almost flipped into the ditch but regained control and sped toward the parking lot. Following her, Shelter saw that the lot was even more jammed with vehicles than it had been earlier in the day. Hundreds of men, women, and children were on the property for Jacob's funeral.

Up ahead, a Hutterite man jumped out of the way of Julie's car at the last second. The vehicle skidded to a halt. Leaving the door open, she sprinted toward the colony's quadrangle. Shelter saw she was now carrying what looked from a distance like a shotgun. He felt a surge of adrenaline. With a pistol and a shotgun, Julie could inflict horrific violence.

The man she'd nearly run over was looking in her direction in disbelief when Shelter pulled up and jumped out of his car. To his left, he saw the commotion was drawing other men from the garage. Shelter held up a hand to them. "Police," he shouted. "There's a person with guns on the property. Get back inside and stay there until you're given instructions."

He turned and sprinted after Julie. Coming here armed and desperate meant that a hostage-taking was a real possibility. Police procedure was to avoid chasing a suspect in a potential hostage situation, for fear of putting lives in even greater danger. It was better to wait for backup, assess the threat and decide how best to deal with it. But Shelter knew Julie well. If he could get close enough to talk to her, he might be able to calm her down and end this right now, without bloodshed.

As he moved into the community, he was met by chaos. Groups of terrified Hutterites streamed past him. "Police!" he called out. "Stay calm. Move to the parking lot." A young Hutterite woman carried a baby and led a school-aged boy by the hand. She peered into Shelter's face, her eyes wide with fear as she skirted him. Behind her stood an elderly man with a bad limp, helping a woman of about the same age. "Where'd she go?" Shelter demanded.

The man jabbed a thumb over his shoulder. "Jacob Waldner's house," he said in a breathless voice as he brushed past. Shelter processed the information as he advanced to where he could see the quad. On one side was the dining hall and the adjoining church. Directly across was the row of two-storey houses, with the Waldner home the middle one of five.

Shelter stopped to assess the situation and his options. He felt a hot wind on his face and heard it whistling in his ears. The excruciating pain in his head hadn't let up. It throbbed with each beat of his heart. He knew that if he passed out again here, it could cost people their lives, but he saw no choice but to push on. He scanned the housing units. Julie had returned to the home of the man she'd murdered. Why?

The Hutterites he'd met fleeing the area would have been only a small fraction of the people who'd come for the funeral. He surmised most of the others would likely be gathered in the dining hall and church. Despite being told by the old man that Julie was at the Waldner place, he couldn't be sure the information was accurate or that she hadn't moved elsewhere. She had the advantage of knowing the property much better than he did. By now, she could be anywhere.

He crossed the quad and, reaching the dining hall entrance, heard the low buzz of voices inside. It was a good sign. Surely people wouldn't be talking among themselves if they were being held at gunpoint. He tried the door and found it locked. He knocked and stepped back. The conversation inside immediately died down, and after a few seconds, he heard a German-accented voice through the door. "Who's there?"

Shelter identified himself, and when the door opened a crack, he found himself looking into Simon Wurtz's eyes. "Thank God you've come."

He opened the door to let Shelter in. The dining tables were crowded with dozens of people. Others were standing in the aisles. From the dishes piled in the centre of the tables, he saw they'd been interrupted while eating lunch. "Julie Klassen is here with a gun," Wurtz said, his voice tight with anxiety. "She seems completely out of her mind."

"She came in here?"

"For a moment. She looked around and then ran out."

"A man told me she went into Jacob and Rachel's place."

A look of horror came over Wurtz's face. "There will be people there to pay their respects to the family."

"How many?"

"I don't know. Many."

Shelter recalled with a shudder that Jacob's body lay in an open casket. He touched Wurtz's arm. "Help will be here soon. Keep the door locked and try to calm the people. Hopefully, this will be over soon."

Leaving the dining hall, he looked at the housing units in front of him. His eyes locked on the door to Jacob and Rachel's home, where the drapes were drawn. Until a communication link was established, there was no way to know what was happening inside. He circled to his left, approaching the units from the south. He took a position where he could watch both the house and the parking lot.

He glanced at his watch. RCMP units should have been there by now, and Traverse wouldn't be far behind. It was too dangerous to approach the house alone. Instead, he would keep watch until help arrived to secure the site and move people to a safe location elsewhere in the colony. Then they could communicate with Julie inside the house and hopefully convince her to give up. He knew the RCMP would bring in a heavily armed tactical squad from Winnipeg and a specially trained negotiating team, but it would take time for them to arrive from the city.

At that moment, the door of the Waldner home was flung open with a loud bang. Men and women poured out of the house. Shelter recognized Jacob's mother being helped through the door by his brother, Amos. They were followed by Jacob's sister and a half-dozen other bewildered Hutterites. Shelter hustled toward them. "Where's the woman?" he called out.

Jacob's mother replied in a high-pitched, panicky voice. "She's got Rachel." A man in his late forties who had been guiding people away from the house interjected in a tense but more controlled voice, "She told us to get out, but she's keeping Rachel with her." Holding his mother's arm, Amos added, "She's completely irrational, screaming and crying."

"We'll handle it from here. Let's get these folks to the garage where you will be safe," he said, pointing toward the parking lot. "More police are coming."

Amos led the terrified group away. Shelter turned to face the houses and saw the Waldners' next-door neighbour sticking his head out the front door. Shelter motioned to the man to get out of the house. He emerged with a woman and two small children and hurried to join the others scurrying toward the parking lot.

Shelter circled to the neighbour's house on the other side. He knocked but got no response. By the time he'd returned to a position with a line of sight to the parking lot, four RCMP officers in bulletproof vests were jogging toward him. Two were carrying rifles. Behind them, he was relieved to see Traverse's car pulling into the parking lot.

He huddled with the Mounties, and by the time they'd made introductions, Traverse had joined the group, giving Shelter a nod. Shelter gave a quick rundown of the situation, explaining that Julie was a suspect in a murder in Winnipeg. "She's a drug addict, and she's armed with a shotgun and a nine-millimetre pistol," he said. "Apparently, she's threatening the life of a Hutterite woman she's holding in the house."

The lead RCMP officer was a beefy sergeant with tattoos on both arms named William Cross. "The emergency response team has been alerted. They'll be here soon."

How soon? It would take time to gather the team and get them to the colony from the city. It was a good sign that Julie had already released almost all the Hutterites. It suggested she wasn't going to try to use hostages as bargaining chips to secure her escape. Cross ordered a pair of Mounties to go to the back of the houses to cover the Waldners' rear door so Julie couldn't make a run for it with her hostage. He sent another officer to check the houses and nearby buildings and evacuate anyone still left inside.

Although he'd never held a formal job as a hostage negotiator, Shelter had received the training and been involved in several hostage-takings over the years. In these life-or-death situations, there was always confusion, huge stress, and pressure on both the police and the hostage-taker. It could lead to rash decisions and violence with devastating consequences.

"I know this woman from way back," Shelter told Cross. "I've got her cellphone number. I'm going to try to talk to her."

"No. We'll wait for our team," the Mountie said in a tone that implied he was taking full control of the hostage-taking. That put Shelter in a tricky position. Winnipeg police had jurisdiction throughout the province, and he had the authority to make this decision. On the other hand, the RCMP had a tactical team en route, equipped with specialized weapons, and an expert negotiator. That counted for a lot if the hostage-taking dragged out for hours, as they often did. But it could take at least another hour for the team to get there. It was critical to establish contact with Julie quickly. The stakes were just too high to wait.

He didn't want to start butting heads with Cross in the midst of a standoff, but he had Julie's number, and there wasn't anything the Mountie could do to prevent him from calling her, short of trying to physically seize his cellphone. These thoughts coursed through his mind as the RCMP officer stood eyeing him with his hands on hips, ready for pushback. Shelter glanced at Traverse, who'd clearly made the same calculations as he had and gave him an almost imperceptible nod that said: *You're right.*

He was about to argue his case with Cross when his cellphone buzzed in his hand. He was surprised to see Julie's name on the screen. "It's her," he said to the other officers. Before Cross could object, he took a step away and tapped the green icon to accept the call.

"Julie?"

"I see those fucking cops out back. Tell them to back off, now!"

"Okay. No problem." He looked over to Cross and covered the cellphone receiver with his hand. "She wants your guys in the back to move away." Cross gave an order into the radio mic clipped to his bulletproof vest.

Shelter spoke into the cellphone. "They've been told," he said, careful to keep his voice calm. He knew it was crucial to get Julie talking, let her vent. On his side, he needed to understand what she wanted and build trust with her. "I want to help you, Julie," he said, the classic opening line taught to hostage negotiators around the world. He put the call on speaker and turned up the volume. Now, the entire team could hear the conversation.

On the other end of the line, he heard Julie gasp for breath and let out a high-pitched keening sound. After a few moments, she said, "You don't want to help me." A sob caught in her throat, and she gagged. When she was able to speak again, she said, "Cops come near this house, and I'm going to kill her. You hear me?"

"I hear you," Shelter answered. He had no doubt she'd carry through with her threat to kill Rachel if pushed. She'd already killed, and she'd do it again unless he found some way to talk her down.

"I've fucked up everything. I want to die," she said.

"I don't want you to die, Julie. And I don't want Rachel to die." He needed to give her a chance to talk it out and hopefully calm down. He listened to her ragged breath, crying and sniffling. Finally, he said, "Where's Rachel? Is she okay?"

That set her off on a tirade. "Why wouldn't she stop whining about that old lady? Every day she was at me about how much pain she was in. Asking why the meds weren't working. Telling Jacob and me over and over that we needed to call the doctor. She wouldn't let it go."

Rachel would have been helping care for Jacob's grandmother. She would have been there hour after hour, watching and listening to the old woman endure the torture of cancer eating at her bones with no relief from pain medication. It would have been equally horrible for Jacob. The memory of those days probably sparked his suspicion of Julie when he finally pieced together the chain of events.

It was hard to imagine what the old woman must have gone through, and it was revolting to hear Julie attack Rachel for her compassion. Rachel had rightly been anguished over the woman's suffering. How else was she supposed to react? He knew Julie's callous desperation was the product of her addiction. She was also probably starting to get dope sick, and that was no doubt making it worse. But he had to conceal his emotions.

"It was a difficult situation," he said, matching his banal words with a calm tone.

"You're damn right it was difficult. She backed me into a corner. I had no choice. I had to end that woman's suffering." She coughed and sniffed loudly. "I'm not a monster. She was almost dead anyway."

Shelter looked to Traverse and shook his head in disbelief. He'd assumed Julie had been talking about killing Jacob, but now she seemed to be admitting to killing Jacob's grandmother.

"Julie, listen to me. I don't want anyone else to get hurt. Let Rachel come out, and we can talk about getting you help."

"Fuck you," she screamed. "Okay? Just fuck you."

"You don't have to go down this road," he said. "If you let Rachel go, we can work it out."

She was crying hysterically again. "It's enough."

"No. Please, Julie. Wait. Listen to me. We have lots of time."

She mumbled and then spoke to herself under her breath, the words unintelligible to Shelter. He sensed she was screwing up her courage to shoot Rachel.

"It's over," she screamed. The line went dead.

THIRTY-ONE

SHELTER BRACED himself for the sound of gunfire. His heart was hammering in his chest, and his breathing was constricted. He fumbled the phone, nearly dropping it. He cursed as he hit the green icon to call her back. Her phone rang, but Shelter was sure it was too late. Rachel was about to be executed.

Suddenly, Julie was back on the line, and he felt a rush of relief. Once again, he heard only her laboured breathing. "Julie," he said. "Listen to me. It's not too late. If you let Rachel go, we can work this out."

She didn't reply for long seconds.

"Julie?"

When she spoke, her voice was panicky and shrill, yet there was also determination in her words. "Here's the deal. I'll let her go if you get in here and swap places with her. You've got ten seconds, or I blow her head off right here, right now."

She slowly started to count backwards. "Ten ...nine ... eight ..."

Cross shook his head violently. "No way! You're not going in there."

"Seven ...six ...five ..."

Traverse dashed to Shelter and gripped his bicep. Shelter looked into the eyes of his partner and friend. "It's too dangerous, Mike."

"Four …three …two …"

"I'm coming," Shelter said into the cellphone.

"Come now, and no gun."

Shelter put a hand on Traverse's chest. "I can't let her kill Rachel."

He handed his gun to him. They both knew from long experience that when Shelter had made up his mind, he wasn't going back on the decision. Traverse let go of his arm and pulled him close. In his ear, he whispered, "Kill her if you have to. Don't wait."

Shelter pulled back and gave him a grim nod. "Thanks, buddy. I've got this."

Cross had manoeuvred to block Shelter's path to the house. "I'm ordering you to stand down."

The Mountie reached for Shelter, but he batted his hand away. "I take full responsibility," he said over his shoulder as he sprinted toward the house.

He knew this was against all police procedure and common sense. There was no guarantee Julie wouldn't kill both him and Rachel. Far from it. But he was sure she wasn't bluffing. She would shoot Rachel. He'd made a quick calculation—perhaps foolishly—that he knew Julie well enough to talk her down. It seemed like the only chance to save the young woman and her unborn child.

As he covered the twenty metres to the front door of the Waldner house, he saw the curtain on the front window flutter and Julie peer out. He turned off the speaker function on his phone and brought it to his mouth. "Can you hear me?"

"Yeah. Get in here now, or she's dead."

"I'm not coming in until you let her go. Otherwise, you've got both of us. I can't allow that. You get that, right?"

Julie went quiet for a second. "All right, but I'll shoot you both if you're not in here the second she leaves."

"I give you my word."

"Get up on the porch."

It was a delicate swap. He had to get Rachel away and trade places with her in the house without spooking Julie and provoking her to start shooting. He climbed the front stairs and said, "I'm outside the door."

"No guns, right?"

"Right."

The door opened a crack. Shelter found himself staring into Rachel's terrified eyes. He scanned her long black dress. There were no visible signs of injury. Julie was stationed directly behind, using Rachel as a shield. "I'm letting her go now. Get in here, or I shoot."

Shelter reached out and took Rachel by the wrist and pulled her gently toward him, keeping his eyes locked on hers and nodding to reassure her. He glimpsed Julie behind, pointing a handgun at her back. Julie reached out and gave the Hutterite woman a hard shove that propelled her past Shelter and down the front steps. Rachel hit the ground running toward the waiting police officers.

Shelter made a quarter turn on the porch to make sure she was safe. He felt himself yanked hard by the collar. He stumbled into the entrance of the house. Julie scuttled backward into the living room. The gun was pointed at his chest. "Shut the door!"

He kicked the door closed with a heel and gave the room a quick scan before focusing on Julie, who'd backed to the other side. It was a macabre scene. She had one hip resting against the coffin where Jacob Waldner's body lay exposed. From his perspective, he could see only his nose and a shock of black hair. It was a strange, surreal moment—the murderer and her victim side by side in the house where she'd also killed Jacob's grandmother.

"Now what, Julie?" he asked. He breathed deeply, deliberately in an effort to keep his voice calm despite the hammering in his chest.

She tried to speak but seemed to choke on her words. Tears streamed down her cheeks and snot ran from her nose before she savagely wiped it away with her free hand. She was shivering, the gun bouncing up and down in her hand. The terror of the situation was being compounded by withdrawal symptoms taking hold of her body.

He took a step toward her. "I can help you. Just give me the gun, and it's over."

"Stop! Get back," she screamed, jabbing the barrel of the gun at him. "I hate you. You dumped me and didn't give me a second thought."

It was a measure of her hysteria and addiction that she seemed to be focused on their failed relationship of many years before. He had no choice but to play along with her delusions. "I'm sorry. I never meant to hurt you."

"Ha! I was broken. I quit nursing school for a semester because of you. Did you know that?" The gun drifted lower as she ranted.

"I had no idea."

She jerked the gun level. "I pull this trigger, and you're gone forever."

He felt drops of sweat sliding down his spine under his shirt and struggled to control his breathing. "Julie. I've got a daughter and a mother. They love me and need me. Your family and friends love you, too. Just let me help you."

"It's too late."

She rubbed her face hard with her hand. Her brow furrowed, and she squinted. Time was short. She was getting ready to act. He had to keep her talking. "I know you. You're a good person. You don't want to hurt anyone else. You just proved it. You let all those people walk out of here. You let Rachel go. You saved her and her baby. Please, Julie. Just give me the gun. It'll be okay."

This seemed to make her pause. Her eyes drifted to the curtained window. When she spoke again, her voice was quieter. "Rachel is a good woman. All these people here are good. They've been good to me."

Shelter sensed he was reaching her. "They care about you, Julie. And so does your family. Whatever you've done, it's not too late."

She focused on him again. "Nah, I think it is."

She shoved the barrel of the gun under her chin.

"No. Wait!"

He saw her finger squeeze the trigger. He flinched in anticipation of the roar of gunfire.

But the explosion didn't come. He blinked. She pulled the trigger again, her finger turning white with the pressure. Nothing. She looked down in panic. With a thumb, she flicked off the safety.

In that moment, Shelter charged her. He covered the space between them in two long strides, dropped a shoulder, and crashed into her. They fell in a heap on the carpet. The gun skittered across the floor. She scrambled to get out from under him. She got an arm free and grabbed the gun.

The barrel swung toward his head. He lurched forward and slapped her wrist. The gun exploded. The bullet ripped past his temple. Plaster fell from the wall. The smell of cordite filled his nose. He struggled to get a hold of her arm, but adrenaline was giving her superhuman strength. She swung the barrel toward him again. He got a leg scissored across her waist. It gave him leverage to pull himself up and straddle her. He grabbed her arm and pinned it to the carpet. The gun fired again, the bullet buried in the wall. He was on top of her now and managed to pin her other arm.

She bucked and screamed and spat, but she was no match for him. He had his full weight on her and his own dose of adrenaline coursing through his body. Finally, she went limp, letting go of the pistol. He looked down into her eyes. "It's over."

Traverse burst through the door, followed by Cross, and another Mountie. Guns raised, they rushed to where Shelter had Julie pinned to the floor and kicked her gun away.

Julie ignored them. Instead, she studied Shelter's face for a moment before turning her head to rest her cheek on the carpet, silent and resigned. He turned her over and handcuffed her. Without speaking, he stood her up and guided her past the other cops and through the front door into the sunshine.

A pair of constables led Julie away toward the parking lot and a waiting cruiser. Cross whooped, clapped his hands, and gave Shelter a wide smile. "Great job!"

But Shelter was feeling anything but elated. The excitement was wearing off. It felt like air escaping from a tire. His shoulders sagged as tension was replaced by deep exhaustion. Traverse read his partner's body language and weary expression. He put an arm around his shoulder and pulled him close. "You had me worried there, buddy. What happened?"

Looking from Traverse to Cross, he said, "Follow me." They entered the house, and Shelter picked up the Sig Sauer nine-millimetre pistol that Julie had stolen from Lanny Butler's farm. He held it up and pointed to a tiny lever on the side of the gun. "She tried to shoot herself, but the safety was on. That gave me my chance."

He ejected the bullet in the chamber, then slid the magazine out of the grip. It was fully loaded. "Lanny Butler told me she had experience firing a Glock. Glocks are just rack and fire. No external safety. So I'm guessing she thought this Sig worked the same way. Or maybe she just forgot about the safety." He handed the gun to Cross.

When they emerged from the house, the RCMP tactical team had arrived. Wearing helmets and full-body protective gear and carrying rifles, they spread out across the colony property, even though they'd no doubt have known the hostage-taker had been arrested.

"Where's Rachel?" Shelter asked.

"We tried to get her into the ambulance," Cross said, pointing to the emergency vehicle in the parking lot. "She needs to go to the hospital and get checked out, but she insisted she wanted to be with the others. She's over at the dining hall."

Shelter and Traverse crossed the quad to where the Hutterites were spilling out onto the lawn. Traverse spotted Rachel surrounded by a group that included Wurtz, Hofer, Amos, and several women. Shelter assumed some of them would be members of Rachel's family who'd travelled to the colony for the funeral. The circle opened to allow the police officers to join them. Wurtz stepped forward and shook Shelter's hand. "Rachel tells us you saved her life. We are very grateful. We will never forget your courage today."

Shelter felt the eyes of the Hutterites on him. His face grew hot, and he was at a loss for words. He gave Wurtz a shy smile and turned to Rachel. "How are you feeling?"

"I'm tired, but I'm okay," she said. "Thank you for what you did."

"I'm glad no one else was hurt. You were very brave. Now, you need to go to the hospital to be examined. You've had quite a shock."

"Yes. All right. What about Julie? Is she okay?"

Shelter was amazed that Rachel was concerned about the well-being of the woman who'd killed her husband, caused unimaginable suffering for her husband's grandmother, and held her at gunpoint in her own home. He regarded her for a moment before answering, "Julie is very ill."

"What will happen to her?"

"She will be charged with Jacob's murder and the other crimes she's committed. She will also get help dealing with her addiction." He didn't mention his suspicion that she'd also killed Jacob's grandmother. He didn't want to add to the distress Rachel and the other Hutterites were feeling. There would be time to investigate the old woman's death.

"We'll pray for her to find peace and healing," Rachel said.

Wurtz nodded in agreement. “It’s time for you to go to the hospital.” He thanked the officers before he and Amos accompanied Rachel toward the parking lot and the waiting ambulance.

THIRTY-TWO

SHELTER SPOTTED Jennifer Kane crossing the street and waved to her from his table in the window of Sid's café. Shelter had arrived early for their 10:00 a.m. meet-up and had already drunk his first cup of coffee while reading the *Free Press* on his phone.

He'd been off work for ten days and seen a psychologist three times. She'd told him what he already knew: he was suffering from a case of post-traumatic stress disorder. It was triggered by shooting the young woman, but it had probably been building over the years that he'd investigated murder and mayhem on Winnipeg's streets. He'd asked his boss, Neil MacIsaac, for stress leave the morning after he'd arrived back from the country.

Entering MacIsaac's office that morning, he'd found the normally anxious and dour MacIsaac in a buoyant mood. The story of how one of his cops had swapped places with a young Hutterite woman and resolved a hostage-taking situation in rural Manitoba was making the national news. The PR team was being inundated with requests to interview Shelter.

Jumping up from his desk, MacIsaac pumped Shelter's hand. "Amazing. Some positive coverage for once. Great work." They'd spoken the evening before when Shelter had given him a bare-bones description of how the hostage-taking had gone down. MacIsaac had commended him in a detached tone. It was different this morning. The media attention and kudos from his higher-ups in the department had woken MacIsaac up to the scale of what had unfolded at the colony.

Shelter had already been congratulated by cops riding up in the elevator that morning, and he'd been cheered when he arrived in the homicide unit. He'd smiled, high-fived his colleagues, and shook their hands, but his overarching emotion was embarrassment. He'd already heard himself being described as a hero on the radio, driving into work that morning. All he could do was shake his head in disbelief. It was a cliché for cops in this situation to say they were just doing their job, but that was the reality. He'd had no doubt Julie was on the verge of shooting Rachel, so he had no other option but to take her place.

"They want to set up a press conference for two o'clock," MacIsaac said.

"Fine, but I can't be there."

"What? You have to be there."

That's when Shelter told him about his difficulty sleeping, nightmares, flashbacks, and anxiety. He left out the part about his out-of-body experiences and loss of consciousness at the Butler farm. His black out had allowed Julie to escape and take hostages. He was lucky it hadn't ended in a bloodbath. It had been reckless to stay on the job. It could've ended up getting people hurt or killed and finishing his career.

He'd resolved not to wait another day before seeing a doctor and getting rest and the counselling he needed. Upon hearing this news, MacIsaac's shoulders had sagged in disappointment, but he'd no choice but to grant him stress leave.

All of Shelter's interview requests were turned down. A deputy chief ended up presiding over the press conference, flanked by an RCMP inspector. Watching the CBC national news that evening, Shelter again felt uneasy when they lauded his bravery. The police press conference was only a snippet in a long report dominated by shots of the colony and a breathless retelling of how Julie Klassen had been charged with first-degree murder in Winnipeg and other counts for the hostage-taking. The reporter ended her piece standing on a country road with the colony visible in the distance behind her. "In a rare step, police sources say the body of an elderly woman who died last month will be exhumed next week as part of the ongoing investigation into her death."

Now, at the café, Kane embraced him and gave him a warm smile. "How's our hero doing?"

"Get outta here," Shelter said with a laugh.

"Seriously, how are you?"

"Not bad. I'm seeing a shrink, and it's helping, but I'm missing Kelsey. She's back in Montreal."

He'd told his daughter a sanitized version of what happened at the colony that evening, leaving out the part about losing consciousness, and playing down how much danger he'd been in. Despite his reassuring version of events, Kelsey was worried about him and volunteered to postpone her return to McGill University for the fall semester, but he'd insisted she go. He didn't want her education to be derailed because of him.

He'd known from the time she'd chosen to go to university in Montreal that there was a better than even chance she would make a life for herself there or somewhere else far away from Winnipeg. Many of his friends had moved away at the same age to Vancouver, Toronto, or Montreal. He'd never given much thought to the impact on their parents, but now, he had to admit to himself that he hated the idea of being so far from her. Still, he told himself he was having the same feeling as parents everywhere whose children left to make a better, or at least different, life for themselves. He could only let her make her own decisions and hope for her happiness.

Once the waitress had delivered their coffee, Shelter smiled at Kane and said, "So, Gabe tells me Julie gave up the whole story."

"It came flooding out of her. She talked for two hours straight."

Traverse had called Shelter a few days earlier to fill him in briefly on Julie's confession, but he was hungry for more information. "Gabe didn't have time to give me all the details. Can you fill in the gaps?"

"What do you want to know?"

"Everything."

Kane looked down at her coffee cup. "Oh, boy. Okay." She took a few moments to gather her thoughts before beginning.

Julie had described her distress at having to listen to Jacob's grandmother lying in her bed, moaning from the pain—pain Julie could have stopped if she hadn't stolen her Dilaudid and replaced it with sugar tablets. The woman's cries for help, the pleading of her family, the doctor's confusion about why the pain management wasn't working—it was just too much for Julie to bear. The old woman was close to death. That meant there'd be no more opioid prescriptions after the latest refill.

It hadn't been hard to steal insulin from one of her diabetic patients and give the woman a deadly injection. She was confident that the death would be accepted without question, a relief for the family and the whole community. There'd be no autopsy to reveal the lack of opioids in her system or the insulin overdose that had mercifully put her into a peaceful coma and then killed her.

If Julie had returned the pharmacist's call and told him she'd disposed of the unused drugs, she might have gotten away with it. "But when Jacob left a voicemail saying that they needed to talk urgently, Julie knew she was in trouble," Kane said.

She'd told herself if she ignored him, maybe he would just go away. Her every thought was about where to get her next fix. It wasn't even about getting high anymore. It was about avoiding the skin-crawling, puking, unbearable shaking sickness that came with withdrawal.

But Jacob had shown up unannounced at her door. He was smart enough to put two and two together—his grandmother's suffering and the missing drugs. Talking to Jacob that day, Julie had been panicking inside. If he reported her, it meant an investigation, prosecution for stealing drugs, and even, God forbid, disinterment of the old Hutterite woman's body and a prison sentence for murder. Scariest of all, it meant being cut off from her supply and a sickness that was worse than death.

She'd asked Jacob if he'd told anyone else about this. No. He wanted to talk to her first. She pleaded with him to keep it quiet, even from Rachel. She pretended to be deeply embarrassed about not disposing of the drugs and told him it could hurt her professionally. She'd straighten it out right away with the pharmacy. He agreed, but she could tell he was suspicious and would check that she'd done what she said she would as soon as he got back from the city. There would be questions. Questions she couldn't answer.

She claimed it had left her with only one option. From a casual conversation with Rachel, she'd learned that Jacob would be leaving for the city in the morning. If she could do it and get back safely, she would have put more than a hundred and fifty kilometres between her and the act. It would take organization, courage, and some luck, but she could do it. She only had one appointment to cancel the next day, and hopefully she'd be back by early afternoon.

She spent time that evening planning it. She knew where Mitchell Grimes kept his handguns, but gunfire would be too noisy in the city. In the end, she drove out to her father's farm and found his hunting knife. "He always kept it razor-sharp, and the blade folded into the handle, so it would be easy to conceal," she'd explained. It would do the job.

Julie knew what road Jacob would take to the city and waited in the parking lot of a coffee shop at a crossroads in Carman. She spotted him easily in the black pickup truck and fell in behind him. She had no idea where he was going or what he had to do in town. She could only watch, wait, and hope for an opportunity. If it didn't happen in the city, she'd have to find another way to do it somewhere, somehow, at the colony or in Krefeld. That would be even riskier.

She'd been surprised when he headed into Saint Boniface. When he turned down the street facing the park, she held back. She knew some houses had video cameras these days. She parked at the top of the street and watched him enter the house. Why was he there? Who was he meeting?

She'd parked a street away. With sunglasses on, a baseball cap low over her eyes, and gloves on her hands, she'd approached the house from the back lane. From the fence, she glimpsed Jacob moving from room to room. He seemed to be alone. She decided to seize her chance. If someone else greeted her, she could make an excuse and quickly leave.

She recalled how she'd concealed the knife behind her handbag and her terror the moment just before she knocked on the door. But it was now or never. There was no turning back. She took a deep breath and gave the wooden door two hard raps. After a few seconds, the door swung open. Shock registered on Jacob's face. "What are you doing here?" he demanded.

She had her story prepared. She admitted to following him in from the country, apologizing profusely for the imposition. She pleaded that she simply had to tell him in person about what had happened to his grandmother's drugs.

He reluctantly let her into the house and led her to the living room. With his back to her, she'd seized her chance. Once it was done, she grabbed his phone and laptop in case he'd recorded his suspicions about her in them and later buried the devices at her father's farm. She made it back to Krefeld without anyone knowing she'd been away.

Shelter shook his head. "What a waste."

Kane pursed her lips and nodded. "A terrible loss for the Hutterites." She lowered her eyes to her coffee cup for a moment. "How long are you off work?"

"You're missing me?"

"Actually, I'm enjoying the break. I'm asking for Gabe." Kane couldn't keep a straight face, and they both chuckled.

"They told me to take as much time as I need. I'm already feeling better, but it's going to be a while."

She took a sip of coffee. "And Penny?"

Shelter wasn't surprised by the question. "We haven't talked. It's over," he said in a tone that he hoped would put a quick end to this part of the discussion.

"Don't you think it's worth another shot, now that you're feeling better?"

He struggled to come up with an answer. "I don't want her to think I'm stalking her."

Kane scoffed. "Get out of here. You were together for over a year, for God's sake."

He considered giving her another perfunctory answer to short-circuit the conversation or at least keep it superficial. It was the same temptation he'd felt when the psychologist asked him a sensitive question—an old reflex to hide his true thoughts and emotions. He knew it was unhealthy, and if he was going to be a better man, he had to learn to resist it. But it wasn't easy.

He started off slowly, not looking at Kane, but down at the teaspoon he was playing with. "I tried to put it back together with her. Penny was the one who said it was over." He paused for a moment, searching for a way to express thoughts he'd had over the past couple of weeks about his relationships—not only with Penny but with Christa, and even Julie Klassen. "With Penny and my other relationships going back to Julie, it's always been like I'm holding back a part of myself, afraid to let go."

"Afraid of what?"

"That's just it. I don't know. The future? Losing myself?" He raised his eyes to meet Kane's.

She shook her head. "That's a story you're telling yourself." She said it gently, but her eyes were intense, focused on his face. "With Christa, you built a life together, raised Kelsey, and you were *so* there for her in the end."

Shelter considered this for a moment. "Maybe you're right. I told Penny I was ready to have a baby with her, but she says she's lost faith in us together."

Kane finished her cup of coffee and gathered her things. "The way you're talking is what leads to a life of regrets. That's not where you want to be. If you love her, talk to her. Give it one more try."

He phoned Penny the next day and left a voice message. Over the next few hours, he checked his phone several times and started to worry she'd simply ignore him. That would be a painful and humiliating end. But as was so often the case when he had these catastrophic thoughts, they turned out to be unfounded. She called him back at the end of the day and agreed to meet him on Saturday morning. He had a hard time deciphering her tone. It seemed neutral, not resentful but not welcoming.

Saturday morning was sunny and cool, about what you would expect for September. Autumn was definitely in the air. Shelter threw on jeans and a sweater over a long-sleeve flannel shirt for their walk in the park. He cycled from his house in the Wolseley district over the bridge at Omand's Creek and the one over the Assiniboine River, down Wellington Crescent to the park. Covering over a thousand acres on the city's west side, Assiniboine Park was where he'd spent a lot of time when he was a boy, riding his bike along the dirt trails that ran through the trees by the river to the park.

Back then, he couldn't care less about gardens, but his mother and grandfather had been devotees of the park's formal English Garden with its carefully tended flower beds and shrubs, meandering paths, and strategically located benches. They'd occasionally drag him and his sister around the garden with them. He'd only awakened to the garden's charm and beauty when he took up gardening, and it had appealed to Penny's design aesthetics as well. They'd visited it at least once a month in the summer and fall for the tranquillity and the evolving colours and aromas as the seasons changed. It seemed like a good place for a talk.

They met at the entrance to the garden, where stood a famous bronze statue of a boy holding a boot, leaking water into a pond surrounded by flowers. They hadn't seen each other in over a month, and as she approached, he was reminded of just how beautiful she was, dressed in a wool jacket and jeans, her jet-black hair pulled back in a ponytail.

She gave him a shy smile, embraced him, and gave him a kiss on the cheek. "You're looking good."

"You too."

He felt his heartbeat tick higher at her nearness. It made him fully aware of the hopes he'd pinned on this meeting. They strolled through the garden, stopping to admire the last flowers of the season and fill in the gaps of what had happened in their lives since they'd last spoken.

Like everyone, Penny had seen the news about the hostage-taking and had sent him a text at the time asking if he was okay. He'd thanked her but found nothing in the exchange to give him hope they could get back together. Now, she told him how proud she was of how he'd handled the situation. He was pleased and glanced in her direction with a bashful smile. He told her about taking time off and seeing a therapist.

Eventually, they found a bench tucked away in a sunny corner where they could talk without being overheard. During their tour of the garden, he'd felt she was open to him. Their conversation had flowed easily, and he'd relaxed into the moment. Now he could feel anxiety rising again. It was time to talk about the future, but before he could begin, she reached into her pocket and pulled out the key to his house. "You should have this," she said, holding it out to him.

He was taken aback. He'd hoped this could be a new beginning. Now he realized she saw it as a coda to their relationship. Struggling to control his disappointment, he said, "I want you to keep it."

"Why?" she asked, studying his face.

"Because I don't want to lose you."

"We talked about it. It's not what I want."

"I don't believe you."

She drew herself back in astonishment, looking at him with wide eyes. "Excuse me?"

"You told me you still love me," he said. "I know you don't trust me when I say I want to have a baby. I understand that. But I've thought about it a lot since we talked. Thought about myself and a baby. It's what I want. I love you, and I'll be there for you."

She leaned her shoulder against the back of the bench and pulled her jacket tight around her as if she was chilled.

She looked off toward the garden path where an elderly couple were admiring a spray of zinnias.

"I'm scared," she said at last. "I want a baby with you so badly, but I need to know you want this just as much as me. The stakes are too high."

"I know you're scared," he said in almost a whisper. "I'm scared too."

She looked down at the key in her hand and rubbed it with her thumb. Finally, she looked into his eyes and dropped the key back into her pocket.

"Let's go."

ACKNOWLEDGEMENTS

Taking this journey a second time turned out to be no easier than the first, and once again, I couldn't have made it without the kind and generous help of so many people.

My sincere thanks to those who patiently answered my many questions about police procedure, Hutterites, farming, and other topics: John O'Donovan, Andrew Mikolajewski, Jake and Judi Janzen, Colin Penner, Sol Janzen, Nadine Kampen, Devin Ross, Craig Ryan, Kelly Hofer, John Lehr, and those who asked not to be named.

I am also grateful to my friends and colleagues who gave their precious time to read and comment on the manuscript at various stages: Mark Abley, Linda Vincent, Paddy Hirsch, Kim Murray, Jeff O'Malley, Alina Pahoncia, Catherine McKenzie, Allister Thompson, Roy MacGregor, and Alastair Gillespie.

My sincere thanks to Linda Leith, Felicia Mihali, Shakiya Williams, and the whole team at Linda Leith Publishing for your faith in my book, and your care in bringing it to the public.

All my love and gratitude to my family. To Catherine, Julia, Alex, and Barbara, thank you for reading the manuscript, commenting on it, and encouraging me to the finishing line. My thanks also to my father-in-law Rodney Rendell-Green and to Mark Rendell-Green and Cheri Tully for your support.

Any errors and oversights are my sole responsibility.

AVAILABLE AND COMING SOON FROM
LINDA LEITH PUBLISHING

Miss Matty
EDEET RAVEL

Sentence
MICKAIL IOSSEL

Christmas Weekend
MONIQUE POLACK

The Unfinished World
MARILYN BOWERING

There's Always More to Say
NATALIE SOUTHWORTH

I Made a Promise I Could not Keep
DAVID HOMEL

Beyond Ken Dryden
OREN SAFDIE

I Can't Believe I'm Old
JANET TORGE

The Roughling
ALEX COSTA

The Faithful
DON MACDONALD